Betrayal from Beyond

The Kier and Levett Mystery Series
Book 6

DEB MARLOWE

© Copyright 2025 by Deb Marlowe
Text by Deb Marlowe
Cover by Kim Killion Designs

Dragonblade Publishing, Inc. is an imprint of Kathryn Le Veque Novels, Inc.
P.O. Box 23
Moreno Valley, CA 92556
ceo@dragonbladepublishing.com

Produced in the United States of America

First Edition April 2025
Trade Paperback Edition

Reproduction of any kind except where it pertains to short quotes in relation to advertising or promotion is strictly prohibited.

All Rights Reserved.

The characters and events portrayed in this book are fictitious. Any similarity to real persons, living or dead, is purely coincidental and not intended by the author.

ARE YOU SIGNED UP FOR DRAGONBLADE'S BLOG?

You'll get the latest news and information on exclusive giveaways, exclusive excerpts, coming releases, sales, free books, cover reveals and more.

Check out our complete list of authors, too!

No spam, no junk. That's a promise!

Sign Up Here

www.dragonbladepublishing.com

Dearest Reader;

Thank you for your support of a small press. At Dragonblade Publishing, we strive to bring you the highest quality Historical Romance from some of the best authors in the business. Without your support, there is no 'us', so we sincerely hope you adore these stories and find some new favorite authors along the way.

Happy Reading!

CEO, Dragonblade Publishing

Additional Dragonblade books by
Author Deb Marlowe

The Kier and Levett Mystery Series
A Killer in the Crystal Palace (Book 1)
Death from the Druid's Grove (Book 2)
Murder on the Mirrored Lake (Book 3)
Revenge in the Rogue's Hideaway (Book 4)
Carnage from the Cursed Crown (Book 5)
Betrayal from Beyond (Book 6)

For my Valiant Husband. Because I'm surprised every time a reader tells me how refreshing it is to see Niall supporting and believing in Kara—and I am reminded each time how lucky I am.

Prologue

Kingston upon Thames

"BACK SO SOON, miss?" Mr. Norrey gave her a nod.

Miss Katherine Prentice blinked at the owner of Kingston Larder and Goods. "Yes. The weeks do seem to pass quickly, don't they?" Moving quietly through the shop, she selected a jar of treacle, a tin of tea, and a sack of dried currants. She hovered over the rack of chapbooks, but reluctantly moved on and took her purchases to the counter.

Mr. Norrey began to pack them into a basket with brisk efficiency. "Going out into the market today, miss? Shall I have this sent out to your cottage along with the goods you picked out this morning?"

Katherine froze. Swallowed. "Yes, of course," she said faintly. "Thank you."

"Enjoy the market, miss," he said cheerfully. "Be sure to stop by Mrs. Hayview's. My nose tells me she's got her famous ginger cake available today."

"How lovely."

The shopkeeper handed over her items and took her payment in exchange. As she was turning away, he looked up suddenly.

"Oh! Will you be wanting to pay for this morning's goods now as well, miss?"

A shudder of dread made its way up her spine. "I... Uh... I...

No, thank you. Not now."

Katherine dashed out of the shop, but did not set out to explore the market as she had meant to. Instead, she headed back the way she'd come, back to the little stone cottage that had become her retreat.

The man's comments—could they mean what she feared they did? She'd been later than usual with her shopping this morning because she kept pausing, losing track of what she was doing. Something felt…off. She kept looking over her shoulder, expecting to find someone there.

The loud bustle of the busy village faded as she hurried along the river path. The Thames grew narrow through here. It rushed by, swollen from all the recent rains. There was only a bit of birdsong to compete with the noise of the current, moving fast and full. The air was crisp, but the sun shone bright.

All in all, it was too light and cheerful to match the shadow that had settled over her.

Had it come at last? The day she'd feared and waited for?

She spotted the evergreen shrubbery and bare branches and shoots of her mother's garden ahead as she rounded a curve in the path. She'd spent the last weeks cleaning the winter debris, readying the garden for spring and summer. The little plot had been her mother's pride and joy. Katherine had made it a habit to come here at this time of year to remember, to care for the garden her mother had loved, and to honor her memory.

The bank leading down to the river was steep at this spot, and it gave out into deep water. Over the years, the path alongside had veered away from the water. The vantage on the turn allowed her a better view of the cottage—and she noticed suddenly that the door stood open.

Her steps slowed. Her heart began to pound. She knew she had closed that door.

The little stone house had been an oasis, a place of comfort and rejuvenation. Now the open doorway beckoned her like the empty, hungry maw of a restless spirit.

A chill crept up her spine. Something was not right. The eerie feeling returned. She started forward again, moving slowly.

But—no. She couldn't do it. Couldn't go in. She considered turning, running back to the village, but she decided to speed up instead. To go past the cottage as if she were in no way connected to it. She kept her gaze forward and her head high. She was moving quickly when she heard a noise behind her.

She turned—and gasped as she discovered the ghost standing directly behind her. Perhaps it was the wrong word, but it felt right. It was the living representation of what might have been.

"Good morning," it said brightly. "You have yourself a charming little place here, don't you?"

Not a ghost at all, perhaps. A trickster. *Enemy,* her heart whispered. It recognized the guile, the threat that lived behind those familiar eyes.

"You should have come to me. Back then, when I invited you." The figure spoke in flat, disapproving tones.

"I did come." She frowned. "I mixed in with the crowd. I listened. I saw you."

A hint of respect showed. "I never knew you were there."

Katherine shook her head. "It was too much hate for me. Too much vitriol. All of you—you had plans to tear everything down, but no word or whisper for how you meant to build it back up." Her nose wrinkled in distaste. "I could see it. You meant only to stir up trouble. To get your revenge, and to line your pockets along the way. That's no way to live."

"No way to live," the trickster echoed her before turning away to contemplate the water rushing by. "You grew up in the city, right on the river. What was that like?"

She gaped. "How do you know that?"

"I know a great deal about you." A side glance. "Not much of it is impressive."

Katherine raised her chin. "I daresay I climbed higher and accomplished more than you, if you take into account where we each started." It had rankled, in fact—when she had discovered the truth. When she had learned about all the vast opportunity and knowledge she'd missed out on.

"Perhaps you are right."

"What was it like, you ask? It was difficult. Unsteady. There were booming times and lean times. My father carried all sorts of people across the river. He moored at the Vauxhall Stairs and ferried the lords and ladies in their fancy dress, hiding behind their gorgeous masks and dominoes. But I preferred the men he carried at the Lambeth Stairs. The businessmen and priests, the supplicants to the archbishop, the clerks and secretaries and speakers and members of Parliament who were heading to Whitehall and Westminster. Those men knew things."

The trickster nodded. "You wanted to know things."

"So help me, I did," she whispered. "When I was young I wanted to know the how and the why of everything, but as I grew older I only wanted to know how to help my father when the steam packets stole his business. I wanted to know why he was forced to add on work for the Customs Office. I wanted to know how we were going to live, who was going to help us when he was injured, fighting in one of their smuggler's raids."

Her enemy turned and met her gaze directly. "Somebody helped you. You went to see *him*, then. After your father was injured. And that's when your parents moved here from the city." It was a statement, not a question.

Katherine nodded. It had been a desperate move, but it had ultimately paid off.

"How did you do it?" The trickster seemed genuinely interested—and perhaps a little impressed. "How did you get near enough to actually speak with him?"

"I watched him. Learned his routines. Hired a group of street urchins to make a ruckus and distract his servants—and I climbed into his coach and waited."

The trickster waited for her to continue.

Katherine's mind went back to that moment. Her heart had pounded then as it did now. "I might have been anyone. A prostitute. An enemy spy. An actress sent by a political rival to start a scandal. An assassin. But he knew, almost the moment he climbed in, sat down, and faced me. He only stared at me, quite calm."

The trickster turned away, crossing to the far side of the path, moving into the green swath beside it. "He must have said something."

"Eventually, he did speak. *Which one are you?* That was all he asked."

Her adversary's head rose at that. Something dark flared behind those eyes. "And what did you answer?"

Katherine threw her shoulders back. "I told him I was the waterman's daughter," she said, her tone deliberately ringing with pride.

Her enemy's lip curled. "The waterman's daughter, so foolish that she never learned to swim."

Before she could answer, the trickster reached into the tall grass and came up with a long oar in hand. Before she could puzzle it out, her enemy rushed her, held the oar high and horizontal and struck her hard with it, pushing her back. The bank dropped quickly away beneath her feet. There was nothing to stop her, nothing to grab on to. Her arms whirled, and she fell backward into the river.

The water closed over her head. She sank down, down, and finally her feet struck the bottom. She pushed off, rising until her head broke the surface and she could gasp for breath. "Help! Help me!"

She'd already been swept a few feet down river. She was going under again. She flailed, fighting the heavy drag of her skirts, trying to stay afloat. Her enemy stalked her, gripping the long oar.

She reached up a hand. "Please!"

The oar extended, heading toward her. She reached toward it and slipped under the water once more. She let herself drift down so that she could push up again. It was a slower rise this time.

When she broke the surface at last, the oar pushed her down again.

No. She tried to grab it, but it was snatched away. She went under again. *No.* She fought, reached out, and found a root extending beneath the water. She gripped it desperately, tried to use it to pull herself closer to the bank, but the oar was there again, the edge sharp against her chest, pushing her away.

She was still being dragged by the current. She watched in horror as she swept by the cottage, her enemy still following, watching, waiting. She couldn't stay afloat. She swallowed river water and panicked, fighting to keep her face out of the water, but her heart was nearly as heavy as her sodden skirts. The rushing water pulled her out further toward the middle. She kept sinking, and it grew harder and harder to push up, to reach the surface. At last, she failed to make it and knew it was over.

The last thing she saw through the watery veil was the trickster, standing high on the bank and smiling down on her defeat.

Chapter One

Bluefield Park
Outside London
Two weeks earlier

T HE DUCHESS OF Sedwick stretched luxuriously, but didn't open her eyes. She was content to melt into the warmth of her husband's embrace and the comfort of her own bed, to listen to the first stirrings of the birds beyond her window and the sounds of the household coming awake past her door.

Home at last. Kara loved their new estate in Scotland. She had relished every minute of their travels as she and Niall had enjoyed a delayed bridal trip through his favorite parts of Europe—but Bluefield Park was *home*. Her heart had swelled yesterday as they returned to the estate where she'd grown up, and it had filled near to bursting at the welcome of their cobbled-together family.

Moving carefully, she turned to gaze upon her husband's sleeping face. He blinked awake and gave her a sleepy grin—and she knew that happy as she was to be at Bluefield, her true home would always be with him, wherever that might be.

Niall pulled her close and kissed her softly before he began to roll away. She reached out to stop him. "No," she protested softly. "I'm not finished."

Grinning, he pulled her close. "Finished with what?"

She framed his face with her hands. "Telling myself how lucky I am."

She felt the truth of it, deep down. Niall's life had been hard, and his heart had been battered, but he'd been strong and resilient enough to allow her to breach the walls he'd erected to protect himself. He'd also been solid and confident enough to not only accept, but to encourage her unique interests and unconventional ways.

Nearly two years had passed since they had first met, and gracious, how they both had changed. She'd been avoiding Society and refusing to conform to the commonly held ideal of feminine fragility. She had buried all of her loneliness and sorrow in keeping her father's businesses running smoothly, and unleashed her creativity into building her automatons.

Niall had been closed and cut off from nearly everyone except for his assistant Gyda and his mentor, the Viscount Lord Stayme. He'd kept his secrets and devoted his energy into furthering his career as a forge artist.

Then had come the Great Exhibition, where they had met as exhibitors and joined together to solve a murder and started down a twisted and sometimes dangerous path that had led them here—married, newly minted as duke and duchess, with secrets revealed and a chance at a quieter, more settled existence.

It was what they both wanted, and she suspected all of their friends and family held the same desire.

"We'll be lucky if Harold doesn't barge in here at any second," Niall said with a grin.

"He seems perfectly well, doesn't he?" Even all of these months later, she still felt a jolt of anxiety when she thought how close they'd come to losing her ward. They had delayed their travels until Harold was pronounced completely recovered, but it had still taken Niall some serious efforts of persuasion to convince her to leave him for weeks on end.

"He is indeed perfectly well, and he put the time we were gone to good use. Turner says his studies have progressed well and it's clear he's spent time with Gyda in the forge. The boy has completely mastered the scrolling jig."

Kara nodded. She had kept her composure last evening when they arrived and tried not to hang on to Harold for too long, but even now she teared up, remembering the joy and relief that had washed over her once she had him in her arms again.

"You did very well, my darling," Niall whispered. "And I promise not to tell how much you worried while we were gone. But I also promised to take the boy along to my consultation with Mr. Blundel. If I don't get moving, Harold will be in here looking for me. He knows we need to get the early train."

"Oh, very well." Kara kissed him and let him go. She watched his muscled form as he rolled out of bed. "Harold will likely pester the man with a hundred questions about his famed wetlands."

"That's one reason I'm happy to take him along. The more Blundel talks about his passion, the more inspiration I'll have for his piece."

"I never knew a naturalist who needed encouragement to talk about his area of research," she said dryly.

Chuckling, Niall pulled on a robe.

"Has Mr. Blundel decided on a set of gates?" she asked.

"Gates and two matching screens to cover the large windows in his laboratory," he answered with satisfaction. After coming back for one last kiss, he went through to his own room. Kara heard the murmured greeting given by Crewe, his new valet, but she turned over and snuggled into the comfort of the bed once more. She was just beginning to doze again when the door to the passageway burst open.

"Rise and shine, slug-a-bed!" Gyda Winther breezed in. "Your lazy days of travel and leisure are over. It's back to work and daily routines now, my friend." Grinning, she shut the door leading to Niall's room, then ran to jump into the bed.

Kara laughed as her friend sprawled beside her. "Go easy," she begged. "We haven't even been home a full day."

"And yet duty lurks outside that door, waiting to pounce," Gyda told her. "Turner is hanging about. No doubt he has a list a mile long for you to go over."

"I'm sure he does." Kara sighed. "And you are right. I should get out of bed and get to it. The Mosemans are coming for luncheon, and Bernard will definitely have yet another list of business matters for me to see to." She grinned at her friend. "But first, I shall give them their presents. I swear, that was my favorite part of our trip, choosing the right gifts to bring back."

Gyda raised a brow. "Really, Kara? The gifts? Your favorite part? Of your *bridal* trip?"

Kara laughed. "Second favorite, I suppose."

"Well, whatever you got them, they absolutely will not enjoy them more than the gift you brought me." Gyda reached out to squeeze her hand. "I cannot tell you how much I love the traditional jewelry."

"I know Harriet will adore the scent we brought her. We found the most wonderful perfumery outside Paris." Kara squeezed Gyda's hand in return. "But I am so relieved that you approve of the jewelry. I did hesitate, because I know they are meant to fasten to a traditional Nordic overmantel, but when I saw the carved tortoiseshell brooches connected by the amber and glass beads—and in that lovely dusky blue that you love—I just could not resist them. I knew they were meant for you."

"I think they must have been," Gyda said seriously. "I lay in the bath last night, imagining the long journey they must have taken to come to me." Her tone quieted. "I am thinking of having a complete traditional outfit made. There is someone I want to show them to, and I think I want to manufacture the full effect."

Kara had been about to roll out of bed, but now she paused. "Someone you want to show them to? I know that tone of yours, Gyda." She fluffed her pillow, leaned back, and raised a brow. "Talk."

Gyda bit her lip. "Kara." It came out in almost a whisper. "I think I have met someone. Someone…important."

Kara drew a delighted breath. "Oh! Do tell!"

"His name is Charles Osbourne."

She couldn't stop her eyes widening in surprise. "But…"

"I know!" Gyda put a hand on her brow. "But he's as beautiful as anyone I've ever been attracted to!"

"Charles Osbourne? Gyda, do you mean *Lord* Charles Osbourne? From the Duke of Stratton's brood?"

"His fourth son," Gyda said with an air of confession.

"Oh, good heavens," Kara breathed.

"I know! The whole thing is ridiculous! Except it absolutely is not. He is not your typical lordling."

"I do seem to recall your saying that the nobility is largely a waste of flesh," Kara said wryly.

"I didn't mean you. You know that. Nor do I mean Charles. He's not like so many of the rest of them. His mind, Kara! He's incredibly knowledgeable, but even better, he is curious."

"Curious? About what, exactly?" Several worrying possibilities occurred to her.

"About everything. It's entirely delightful, how much he knows and yet how much he still wishes to learn. He's especially interested in craftmanship and creation."

Kara relaxed. "Well, then. He must find you fascinating, my dear. Your artistry is undeniable."

Gyda flushed with pleasure. "That means something coming from you." She made a face. "I'm just…bowled over by him, Kara. I cannot stop watching him, listening to him talk. He has such passion and initiative."

"As do you," Kara reminded her.

"We do have that in common. His enthusiasm fascinates me, but it's more than that, as well. I'm not sure I've ever felt this way about anyone."

Kara took her friend's other hand and squeezed them both. "I'm so very happy for you."

Gyda pulled her in for a hug. "Thank you. I couldn't wait to tell you." Pulling back, she grinned. "And thank you for not immediately voicing your reservations. I know you have them. I do as well. There are a good many reasons why a relationship will never work between us. I list them to myself daily. And yet...I cannot help but hope for one more day, every day."

"Oh, Gyda. That is truly all any of us can hope for. One day at a time."

"No. You and Niall have promised each other a lifetime. I want that. Someday."

"You know you will have all of my support. And Niall's. All we wish is for you to be happy."

"I do know it. And I'm happy." Gyda let go and threw herself back against the pillows once more. "*So* happy. And afraid."

"I know just what you mean, my dear. But my advice is to let the fear go. It doesn't help keep you safe, in any case."

"I'll do my best." Gyda bit back a laugh as a creak sounded in the passage outside. "Is that Turner? I think he's growing impatient. I will let you start your day. But Kara? I am very glad you are back."

"Thank you, my dear." Kara smiled. "So am I."

IT WAS A productive meeting. Mr. Blundel approved of Niall's preliminary plans. His enthusiasm as he made suggestions for additions and changes sparked Harold's curiosity, and the boy's questions spurred the naturalist on to even more valuable descriptions. In the end, the meeting went on twice as long as Niall had expected, but was more than twice as useful. Everyone was content as they parted ways.

Niall checked his pocket watch. "What do you say to heading over to Stayme's?" he asked Harold. "He'll likely be heading out to Bluefield today. We can ride with him."

Harold paused long enough in the recitation of marsh animals he now knew he *must* see to agree.

Niall hailed a hack, and they set off for Mayfair. He made a few notes as the boy waxed enthusiastic about the prospect of a visit to Mr. Blundel's fens, but after a while, Harold grew silent.

Niall looked up to see the boy pressed up against the window. "Is something amiss?"

"No." Harold sighed.

Niall waited.

"It's just… Sometimes it feels odd."

"What does?"

"Riding inside a hack instead of hitching on to the back and dropping off before you're found out."

"Ah."

"Sometimes when I see the street rats, it makes me wonder about my old crew."

Niall put aside his pencil. "Do you not see them now and again? I would have thought you would run into them in Covent Garden when you help out Maisie with deliveries." The boy still enjoyed helping out at the pie shop where he lived when they had coaxed him off the streets.

"Not so much anymore."

Niall wondered if a fair few of Harold's old crew might not have survived the harsh conditions of London's streets. He kept the thought to himself and gazed quietly out the window for a long moment. They had reached the first of the cleaner, quieter streets of Mayfair before Harold spoke again.

"Niall?"

"Yes?"

"I truly am recovered. Dr. Balgate said so."

"I know. And I think you know how relieved and happy we are." Niall himself was still furious, as the poison that had endangered the boy had been meant for him. But justice had been served, and he had to let his anger go. Or so Kara kept telling him.

"Before I got ill, I asked Kara if I could take lessons." Harold paused. "The sort of lessons she had when she was younger."

"Oh." It was no small request. Kara's lessons had been extensive and varied—not to mention unusual and, in part, illegal.

"She agreed," Harold reassured him. "But that was then. I'm worried she might not still feel the same."

Niall held his breath a moment. He let his gaze wander over Harold's anxious expression. The lad was growing up. He'd noticed Kara's worry, and instead of resenting it, he was being careful of her feelings.

Pride swelled Niall's chest.

"It is very good of you to take her feelings into consideration. Not to mention, it is very mature of you. Well done, Harold." Niall paused. "I think, if you were to ask again, that Kara would first say that she doesn't wish for you to worry about your safety, or hers, or mine. I would agree that we want you to know that it is our responsibility to protect you, not the other way around." He held up a hand as the boy's expression grew stubborn. "However, I think we both can understand the wish to learn, to prepare, to ready yourself for all of the sorts of obstacles life might throw at you." He nodded. "If you ask again, I am sure she will agree." He gave a half-smile as Harold sighed in relief. "But if I were you, I would come up with a list of the lessons you would like, and prioritize them, with reasoning included. You know she respects a measured argument."

The boy laughed. "I will." His attention was drawn to the window again as they turned into the wide lanes of Berkeley Square. "We're here!"

Niall paid the driver while Harold ran ahead to the viscount's door. It opened just as Niall caught up to the boy, but not before he noticed Harold's attention fixed on Stayme's slightly naughty door knocker.

The lad truly was growing up.

Watts, the viscount's butler, welcomed them.

"Is he in his study?" asked Niall, familiar with his aging mentor's compulsive habits.

"No, Your Grace." Watts was entirely too staid to roll his

eyes, but his tone got his point across. "Lord Stayme is in the blue bedroom at the moment."

"Do you have houseguests?" Niall knew the blue room was meant for guests—not that the viscount ever entertained any.

"No, sir. He's had the telescope moved in there."

"Is he harassing the gardeners again?"

"Not that I am aware of." Now the butler's tone intimated that the old man's antics were worse. Worse than Stayme's unfounded conviction that he knew more about gardening than the men hired to care for Berkeley Square's central garden?

"I'll go up."

"If I may suggest it, Master Harold might wish to go down to the kitchens," Watts said. "Cook has just made a batch of treacle scones. They are likely still warm."

Harold shot a questioning glance his way, and Niall nodded. The boy headed for the green baize door that led to the servants' stairs as Niall exchanged a glance with the butler and headed upstairs.

"Something is afoot," Stayme announced when Niall entered the guest room. The old man sat at a table at the window. His prized telescope sat upon it, aimed out the window at the front of the house. The viscount was scribbling busily in a journal.

"What's afoot?"

"Someone is watching the house."

"Someone is always watching the house. What are you mixed up in now?" The viscount was one of the foremost dealers in that most valuable resource in games of power—information.

"That's just it. Everything is relatively dull right now. The Whigs and the Peelites are settling into their coalition government. Palmerston, turned home secretary, has shifted his focus inward, though he cannot keep from commenting loudly on foreign affairs. That leaves things mostly quiet at the moment. And yet I have a watcher. An intriguing specimen, too."

"Intriguing?"

"Yes. It was a man stationed in the garden at first. He looked like any aging clerk, sitting with his newspaper, but he sat out there a little too often, for a little too long. I made a detour around the square one morning, to be sure to get a good look at him, but then I shrugged it off. As you say, there are those out there who like to keep track of me."

Niall grinned.

"But after I did that, I noticed the clerk didn't come back. However, a gentlewoman did. She made a show of wandering the garden and reading her novel, and she made sure not to sit in the same spot, but she couldn't fool me. I went out to harangue the gardeners and set them to trimming the trees before the spring thaw, so that I might get a good look at her." The viscount raised a brow. "And guess what I noticed?"

"I couldn't possibly." Niall went to the room's other window and peered out, but he saw no one lurking in the garden.

"The aging clerk and the gentlewoman were the same person," Stayme said grimly.

"Are you sure?"

"Yes."

"Perhaps they were related. Siblings?"

"I considered it, but no. I began to truly watch the watcher, and I'm convinced—they are the same person, and that person is female. I gave no indication of anything amiss, but I called in one of my own best people and set him on her."

"And what did he find?"

"Well, it took a full morning for her to notice him."

"Your man must be good."

"He is."

"Who do you think sent her?"

"I hadn't the faintest notion. Until…"

"Until?"

"When she noticed my man, things got strange."

"Strange?"

"She acknowledged him. Walked right up, winked at him, then set off."

"He followed, I presume?"

"He did, and he said it was damned hard to keep her in his sights, despite her skirts. She knows a trick or two. He managed to keep up with her—until she disappeared into one of the rookeries."

Niall stilled.

"Yes." Stayme looked grim. "He lost her near Seven Dials."

Niall closed his eyes. "Surely it is not her, Stayme. We heard she was last spotted in Austria, right before we set out on our bridal trip."

Petra Scot had been the woman who made public Niall's family secrets—that his mother had been the illegitimate daughter of King George IV and his illegal wife, Maria Fitzherbert. She had meant to use his story to stir up religious unrest and anger against a corrupt government and a ruthless royal family. She'd wanted his story to be the tinder to start a fire of rebellion and rioting. She'd said she'd wanted leverage to influence change in England's foreign policy—and had even convinced several unsavory factions of a few foreign governments to back her plans.

Niall knew the truth, however. Petra had merely wanted money, and a bit of revenge against the royal family and all of those who had mistreated her own mother—the disgraced Queen Caroline. When Niall and Kara foiled her plans, she'd added them both to the long list of those she meant to seek vengeance upon.

"I never saw the Scot woman, myself," Stayme said bitterly. "Only her lackeys." He'd been abducted and held captive in an attempt to force Niall's cooperation. "But I've heard her described. Dark hair and eyes. Slope of a nose. She was the right age, too."

Niall sighed. "I think it's far more likely that this woman was sent by one of your enemies, rather than mine. Petra is far too crafty to allow herself to be seen." He didn't want to believe Stayme was right. They had all had quite enough danger and intrigue. He just wanted to settle in with Kara and make his art— and perhaps a child or two. Or ten.

"You might be right. But we should both keep our eyes and ears open. And there is something else you should know."

Niall waited.

"She sent a new watcher after she was found out. Disguised him as one of the gardening apprentices. It might have worked, too, if I was not familiar with all of their staff." Stayme stood. "But the boy left, faster than a shot, the moment you and Harold climbed out of that hack."

Niall cursed under his breath.

"Niall? Lord Stayme!" The echo of Harold's pounding footsteps reached them before the boy himself. He skidded to a stop in the doorway. "Good morning, sir! Are you coming to Bluefield Park today?"

"Of course I am," the viscount said gruffly. "I would have been there yesterday, had I known just when they meant to arrive." He shot a dark look at Niall before ruffling the boy's hair. "Watts likely already has my luggage strapped to the coach."

"He said so," Harold confirmed. "Cook made us a basket, too, but she says I'm to just eat the roast chicken. Three scones are enough, she says."

"Aye, lad. Some meat will put some flesh back on your bones." Stayme had been nearly as upset as Kara and Niall when the boy had been poisoned.

They trooped downstairs, and Stayme stopped to give his secretary a few last instructions.

Watts sidled up to Niall. "He wasn't exaggerating?" he asked quietly.

"I'm afraid not."

Watts absorbed the news. "I'd hoped he was just bored."

"It might be nothing, but you should alert the staff. Be careful, even when he's with us."

"We know what is expected of us, sir."

"I know you do."

Stayme's traveling carriage rolled up outside, and they were soon all bundled inside and on their way. Harold leaned toward the window, looking back for a long moment. He turned to look over his shoulder at Stayme. "Sir? Why do you have a naughty door knocker?"

Niall had never once seen such a look of surprise on the old man's face. The viscount cleared his throat. "I'll tell you why, boy. It's because I was once a young man myself." He barked out a laugh at Harold's dubious expression. "It's true! And I tell you, in my day we were not so prim and prissy as the gentlemen today like to think themselves. We ran *wild*. We lived hard. I could raise your hair, if I told you some of the tales of our exploits."

"Tell them!" Harold urged.

"When you are older, I shall," the viscount vowed. "But for now, I will tell you that when I was a gentleman about Town, getting up to every escapade, I promised myself I would never turn into a cold fish, a pompous prig with no taste for adventure, laughter, or fun. I vowed never to forget to relish the joy to be found in wine, women or a game well played." He looked Harold directly in the eye. "And by God, I kept that vow. I keep that knocker to remind me of it." He pointed a finger. "If you learn nothing else from me, boy, let it be this—keep the promises you make yourself. For if you cannot be true to yourself, how can you ever honor the others in your life?"

Niall pursed his lips. Stayme had told him something similar when he was younger. And those words had been on his mind on the day he wedded Kara. He'd pledged himself to her that day. But he'd also made a promise to himself—that he would keep her and their loved ones safe.

As Stayme said, he meant to keep all the vows he'd made that day.

Chapter Two

K ARA MANAGED TO get a great deal done, both with Turner and with Moseman, the man who acted as her right hand in running the businesses and factories she'd inherited from her father. She had a lovely luncheon with him and his family, then managed to convince them to stay after Niall and Harold returned with Lord Stayme in tow.

They shared news, much laughter, and a little gossip. Miss Harriett Moseman, as predicted, adored her French *parfum*, and continued to practice her fledgling skills at flirtation upon Niall. He bore it well and treated her gently. After a sumptuous afternoon tea, the Mosemans departed, and Stayme went upstairs to his rooms to rest. Kara went looking for Niall, but couldn't find him, not in the house or even out at his forge.

"Turner, have you seen Niall?" she asked when she returned.

"No, Your Grace, but I heard Crewe mention that the duke went out for a walk."

"Oh," Kara said, surprised. "Very well, then. It gives us a chance to chat, doesn't it? Will you join me in the ivory sitting room?"

"Of course."

They settled into the little room that she'd always regarded as a combination of office and private retreat. She poured a snifter of brandy for Turner and a bit for herself. Turner sighed as he sank into the plush leather chair. Kara got comfortable on the settee and smiled at him over the top of her glass. "Just like old times, isn't it?"

Her butler, friend, and assistant permitted himself a rare, conspiratorial grin. "So it is." He took a long drink. "But on the whole, I prefer these times." He raised his brows. "You are not nearly so lonely now as you were back then."

"I may have felt lonely at times, but I was never *alone*," she said fiercely. "I always had you."

"And so you always shall." He lifted his glass.

"Who could have predicted such a turn of events?" she marveled.

"No one," he said with firm decisiveness. "There could have been no prediction of such a tangled path."

"It ended well, in any case—and that's my romantic life sorted. Now, what of yours? I trust you had the chance to spend a little more time with Mrs. Canning while we were gone?" Turner's affection for the housekeeper of nearby Wood Rose Abbey—and hers for him—was the stuff of much local gossip.

"We spent an appropriate amount of time together, as we always do," he answered primly.

"But Turner, we've all grown busier over the last couple of years—"

"I wouldn't want it any other way."

"Nor would I, but I would never wish to take away your personal time." At his stubborn look, she changed topics. "How is Tom coming along as underbutler?"

"The young man is learning. He is enthusiastic. It was a good idea to promote him."

"Excellent. You are satisfied, then?" She knew he would understand all that she was asking.

"In every way," he said gently.

"Good." She sighed in relief and leaned back against the cushions. They sat in comfortable silence for a few minutes. Kara let her mind roam back over the day. "Did you think Niall looked a little…tense this afternoon?" she asked suddenly.

Turner thought it over. "No. Not that I noticed."

"Hmm. Good, then."

A smile played at the corner of the butler's mouth. "Perhaps he is just loath to give up the relaxation and ease of your travels."

Kara fought back a blush. "Perhaps." She thought about it. "I know how to fix that. Will you have the fires lit in my laboratory tomorrow morning and have our breakfast served out there? Just the two of us? He always enjoys that."

"Of course."

"I haven't even set foot in the lab since we returned. Has Harold made any progress on the Green Man?" She and her ward had dreamed up the design of the automaton after Harold found a Green Man sculpted into a fountain at their new estate in Scotland.

"No. After his schooling, he's been spending most of his time with Gyda in the forge." Turner lifted his shoulder. "I believe he's been waiting for you."

"Well, we will get back to it, then."

Turner drained his brandy and stood. "And that is exactly what I should do. First, I'll go and tell Cook about your plans for breakfast."

Kara finished her drink as well. "Yes, I think I'll see what Harold is doing. Perhaps he'll want to begin again on the Green Man."

She found the boy in the schoolroom, draped over a desk. "What are you working on?" she asked as she entered.

Harold jumped and draped a protective arm over the paper in front of him. "Oh! You startled me."

"Niall mentioned you were interested in Mr. Blundel's work on cataloging the wildlife in his wetlands. Are you researching the subject?" The boy often enjoyed digging into the topics she and Niall used in their art.

"No." Harold stood and placed himself between her and the

desk. "I am, ah… I am working on something, but I'm not quite ready to show it to you yet."

"Oh." Kara stopped, surprised. "Of course. I don't mean to pry."

"No! You are not prying. I just want to sort everything and get organized before I share it."

"Of course," she repeated. He sounded so…grown. It gave her a pang. "I'll leave you to it, then." She turned to go.

"Kara?"

She turned back just in time to catch him as he hurled himself into her arms.

"I'm so glad you are back."

She ran her hands through his hair and pressed her cheek to the top of his head. "So am I. Let me know when you are ready to begin working on the Green Man again."

"Tomorrow?"

"Excellent." She left him and paused on the landing of the main staircase, her heart full and her mind busy. Harold was growing up. They had tried to give him opportunities to explore different skills since he had come into their care. It would be up to him to choose his path, but she couldn't help but wonder which direction he would take.

And where was Niall? She drifted downstairs to see if he'd returned.

"I haven't seen the duke," the maid, Prudence, told her. "But Lord Stayme announced that he is tired and not at all hungry after such an extensive tea. He has asked for a tray in his room tonight. Shall I bring one up for you as well?"

"No, thank you. I find I'm not hungry either. I'll wait for Niall."

Prudence curtsied and set off. Kara drifted upstairs. She sat down with her correspondence until her eyes grew tired, then she rang for her dresser and readied for bed. Yawning, she curled up in a chair before the fire—and woke, much later, to find Niall kneeling before her.

"Kara?"

Smiling sleepily, she reached for him. He gathered her in his arms and took her to the bed. "Where have you been?" she asked as he climbed in next to her.

"I went walking and stopped to chat with the gardeners." He smoothed her hair on the pillow. "I remember the first time I saw you in these rooms."

"It was you sitting in that chair back then," she said sleepily. "I walked in and you scared the life out of me."

He chuckled. "You showed no sign of it."

"Well, I couldn't, could I?"

"I was frightened for you," he said, his voice low. "Do you remember? That night I saw someone come through the gate hidden in the hedge, beyond the laboratory."

She nodded and yawned.

"How many people here at Bluefield know about that door?"

"Turner, of course." She yawned again. "The head gardener, too, and likely his son." She forced her mind to focus. "Turner may have shared it with young Tom." Her brow furrowed. "I wouldn't be surprised if a couple of the footmen knew. It's not as protected a secret as the tunnels are. My father used to say that letting a lesser secret out kept people from looking for more."

Niall pursed his lips. "Those who know about it do not use it, though, do they?"

"No. My father would use it occasionally, to avoid visitors he had no wish to see. I used it for the same reason a time or two." She gave him a sleepy grin. "But not since that night, when I found you here."

"Someone has used it recently," he said quietly.

She frowned. "How would you know?"

"I twisted a thin piece of twine at the bottom of the gate, so that I would know if it has been opened."

She blinked. "When did you set that up?"

"Back when I first moved into the loft above the forge. It seemed like a good idea, to keep track of something that was supposed to be secret. The twine was never shifted, however. I checked it again before we left on our tour. It was intact then. It isn't any longer."

"But the gate is hidden in the hedge. It could have been disturbed by weather, or by a bird or an animal."

"Perhaps."

She could tell he didn't believe it. She started to rise up on one elbow, but he shifted his gaze to the chair again. "You might have thrown me a bone, that first night in here," he said dryly. "As I recall, you had already bested me once that day."

She made a face. "No. I could not have made any of it easier on you."

"Why not?" He lowered his tone to a whisper. "Didn't you *like* me?"

"Oh, I liked you. And that is precisely why I had to challenge you. I wanted to keep you interested." She looped her hands around his neck. "Did it work?"

"I was interested."

"Was?" She pouted.

"I was interested back then." He kissed her. "Now, I am spellbound."

"Just the way I like you," she murmured.

He moved over her and kissed her again. Perfectly willing to abandon the discussion of the gate, she sank back and set about freeing the buttons of his waistcoat. Impatient, he tore at the thing. Buttons went flying about the bed, but Niall ignored them, focusing instead on a long, slow caress that started at her ankle and trailed upward, rucking her night rail high and banishing any further worry from her mind.

KARA WOKE EARLY the next morning. Dawn was just a hint of pink in the sky outside her window. Rolling over, she found the other side of the bed empty. She sat up. "Niall?"

His spot beside her was still slightly warm, but he wasn't to be found in her rooms or his. A niggle of worry set her to dressing. All that talk of the gate last night, and now this. The last time he'd stayed out so late and left so early—when he wasn't deeply involved in a project in the forge—it was because he'd been patrolling the grounds, watching for trouble.

Surely they had not been home long enough for trouble to find them? Perhaps he'd begun work on Mr. Blundel's gates. She finished shrugging into one of her simple laboratory gowns and went to check the forge.

It was cold and closed. Unease settled in her belly. She headed for the lab. It was still locked. Turner hadn't yet sent anyone out to light the fires. She let herself in and stood in the cool dark a moment, breathing in the slightly metallic scent of one of her favorite places in the world. Once her eyes had adjusted, she moved to the first hearth, the one near her workbenches. Luckily, the fire had been laid out already. It took her a moment or two to get it going, but once it was starting to crackle, she moved on to the second, near the table and chairs where she and Niall often breakfasted together.

In the growing but dim light, she noticed something sitting on the table. A box—the sort that might come from a bakery. Perhaps Turner had been out here after all?

A thought—more a memory, really—occurred to her. Her heart began to pound.

She approached the table slowly. Carefully. Reaching out a hand, she flipped the box open.

Butter biscuits.

Her stomach dropped.

The laboratory door opened and she crouched, bracing herself for a fight.

"Kara?"

"Niall," she said in relief.

He heard it in her tone and came quickly. He searched her

face and then noticed the opened box. He only looked puzzled—but then understanding flashed. "Are those—"

"Yes."

"From—"

"Yes." Fear and resentment rose within her. They mingled to make her feel physically ill. But she straightened her back and pushed them aside with a wave of determination. "I think we had better call Wooten."

The door creaked again, and they both spun to face it.

"Here you both are." Turner sounded as relieved as she felt. "You are needed in the main house. Inspector Wooten has arrived."

THE INSPECTOR SIGHED and held up a hand. Wooten was a familiar figure. A tall man with a kind face and unusually long arms, he had been helpful when Kara was wrongly accused of a murder that took place at the Great Exhibition. Niall liked the man. They had worked with him on and off since then. Right now he wore an expression of slight exasperation that they had pulled from him more than once before.

"Hold just a moment." Reaching into his pocket, the inspector pulled out the notebook they had seen him use numerous times on other cases. "You tell me what has put you both in a tizzy, then I will share my news."

"Oh dear. Our apologies, Inspector Wooten," Kara said, contrite. "We've set upon you with barely a civil greeting. It is good to see you again, sir. I see Turner has made sure you have tea."

"I've sent for a tray of crumpets as well, Your Grace," Turner said.

Hang the tea and crumpets. Niall wanted to shout it. Petra Scot was back, and he had a cold knot of dread sitting in his chest.

Wooten sat poised, waiting.

"Petra Scot." Kara drew a deep breath. "She's been here. At Bluefield."

"What?" A gasp came from the parlor door, where Gyda stood, with Stayme trying to push past her.

"Come in, come in." Niall beckoned them. "We are all in this up to our necks, and it will save time trying to repeat everything later." He knew he sounded irritable, but it was nothing to how he felt.

"It started yesterday, with Stayme." He nodded as the viscount took the armchair by the fire. "Tell them."

Stayme told his tale with dramatic flourish. Wooten, used to the old man, merely let him go on, taking notes all the while. He asked a couple of questions, then turned to Kara. "Now, tell me about this morning."

"Last night," Kara corrected him. "Niall, tell him about the gate."

Niall explained. Wooten made notes again.

Kara took up the tale. "Then, this morning, I went to my lab and found a box of butter biscuits waiting for me on the table."

Gyda grasped the significance even faster than Niall had. "Not from Eliassen's?"

Kara nodded, and Gyda looked grim.

"It wasn't you who left them there?" Wooten looked to Turner, who shook his head. "Or the cook?"

"No one from our staff has been in the lab since the duke and duchess departed on their trip," the butler assured him.

"The biscuits are significant because they came from Eliassen's Bakery, where I first met Petra face to face," Kara told the inspector. "She tried them on my recommendation." She pressed her lips together for a moment. "And on the night that she was captured, I arrived at her lair with a box of them to leave as a calling card."

"You mean, before all hell broke loose and you burned the place down and dismantled her entire organization," Wooten said dryly.

Kara shrugged.

"She's playing with us," Niall growled.

"Wait," Gyda protested. "I thought she was spotted in Vienna not so long ago?"

"We don't believe she was there for long," Wooten said. "She has not been welcomed abroad. Her former allies have labeled her a failure and abandoned her and her League of Dissolution. She has found no place to land, it seems, and has been chased out of several spots in Europe. We know she is definitely back in England now, though."

"And likely in a temper," muttered Stayme.

"Just so," agreed Wooten. "It's why I came to warn you. Since her escape, her road has been rocky and treacherous." He glanced at Niall, then at Kara. "You two are high on her list of people to blame. We cannot know if she came back for vengeance, but I think we must act as if she has."

"If your people have spotted her, why hasn't she been picked up?" Gyda asked tartly.

"She is slippery," Wooten said on a sigh. "But we are looking for her. It should not be long before we have her. She's burned as many bridges here as she has abroad."

"Which means she might be getting desperate," Niall bit out. "It will only make her more dangerous."

"You are right." Wooten sounded solemn. "I wanted to tell you all to be careful. You are all already gathered here. Perhaps you should stay here together for a few days."

"She's already breached Bluefield's defenses once," Stayme griped.

"It won't happen again," Niall vowed.

"I trust that it won't." Wooten sounded damnably calm. "Stay here. Stay alert."

"What about William Barnstaple?" asked Kara. The man had been Petra's second-in-command when she was wreaking havoc with the League of Dissolution. "You believed he was the one who freed her from government custody, didn't you? Perhaps she is collaborating with him again."

"We've seen no sign of him since her escape. If he is in England, then he is well hidden."

"Which raises the question—why is she not well hidden as well?" Kara asked. "Certainly, she has the skills for it. Why flounce about and let us know she is back?"

"Because she wants us to know she is coming," Niall answered grimly. "She wants her revenge, and she's telling us she's started the game."

"It's hardly a game," objected Kara.

"To her it is," Gyda chimed in. "We've already beaten her at it once. We'll do it again."

Niall hoped like hell that she was right. He stood. "Turner, gather the footmen. I'm going to set up a schedule so that someone is always on watch. Kara, have the housekeeper ready some rooms. We will need a few extra men."

A knock sounded on the parlor door. "Excuse me, Your Grace." Tom, the underbutler, looked pale when Niall yanked it open. "But this has just been discovered fixed to the front door." He held out a folded paper.

"Just now?" Niall asked, taking it. He opened it and read what was written inside. Anger bloomed on his face. He thrust the paper back to Kara and pushed past Tom, heading for the front of the house.

He heard Kara read the finely printed message out loud.

Enjoy your biscuits.
While you may.

Niall was already moving toward the front door, but he heard Wooten speak. "It wasn't on the door when I was admitted."

The inspector was on his heels in moments. "She might not have placed it there, herself," he said as Niall yanked the door open.

Niall gazed over the empty drive and carefully tended

grounds. "Perhaps not," he said quietly. "But either she or one of her minions stood right here, just moments ago. While were sipping our damned tea."

"She's goading you."

"It's working." He sighed. "I'm going out to scout around, but I already know I won't find anything. You should go back to the parlor, Wooten. Tell them I'll return shortly." He paused. "We brought you and Mrs. Wooten something back from Oslo. Kara will wish to present it to you before you go. Please keep us updated. We will do the same." He strode out.

Niall moved quickly, searching amongst the outbuildings and gardens and along the wooded sections of the estate. As expected, he found no sign of an intruder.

Such a short time, but he'd already become used to living without the weight of secrets and dread. Now they felt twice as heavy as he shouldered the burden again. But shoulder them he would. Petra Scot may have made the first move in her game of vengeance, but Niall meant to win.

Chapter Three

F OR A WEEK, they all lingered easily enough at Bluefield Park.
Between them, Niall and Stayme turned the estate into a
fortress. Guards manned the entrances and patrolled the
boundaries at variable schedules. The hidden gate was securely
padlocked. "No one is getting through here without making a
significant racket," Niall said with satisfaction as he fastened the
last chain.

Kara thought it was going a bit far, but her husband—how
she enjoyed saying that, even to herself—convinced Turner that
they should go together to inspect every inch of Bluefield's secret
tunnels. They were all clear, as Kara had insisted they would be,
but it eased Niall's nerves to be sure.

They kept themselves busy for the week, and even for a few
days beyond.

Kara and Harold finished the design for the Green Man automaton. Kara got him started on the initial framing and let him
carry on while she drafted a plan for the project for her next
client. It was a picnic scene, complete with figures eating tiny
sandwiches and strawberries, a thieving squirrel, and a child
holding a kite that lifted aloft, as if on the wind.

Gyda kept both herself and Kara's lady's maid, Elsie, busy.
They were sewing an elaborate traditional Nordic dress to go

with her new jewelry.

Stayme kept a couple of trusted couriers running ragged as he conducted his business from Bluefield. When he wasn't working, he buzzed around the rest of them and their projects, offering advice, criticism, and praise.

Niall fired up his forge and started on his marshland-themed gates, but he kept pausing to check in with the patrols and read over Wooten's updates, which arrived every couple of days.

"Still nothing!" he exclaimed. Kara could feel his frustration as he handed her the latest missive. They were approaching the middle of the second week. "How can Petra have disappeared so completely?"

"Perhaps she has left the country once again?" Turner ventured.

"I've had no word of it," Stayme said. "And I've had people watching."

"They cannot watch every ship that leaves every port," Kara said with a sigh. "Not even your net stretches so fine."

"Perhaps she's just lurking around here, waiting for her chance," Gyda mused.

The thought sent a shiver down Kara's spine. "If she is, then I hope she is seething in frustration." She squared her shoulders. "And I am happy for her to continue to do so."

Gyda's words stayed with Kara all day. In the evening, she decided to dissipate some of her nervous energy in her gymnasium.

It was a special room fashioned from a walled-off section of the ballroom. The place had been designed by her father and some of the consultants he had hired to train her when she was young. Much of the ballroom décor was hidden behind equipment, and parts of the wooden floor were covered in mats. She had spent many hours in here back then, and kept up a good bit of her training even after her father's death, but it had been some time since she'd used it.

She roamed idly about a moment, lighting the lamps. The

one mirrored wall reflected the light, making the space bright—useful for studying one's opponent. She swished a fencing foil back and forth a few times, but she had no partner to spar with.

Her thoughts went back to the last time they had matched wits with Petra Scot and her followers. There had been some physical encounters then, as well. The recollection led her to assemble a rough circle of wirework dummies. They were a varied lot, padded out to represent opponents of different heights and sizes. It had been a trick taught to her by an Irish fellow, a master of the *shillelagh*, a club or walking stick sometimes called a fighting stick. The instrument was very useful for defending oneself, and Kara had been trained to use it to fight off an attacker.

She had several sticks of varying sizes and lengths in a rack on the wall. She took down her favorite, stepped into the circle, crouched into a fighting stance, then began to move. Whirling, striking, and jabbing, she hit one opponent in the throat, the next in the kidney. *Spin. Strike. Knee. Groin. Head.* She pushed herself hard. *Think. Strategize. Hit.*

It had been too long, she realized. She tired too quickly, although her aim remained true. She stopped, panting, and resolved to get back to her training more often. Still breathing heavily, she eyed the rope that hung from the high ceiling.

She hated that rope. It had taken her a ridiculously long time to conquer it and consistently reach the top. She winced at the thought of tackling it again, but avoiding the hard things would be of no help. She pulled in a great gulp of air, grabbed the rope, closed her eyes a moment, then jumped high and began to climb.

Her arms grew tired. It took her a moment to remember just how to lock the rope with her feet so that she could use her legs. So slow. But she gritted her teeth and pushed on. When she reached the top, she braced herself with her feet, threw back her head, and sucked in celebratory air. She hung there for a triumphant moment before going carefully back down, hand over hand.

When she reached the bottom, she was startled by the sound of rapid clapping. Harold rushed in, his eyes shining. "Gor! That was somethin'!" In his enthusiasm, a bit of his old street accent crept back. "Kara! I can't believe you can do that!" He looked around, clearly entranced. "I didn't even know this was back here!"

"That was rather by design," she admitted.

"But things change."

She looked up to see Niall following the lad in, carrying a laden tea tray.

"Come," he said. "Pull out one of those mats and we will have a picnic."

Kara moved to arrange the space. Niall set down his burden, then poured water from a tall pitcher. "Water first, then tea."

She saw he had also brought a plate of her favorite cream-filled pastries. Raising a brow, she settled next to Harold. "This smacks of a conspiracy."

"A small one," Niall admitted. "Young Harold has a proposition for you."

"Does he?" The water was cool, and her curiosity was piqued.

Harold looked nervous. Also, he was not attacking the pastries, which was a sure sign that he was preoccupied.

"I…I want to take lessons," he blurted.

"Beyond the Latin and mathematics that you are studying now? What subject is it that you would like to explore?"

"I want to *train*, Kara," her ward said, excited. "Like you did! Like what you just did with that rope. Fighting, climbing, escaping, hiding. I want to learn it all, just like you."

The request hit her like a blow. All of her nervous anxiety rushed back. She felt such a *failure*. "Oh," was all she managed to get out. She had to blink back tears.

"Kara," Niall said with concern.

Harold looked aghast. "I didn't mean to upset you!" He drew a deep breath. "They still talk of you, you know. In the city, throughout Covent Garden, in the alleys. The rich nob's daughter who can slip through the streets unseen, scale a wall like a monkey, and take down a street thug with one blow. I want to learn it all too." He took her hand. "I want to be like you."

She bit her lip, hard. "When I took you as my ward, Harold, my greatest wish was for you to live a life in which you didn't have to learn those things."

"I don't have to. I *want* to." He looked stubborn suddenly. "Back on the streets, when I was cold and hungry and the runt of the crew...back then, if I could have picked any life I could have—any at all—I would have picked *this*." He smiled tremulously. "Here. With you and Niall. And Gyda and Turner and Stayme. Watching you and learning from you—how to act, how to be a family, art, and forging, and mechanics, even Latin." He made a face.

Kara squeezed his hand. "I was always fearful, watchful, on edge, as a child."

"Yes, but it worked! Those men came for you and you escaped. Four times!"

"Three times," she said. "Three times I evaded them."

"Only because you were not ready the first time."

"I never wanted you to live in fear, Harold." Niall made a noise, and she rolled her eyes at him. "Yes. I recognize the absurdity of such a statement, given that the lad was so recently poisoned. Not to mention our current predicament. I'm sorry, Harold."

"I want to do my part," the boy insisted. "I want to help protect the family."

The family. Her heart eased a little to hear him say it. Yes. They were a family. And he deserved equal footing in it.

"I would feel less afraid if I could do some of the things you can," the boy cajoled.

"I understand." Her gaze met Niall's. "I assume you have already encouraged him in this?"

Her husband shrugged. "I told him you would decide. But I don't believe it will harm him to learn. It's not going to attract trouble, Kara."

"No, there's no need of that. It finds us all on its own." She sighed. "I know you are right." She eyed Harold sternly. "If I agree, you will have to abide by the same rules I did. That means studying first—and if you fall behind in your lessons, then the training will pause."

Harold nodded eagerly.

"And one more thing."

He waited.

"You must study fencing. I need a sparring partner."

"That's all? I can do it?"

She nodded. "You can."

He launched himself at her and hugged her tightly around the neck. "Thank you! Thank you!"

"You are welcome." She held him for a moment. "We will make arrangements. But for now, sit back and pass me those pastries."

❊❊❊

THE INTERLUDE LED to Harold's satisfaction, but a couple of more days of their isolation stretched out and began to lead to frustration for the others.

"I'm going to go and speak with Wooten myself," Niall announced as they sat in the parlor one evening. "There must be something else we can do to find the damned woman. Perhaps I will also go and consult Towland. I'll have him set the members of the Druidic Order to investigating."

"I'll go along," Stayme chimed in. "There are files that I must have, if I'm to extend my stay here."

"I'll take the train into Town with you both," Gyda said. "Charles writes that he has good news and something to show me."

Nerves flaring, Kara stood. "I am not sure," she said, pacing to the hearth and back around again. "Perhaps it is too soon."

"We cannot stay locked up here forever," Gyda told her. "For all we know, Petra could be on the Continent again, or on her way to the Americas. She'd be laughing at the thought of us holed up here, hiding from nothing."

Kara couldn't explain the dark foreboding that clawed at her every time she thought of that note. "I don't think we are hiding from nothing."

"Stayme and I will stay together," Niall said, frowning. "We will take every precaution. But Gyda—"

"Let me send a note with one of your couriers, Stayme," Gyda interrupted. "I'll have Charles pick me up at the train station. He's the son of one of the most powerful men in the realm. I'll be safe as houses." She sighed. "It's been too long since I've seen him."

"I still don't like it," Kara objected. She couldn't stop pacing.

"We cannot keep at this stalemate forever," Niall said grimly. "But we must all be very careful. Prepared." Standing, he drew Kara into his arms. "You and Harold will be safe here. But you must stay alert as well."

Nodding, she burrowed further into his arms.

Chapter Four

THEY ALL LEFT early the next morning. Kara and Harold breakfasted, then went together to the laboratory. A shiver shook Kara as they passed the forge, gone cold and quiet for the first time in a while.

"I think I remember all the gears and sequences needed to make the Green Man's arm raise his sword," Harold said as he donned an apron over his clothes. "I'll start on the arm and show you before I attach it."

Kara smiled. Harold liked to include a sword in all of his automaton figures, because he could forge the blade with Niall. She couldn't object to his urge to combine their arts.

They spent a quiet, productive morning, then paused to take luncheon back in the house.

"Mr. Welk is due to arrive this afternoon," Turner reminded them as he placed a platter of cold ham on the table.

"Oh, yes." Kara had forgotten that today was the day the mathematics instructor visited Harold. "Do you have the problems he left for you all worked out?" she asked.

"Yes, although the last one took me a good long time, only because I'd left off a null sign," Harold confessed. "I had to go back, and then I realized."

"Good for you, for figuring out where you went off track.

That is a skill that will translate into many aspects of life." Kara smiled at Turner. "And if Mr. Welk is due, then that means it is your half day today. What do you have planned for your afternoon off?"

The butler hesitated. "Perhaps I should delay my plans until tomorrow, seeing as the others have not yet returned."

"Delay what plans?" Kara raised her brows. Turner could be remarkably non-forthcoming about his private time.

"Well, the Camleighs have left for Shropshire, on a visit with their eldest daughter."

The Camleighs were the family at Wood Rose Abbey. "Ah, so you and Mrs. Canning have an afternoon together? Of course, you should go."

"I don't like to leave you…" But Turner sounded hesitant.

Kara's anxiety spiked a bit, but she heard the note in her friend's tone. He *wanted* to go. Turner had a life of his own. She'd had to remind herself of that since she was a girl, and she hated the thought of her troubles interfering with it. "Nonsense. What did you have planned?"

"Perhaps just a stroll into the village."

"Then you'll be right here in the neighborhood, won't you?" She brightened. "Actually, you might wish to take my little chaise. You and Mrs. Canning can drive out. That seems…" She glanced at Harold and stopped herself before she said *safer*. They were still doing their best not to alarm him. "…better? Doesn't it?" she finished.

"Perhaps I should just stick close to Bluefield," Turner said.

"Well, you are always welcome to invite Mrs. Canning to spend the afternoon here." Well aware of the rivalry between Turner's love interest and her own housekeeper, she doubted he would agree to that suggestion.

He pursed his lips. "Perhaps you are right. A drive might be just the thing. Thank you, Your Grace."

"Just keep alert, will you?" she asked with a raise of a brow.

"Of course."

After luncheon, Harold went to prepare for his mathematics lesson while Kara settled into the ivory sitting room, at the drafting desk in the corner. She set to work sketching out the mechanism that would unfurl the kite on the picnic automaton. It was the most complex part of the piece. She had done something similar before, but on a much larger scale. Adjustments would have to be made.

Time passed, but she scarcely noticed, she'd become so lost in the connections and their mechanics. She jumped when a footman knocked upon the door and thrust it open at the same time.

"Your Grace! Can you come? One of the guards says there is a woman at the gates. They will not let her through, and she is in a lather!"

Kara's belly clenched. A woman? Surely it was not Petra Scot? But who, then?

She stood. "Is Mr. Welk still here?"

"Yes, ma'am."

"Good." She strode out into the passage. "Make sure he stays upstairs and keeps Harold occupied. Take him aside to explain, if you must."

Tom was waiting for her in the entry hall. "I'm going with you," the underbutler declared. "Please don't try to stop me, Your Grace. You know it's what Turner and the duke would both insist on."

"Thank you, Tom," she said, grateful for an ally. The young man had proven useful in the past.

She rushed out and followed the drive down to the gate. As they drew near, Tom positioned himself in front of her. She craned her neck to see around him. She could hear men talking loudly and feminine...sobbing?

She stepped around Tom, then rushed to the gate. "Open it! Open it!" she called. "Mrs. Canning?" Dread threatened to choke her as the disheveled housekeeper fell into her arms. "Are you all right? Where is Turner?"

"Oh, Your Grace! Thank the heavens above! That's what I've been trying to tell these men. Please, tell them to come! Turner has been hurt!"

※≫✕≪※

IT HAD BEEN a frustrating trip for Niall. Wooten had been unable to provide any new information about Petra or her whereabouts.

"We thought we'd found William Barnstaple, but it turned out to be *Billy* Barnstaple, a fifty-year-old manager in a tannery in Bermondsey." The inspector shook his head. "Either she's left England again or she's tucked herself well away in a hidey-hole."

"She must be up to something nefarious. Surely she did not come back only to harass Kara and me."

"Oh, I'm sure she has something else up her sleeve. I just haven't figured out what it is. Yet." Wooten cast a sidelong glance his way. "We have interviewed the educators who raised her. They were no more thrilled than you to hear she is back, but they haven't seen her or heard from her."

"She already ruined them," Niall said. "She confessed as much to Kara. It was one of the first acts she pursued, along with her fellow founding members of the League of Dissolution. No. She's a planner, that one. I'd wager she's got some new scheme in mind. She's likely just playing with us in the meantime."

"Not everything burned in that fire in Seven Dials, you know. We recovered some of the League's files. They were investing." Wooten consulted his notebook. "In railways, metal plating for ships, and something called the Submarine Telegraph Company."

"Yes," Niall said bitterly. "That was their aim. Start a war and profit from it. She admitted it without compunction."

"Companies like that are no strangers to their large investors," Wooten said. "I have men talking to each of them, hoping there might have been some contact."

"Investments will likely lead you to Barnstaple. He was the

one who was good with numbers and strategy."

"I strongly feel that finding him will lead to her," said Wooten. He sounded confident.

"I hope you are right."

Niall had worse luck with Arthur Towland. His friend was the senior member of the Order of Druidic Bards. He was also a police court magistrate, and today he was sitting on the bench in Marylebone, inaccessible to visitors. Niall left him a note, inviting him out to Bluefield, then he and Stayme went to Berkeley Square, so the viscount could consult his staff and gather his files.

"Guts and garters, boy, your leg is moving faster than a piston on a steam engine," the old man said as he filled a box at his desk.

Niall stood to stop his leg from twitching. "I cannot help it. I was on fire to come into Town, and now all I can think of is getting back to Bluefield."

"Well, help me with this last box and we'll go," Stayme replied.

It wasn't too long before they were moving through the village of Ambleburrow and turning onto the lane that led to Bluefield. Niall found his leg jumping again as they grew closer.

He let loose a sigh of relief as they approached the gates, but as he shifted to the window, he realized they were already open. One of the posted guards was in the process of closing it before he realized who they were and started back again.

Niall put down the window. "Where's the other guard?" He'd specifically asked that they watch in pairs.

The man looked visibly nervous. "Beggin' your pardon, sir. He's gone on to help the duchess. I know there's supposed to be two of us here, but Mr. Turner's been hurt, you see. It looks bad."

"Go!" Niall called to Stayme's coachman. "Now!" He fell back as the carriage leapt forward. The drive suddenly seemed interminably long, but they made it to the front of the house. Niall jumped out before the carriage had even stopped moving.

"Kara!" She was there, her face pale and drawn as she directed several men in unloading a pallet from the back of a wagon.

Turner lay upon it, unconscious. He looked old and frail in a way that Niall had never seen. "Are you all right?"

She nodded wearily and leaned into him. "I'm fine. It's Turner and Mrs. Canning. They were in an accident. She's bruised, but only Turner was seriously hurt."

"He doesn't look good at all."

"I know," she said, worry written across her face. "He's been unconscious since we found him. There's a large lump on one side of his head. I think he has broken ribs, too." She drew in a shuddering breath. "I've sent for Dr. Balgate." She raised her voice. "Keep the pallet level, please! I want him carried up to the guest room next to my rooms. Do not remove him from the pallet, just place it on the bed. Do you need more men to help keep it level and steady?"

"I've got it." Niall stepped in to help. Between them all, they maneuvered past the crowd of gathered servants and a weeping woman he did not recognize. Working carefully, they got Turner upstairs and into the designated bedroom.

"Blankets!" Kara called, following them in. "I want him kept still and warm until Dr. Balgate arrives. I'll need warm water and towels. Hot tea and a decanter of brandy. Robert"—she pointed at one of the footmen—"go out to the icehouse and chip a good-sized bucket of ice. Bring me a full bowl and keep the rest ready in case of fever."

She started to drag a chair closer to the bed. Niall went to move it for her, laying a hand on her shoulder as she sat and took the butler's hand.

She glanced up at him. "Shouldn't he have woken up by now?"

"I don't know. Wait until Balgate sees him before you start worrying." He crouched beside her. "What happened?"

"It's my fault," she said in an agonized whisper. "It's his half day. I encouraged him to go out, as he'd planned. I offered my chaise, thinking it would be safer than walking out with Mrs. Canning. Someone was lying in wait, though. They hid in the wood that crowds the bend in the road on the way here from the village. They fired a gun right there, just as they passed. Mrs. Canning said it was a roar like thunder. The horse went wild, thrashed about, and came partly out of the traces, then dragged the chaise half-cocked down the road. It overturned, and they were both thrown. Turner suffered the worst of it." She hid her face. "I should never have pushed him to go."

"This is not your fault," Niall said sternly.

"He was wavering. He offered to stay with me and Harold. I encouraged him to go. I didn't want him to miss his personal time because of our troubles."

"You will not take this on yourself," Niall told her. "This was Petra. Or one of her minions. Any fault lies with her."

"I wish he would wake up," she whispered.

"Mrs. Canning?" Niall said suddenly. "She was downstairs? Weeping?"

"Oh, yes. Would you see to her, Niall? I don't want to leave Turner."

"Of course." Grateful for something useful to do, he stood, only to be pulled aside by Elsie, Kara's personal maid.

"Your Grace, would you have a more comfortable chair brought in here?" She gestured toward Kara. "It's my guess we will scarce be able to drag her away."

Niall agreed. He spoke to a footman, then headed downstairs in search of Turner's lady friend. He found that the staff had taken the woman in hand. He found her in the kitchens with hot tea and several sympathetic shoulders.

"Mrs. Canning?" he asked gently. She jumped to her feet, along with the others. "Sit, please," he said to them all. "I thought I would offer to escort you home," he told the visibly shaken woman.

Her face collapsed in relief. "Oh, thank you, indeed, Your Grace. I was dreading the walk." Her lip trembled. "Turner? He will be...?"

"We have the duchess's own doctor on the way," Niall reassured her. "Dr. Balgate cured Harold when he was very ill indeed. I have every confidence that he will do the same for Turner."

The housekeeper nodded gratefully. She looked around. "I hope someone will send news of his recovery?"

She departed amongst assurances. Niall saw her to his own coach, then took John Coachman aside. "Keep your eyes peeled and the horses under a tight rein," he said, low.

"Aye." John had clearly heard the details of the accident.

As they set off, Niall asked Mrs. Canning to point out the spot where the incident had occurred. She agreed, but held her silence as they traveled, even when they passed a couple of grooms bringing the battered chaise back home. As they grew closer, she leaned forward and indicated the spot.

"I do hope you will be able to catch the villain who did this," she said. "It's not right, setting out to harm someone who has done nothing to you."

"I mean to," he answered. "I mean to put a stop to this."

Niall delivered her safely home before directing John back to the scene. There were scuffs in the lane from where the chaise had been dragged, but nothing in the spot where the shooter must have lain in wait. He widened his search and eventually found half a boot print in a soft patch of dirt.

"I couldn't even tell if it was a man or a woman's boot," he told Stayme later, as they lurked on the threshold of the guest room. "Just middling sized, with no distinguishing features."

"I told you, she's good, that Scot woman." The viscount shook his head. "Neither she nor her hirelings are going to make this easy on us."

"What did Balgate say?" Niall asked. He could see that the doctor had visited, as the pallet was gone and Turner had been thoroughly washed and dressed in a nightshirt.

"He wanted to know when we are going to stop making him dance on the end of our stick," Stayme said wryly. "He confirmed the broken ribs and wrapped them. He praised Kara for her quick thinking with the ice, which is apparently something they found useful when they were working with his amputees. Balgate thinks Turner will awaken when the swelling on that lump goes down. He's down in the stillroom, brewing up a poultice to slather on it."

Sighing, Niall entered to crouch down next to Kara. "Come down and take some dinner? Stayme will sit with him while you get away for just a few minutes."

"No, thank you," she replied absently. "Elsie will bring me a tray."

"My love—" he began.

She stopped him with a hand to his arm. "Please, Niall." She rested her head on his shoulder. "You already know what I'm going to say."

"Yes." Her loyalty to Turner was unshakable—with good reason. "He never gave up on you."

When Kara had been kidnapped as a child, even Scotland Yard had been unable to uncover the villains. It had been Turner, a footman at Bluefield Park at the time, who had put together the clues. When the police ignored his theory, he risked himself to save her.

"I'll stay here," she said. "I want to be here when he wakes." Niall's stomach gave a loud rumble, making her smile. "You two go and have your dinner."

"I'll come up and sit with you once we finish."

"Good."

He kissed her hand and went down to dine with Stayme. They were just finishing when a pale-faced Prudence entered.

Tom stepped forward to intercept her. The downstairs maid usually had no place in the dining room, but Niall waved him off.

Prudence gave a curtsy. "I do beg your pardon for interrupting, but Your Grace, this was just found on the front door." Hand shaking, she extended a folded note.

Alarm and anger kindled in Niall's belly as he took it. They burst into full flame when he read the note. Raising his head, he handed it to Stayme, then gave both the servants a hard look.

"Not a word of this," he growled. "Is that understood? Tell no one about this, for now. I don't want Kara to know anything about it until Turner is awake and stable."

Standing, he looked to Stayme. "Keep a sharp eye on things here, won't you? I have a few calls to make in Town." He paused and looked back at the viscount. "Wait a moment. You have people trained to dig in and ferret out secrets. Let's put them to use." He leaned in and spoke low near Stayme's ear before straightening again. "Find out all you can, will you? We might need a bit of leverage."

Chapter Five

FOR NEARLY TWO days, Kara kept her vigil beside Turner's bed. Twice, she thought he was about to awaken. He would move purposefully, grimace, but then fall back, inert once more.

She decided to take it as a hopeful sign. Because she could not bear for it to be anything else.

She intermittently applied cold and Balgate's poultice to the lump on Turner's head. She made sure he was kept warm and clean. Occasionally, she would prop him up and try to dribble a bit of honey-laced tea into him.

Niall and Elsie kept her supplied with trays of food and endless mugs of tea. Everyone else visited, sitting beside her, talking in whispers of how they would spoil Turner when he finally woke.

"I'll make him scads of clotted cream," Cook promised. She'd come up for a *quick peek in,* as she put it. "And I will not say a word about how thick he loads up his scones."

"When he wakes up, tell him I have kept up with my studies," Harold urged in a whisper. "And tell him I have finally learned how to move my feet without thinking about it too hard, when I am fencing!"

"Tell him I've kept all the grates spit-spot clean," Prudence said when she came to fetch Kara's tray. "He has no cause to worry about the downstairs rooms."

"They are all too nice," Gyda declared. "When he wakes up, I am going to tease him about how far he is willing to go to make Mrs. Canning worry about him."

Niall, wisely, merely sat beside her in watchful silence.

And at last, late on the second night, just as Kara had been about to lie down on the cot she'd had brought in, Turner stirred, sighed, and opened his eyes. Heart pounding, she reached out to take his hand. "Well. Good evening to you." She had to blink back tears of relief.

He noticed the tears. "Evening?" he rasped. Alarmed, he tried to sit up, but gasped in pain and fell back.

"Easy," Kara warned. "You have some broken ribs."

"What? What happened?" His voice gave out, and she poured a cup of barley water that Balgate had left.

He sipped at first, but then drank thirstily. Handing it back, he frowned around at his surroundings. "Where—? The guest room?"

"Yes. The one right next to my rooms. We are at Bluefield," she reminded him. "I know you would likely prefer your own bed, but there is not enough room to maneuver in that monk's cell you call a bedroom."

"What's happened?" Turner reached up to gingerly touch his head. "Oh, yes. The chaise. I'm so sorry! There was a shot. It spooked the horse." His eyes widened. "Mrs. Canning? Is she—?"

"She's fine," Kara soothed. "Just a little bruised. She'll be so relieved to hear that you've awakened."

He blinked and looked around once more. "How long?"

"Two days, nearly."

"Good heavens," he whispered. He scowled at her. "You have not been sitting here all of that time, have you?"

She merely raised a brow at him.

"Miss!" he said, then shook his head. "Your Grace, I mean."

"You are not to worry. Balgate has been here. He'll be back in the morning. You had a knock to the head, but he crafted something noxious to cover it with, and it seems to have finally done the job." She squeezed his hand. "You will have to play the invalid for a while. I know you will hate it, but needs must."

"No. No. Two days? There must be a hundred things that need looking after."

"The ship is not the same without you at the helm, but we will get by. It is your recovery that is important now."

Turner relaxed a little at this reassurance. But then his eyes narrowed. "This is the work of that woman, isn't it? Petra Scot."

"We assume it must have been her or one of her lackeys. But there's been no further sign of her since." She waved a hand. "Forget her. Now is the time for you to drink the rest of that water and rest. If you tolerate it well, perhaps Balgate will allow you a bit of breakfast in the morning."

He drank the rest down, and that seemed to exhaust him. Turner lay back and was soon asleep again. But she thought it was just a natural sleep, at last.

Sighing in relief, she sat back and watched him for a while before turning to the cot, feeling lighter and more hopeful than she had since the accident.

The next morning was a flurry of activity as Turner awakened early and the good news spread. Kara finally left him in Balgate's care. She had a long bath and a decent breakfast. She sat with Harold a bit before she took care of a few things she had neglected. It was nearly noon when Niall took her aside, leading her to the ivory sitting room and shutting the door.

Her heart dropped. "What is it? Has she struck again?"

Niall handed her a folded bit of paper. "This was found on the front door. The same evening as Turner's accident."

She steeled herself, then flipped it open.

I owed you that one, Kara Levett
For Clémence

Kara drew a long, shuddering breath. Shaking, she covered her mouth with a hand. "She's not going to stop, Niall," she whispered.

"No," he agreed.

"We—" She stopped, cocking her head. "Listen. Do you hear shouting?"

They both jumped as someone pounded on the door. "Your Grace! Your Graces!"

Kara leapt to her feet, but Niall beat her to the door.

"A fire! There's a fire!" the maid said, breathless.

Niall was out and running.

Kara grabbed the maid, who had fallen back out of the way and now stood staring off after him. "Where?" she demanded.

The girl sucked in a breath. "At your laboratory, Your Grace."

"Harold? Is he still upstairs?"

"Aye, I believe so, ma'am."

Kara took off. *Damn these skirts.* But she lifted them high and flew as fast as she could out the front, over the drive, and along the path, past the forge, on toward the lab.

A crowd had gathered at the far front corner of the building. Groomsmen and stable lads, mostly, along with a few gardeners—and Niall.

He nodded reassuringly as she pulled up, breathing hard. "It's all right. It's out already. One of the stable lads spotted the smoke. They dealt with it quickly." He rested a hand on a young man's shoulder.

Kara straightened. "Zachariah, isn't it?"

The stripling, just on the verge of manhood and gangly with it, nodded shyly.

"Thank you." She looked over the collection of buckets, a pile of wet and steaming horse blankets, and the black, charred corner of the building. "Thank you so much. Your keen senses and your quick action have saved the day." She glanced around, meeting the gaze of everyone there. "Thank you all."

The young man shuffled, wringing his hat in his hands. "We know how much your laboratory means to you, Your Grace."

"It does, indeed. But your safety and the well-being of all of us here at Bluefield Park means more. There are chemicals and cleaning agents inside that could have sparked an inferno. The fire could have raged on or sparked and spread to the other outbuildings. You all prevented that, and I'm so grateful."

Niall stepped forward and addressed them all. "We are under siege, lads. I know you've heard we have an enemy working against us. It is clear these people do not care who they harm in their quest for vengeance." He looked at the damaged corner of the building, at his wife, and back at the group of men. "Today you've stolen their victory. Well done, all of you."

Someone gave a whoop.

"We've all got an eye out, Your Grace," said John Coachman. "They shouldn't have got here at all." He shook his head. "It won't happen again."

Murmuring darkly, the men broke off, leaving in groups.

Kara stood, staring at the smoke marks and the bit of damaged building.

"It will be a quick repair," Niall said. "We'll just have to make sure we brace everything well."

She nodded. "They really did save the day. I doubt there is a mark on the inside." She looked up at him, the ire inside her rising. "Niall, you know what this means. We cannot go on like this."

"Wooten—"

"Wooten will do as he must. It hasn't led to any results yet, has it?" She shook her head. "No." Fury simmered in her belly and sent tendrils creeping up her spine. "We are done. No more waiting for her to come to us." She looked at Niall with determination. "We cannot let her harm anyone we love, not again. We have to find her. Even if we do it ourselves."

Relief washed over her when he nodded his agreement. "That was my thought exactly."

KARA WISHED TO hold an immediate meeting and begin planning right away, but Niall convinced her to wait until Gyda returned. His friend and assistant had seen Turner this morning—and teased him mercilessly—before going into London once more. She had spoken of a meeting between Lord Charles Osbourne and some of her friends in the city's artistic community.

Grumbling, Kara agreed to wait. She went to wash away the smell of smoke before she settled at her desk, writing a growing stack of letters. She sent them out with a courier, grouched a little more upon learning Gyda was still away, then retreated to her rooms with her maid, Elsie. While she kept busy working on her converted skirts, adjusting them for ease of movement and adding hidden pockets for useful implements, Niall retreated to the study, where he went through the post and sent out a few more private messages.

Feeling restless afterward, he collected Harold and went out to the forge. His arm had been injured on their last adventure, at his new estate in Scotland. It was recovering, and the bridal trip had provided a nice rest for the healing muscles, but it was time he started getting it back in working condition, and since he needed a distraction…now was as good a time as any.

"Put your mind to work," he told Harold as he set about forging long stems and leaves for the wetland-inspired project. "I'd like to get some real texture on the cattail heads we mean to put in the foreground."

"How about we heat them and take a wire brush to them?" the boy suggested. He was shaping tree branches at his own, smaller anvil.

"That will work, but I've a mind to make it more realistic. I'm turning it about in my head, and I hoped you would do the same."

Harold nodded and went back to work.

After a couple of hours, Niall's arm began to ache. He called a halt and took Harold back to the house so they could both bathe. Niall was just finishing up and getting dressed when Stayme burst in.

"It's not as strong as we might have hoped for, but it's something," he said, waving a paper.

Niall took it with a questioning look.

"It's the report you requested," Stayme explained.

Niall read it over, frowning deeply as he went further. "Odin's arse, but people can be the very devil, can't they?"

"So they can, but at least we can use it against him."

"Yes. Put it together with the other information we've gathered, and it might do the trick." He glanced out the window at the afternoon light. "Where the hell is Gyda?"

"Must we wait for her?" Stayme grumbled.

Niall shrugged. "It's too late to make this particular call, in any case."

"If she doesn't return by morning, we should move ahead," the viscount insisted. "The timing regarding the man's request to the Crown is crucial."

Niall agreed, but in the end, it wasn't necessary. Gyda returned to Bluefield late that evening. She blew in looking breathless and happy, just as Niall convinced his wife to sit down with him in the parlor.

"Niall! Kara! It's so exciting! It's happening!"

Kara sat up straighter. "Here you are at last! What's happening?"

"Charles has found a suitable space. He can move ahead with his plans!"

"Plans?" asked Niall.

"It's all coming together." Gyda dropped onto the settee with a happy sigh. She grinned at Stayme as he entered and closed the door behind him. "I told you that Charles is very interested in the idea of craftsmanship and creation. He wants to establish a museum dedicated to the creative process, to the design and construction of both art and functional objects, even industrial works. He believes it all has beauty and value. He believes that artists, craft masters, and inventors should be celebrated. He wants to display selected works and also incorporate an interactive element to the place as well, so that ordinary people might see creation in progress—just as you did, Kara, when you worked on your automatons at your spot in the Great Exhibition."

"The attendees were fascinated seeing her at work," Niall said.

"Exactly!" Gyda said. "People might be inspired. Who knows what might come of it? At the very least, they might become more appreciative, seeing the artistic or inventive process in action. Charles has been in contact with various critics, masters, and artists. I told him that you might put him in the way of inventors or industrial specialists, Kara." She turned to Niall. "And you will never guess just who Charles means to work with."

He raised a questioning brow.

"Your friend—Ansel Wells. Did you know that he has opened a gallery?"

"What? No. How?" It hadn't been so long since Niall had spent a few nights on Ansel's sofa, in his suited-to-a-starving-artist single-room flat.

"He received an inheritance and bought a bang-up building with plenty of light and a charming little studio attached for his own painting. He's very interested in helping Charles. They mean to use the gallery space to begin the museum, and Ansel is eager to recruit artists to be featured there."

"It sounds intriguing," Niall admitted.

"It will be *glorious*," Gyda corrected him. She peered around at the three of them. "I thought you would be more excited about the idea. What is it? Is Turner...not mending?"

"Turner is fine," Niall assured her.

"Balgate says he can get out of bed after a few days," Kara told her. "His ribs need time to heal."

"What is it, then?" Gyda demanded. "That Scot woman?"

Niall explained about the fire and showed her the note.

"The wicked cow," Gyda breathed.

Kara leaned forward in her seat. "She's tried to kill Turner in revenge. I did subdue Clémence Wilkes with her own ether, that day in the labyrinth in Seven Dials, but she was awake, lucid, and on her feet when Petra went into a raging temper. Miss Scot caused the fall and the blow to her friend's temple that killed her, yet she blames me." She scowled. "It is a warped and immature mind that cannot accept one's own faults and mistakes. I have plenty of my own sins to answer for. I won't take that woman's on as well."

"The thought that worries me is that, having failed, she may try again," Niall said.

"Worse, now we know she continues to plot additional revenge. She could go after any of you next."

"We already knew we were all in her sights," Stayme said wryly. "She likely holds us all responsible for her woes."

"I've sent notes to Moseman and to the executives in charge of my factories and other holdings. They need to be wary of sabotage. She might try to dismantle my organizations if she blames me for the loss of hers."

Kara folded her arms, and Niall took a moment to appreciate that familiar look of determination.

"We cannot sit here and wait for her to strike again," she declared.

Gyda straightened. "I should say not."

"Wooten's progress has been slow. Too slow. We need to find her ourselves," said Kara.

Stayme looked interested. "And do what with her, should you find her?"

Niall had been pondering the same question. "We'll turn her over to the Crown, if possible."

Kara pursed her lips. "And we will do what is necessary, if it is not."

"Now we are getting somewhere." Stayme pointed at Kara. "Finding the Scot woman is the first problem, but you have another."

"What is that?"

Niall knew what the old man was going to say. "The note. The second one left on the door. And the fire. Someone set it."

"Indeed." Stayme looked stern. "Neither Petra nor her lackeys should have been able to penetrate our defenses twice." He shook his head. "No. You have a traitor here at Bluefield."

Kara's face fell.

"Who?" Gyda demanded.

"I don't know. Yet. But I will find out," the viscount vowed. "Turner can help me. It will keep him occupied as he recovers."

Kara looked crestfallen. "I hate the thought that someone here might have worked against us. And to go so far as to set that fire?"

"Let Stayme handle that," Gyda said. "We must cut the head off the snake. That means concentrating on finding Petra Scot." She grimaced. "But how?" Shooting a look at the viscount, Gyda raised a brow. "I assume you've been at work on it?"

"I have." Stayme glanced at Niall. "*We* have."

"I've been thinking about it all day," Kara said. "The woman is diminished and alone. Who do we go to when such circumstances strike us? We go back to the beginning. We go to family."

"Except we know that she has none," Gyda objected. "Wooten already checked with the couple that raised her. Clémence is dead. Barnstaple has disappeared. Isn't that what the inspector said?"

"There were more than three children involved in that educational experiment," said Kara. "Five of them were raised together."

"You are thinking exactly as I have been," Niall told her. "I remember what she said that night, when she was speaking of her life. Five children in the experiment. Barnstaple was a merchant's bastard. Clemence was the child of a slave, while Petra was a royal by-blow. But there were two more. A nobleman's natural son and a babe from the streets. The first three were the ones who excelled when granted the boon of a fine, extensive education. The other two she implied were…ordinary."

"The other two did not seem to be involved in the League of Dissolution, either," Kara recalled. "But Petra seems the type to keep tabs on anyone and everyone who might somehow become useful to her."

"So, she might be holed up with one of them?" Gyda asked. "But how do we find them? We don't even know their names."

"No, but Petra did tell me the names of the couple who ran the experiment. The pair that raised her."

"Didn't Wooten say they were uncooperative?" Gyda frowned, trying to remember.

"He did," Niall confirmed. "I asked the inspector to go back to Matthew Hanlin and find out the names and directions of the other two children. Mr. Hanlin declined to share the information."

"Bastard," Gyda grumped.

"Which is why we've been doing a little digging of our own." He held up the report that had come in just this afternoon. "We have something that might help."

Kara took it, and Gyda came to sit beside her. Together they read through the report, then looked up with matching frowns.

"The girl first," Kara said. "I want to find the girl first."

"We need the two boys. We've found a vulnerability to use against Hanlin, but it is time sensitive," Stayme objected. "We need to move on him quickly."

"No." Kara stood firm. "She will be the sort of leverage we will need to force his hand. Find me the girl."

Chapter Six

"**B**EGGIN' YER PARDON, ma'am, but if it's to Walworth ye wish to go, might I ask that we consider takin' along a footman?" John Coachman shifted uncomfortably in the gravel drive. "The area is likely safe enough in the daytime—in normal conditions. And 'tis early enough." He glanced at the sun, just over the horizon. "But still, we ain't operatin' in normal conditions right now, are we?"

Kara looked to Niall. "Is that area really so bad?"

Her husband shrugged. "I have no experience with the place, but I trust John's opinions. And he's right about our situation." He looked toward Tom, who stood at attention at the front door. "We'll take one of the guards at the gate, but could you please send one of the footmen down to take his place?"

"Yes, sir." Tom headed inside. John took his place on the bench. Kara allowed Niall to hand her into the carriage, and they started off.

"I'll have to speak with Stayme about hiring a suitable man to accompany us, at least until this mess is over," Niall said as they stopped to take up a guard.

"Better to be safe." Sliding over to sit next to him, she leaned in, happy to absorb a bit of his warmth—and his strength. In her mind, she rehearsed the arguments they meant to make with

Matthew Hanlin and his wife, Sarah.

After a while, Niall heaved a long sigh. "I'm sorry, Kara."

"For what?" She tilted her head back so that she might see his face.

"Petra is a complication from my past. It's just so damned frustrating. Even with the secrets of my family connections out in the open, still, they keep creeping in, stirring up trouble."

She pressed against him. "Don't be ridiculous. We've both had specters from our past rise up to cause trouble."

"Yet somehow my specters seem to materialize larger, more solid, and armed with sharper teeth," he said wryly.

"Nonsense. And do not forget, some of our exploits have originated with neither of us."

"And yet we are sucked into the mists, just the same."

Kara sat up. "Must I remind you of what you said to me at our wedding? Our life is sure to be a whirlwind."

He raised her hand to his lips. "But the rewards are beyond worth it."

"A thousand times worth it." She reclaimed her hand and traced a finger down the sculpted line of his jaw. "Since we first met, you have shown me in a hundred ways your strength, your kindness, the courage of your spirit. I believe in you, Niall. Just as you believe in me."

"As we are forced to believe in specters?"

She gave him a smile, but it trembled a little at the force of her emotion. "No one has ever made me feel so comfortable in my own abilities, so able to take on the world. Together?" She waved a hand. "Specters don't stand a chance. We can move mountains."

"A mountain might move more easily than Petra Scot," he mused.

"Gyda was right. We've beaten her once. We will do it again." Her eyes narrowed. "We must."

"You are right." He sighed again. "I was just hoping for a bit of peace."

Kara sat back, thinking. "Perhaps we are not meant for peace."

He groaned.

"It might be true," she said. "Perhaps our lot is adventure and intrigue—"

"And madness. Don't forget the madness."

She pulled a face. "Madness might be too strong a word."

He huffed out a laugh and began to tick off fingers. "Murder, mayhem, international conspiracies, fires, pistols, cemetery guns, poisoned artifacts—"

"Fine, fine!" She took his hand and kissed it.

"I wasn't even finished," he complained.

"Madness is just the right word, then. I concede it. But as long as it comes with love and the ability to do some good in this world…" She shrugged. "As long as it comes with you, Niall Kier, Duke of Sedwick, then I can accept it."

Laughing softly, he kissed her forehead. "Very well, then, Kara Kier, Duchess of Sedwick. We will conquer the madness together."

She leaned into his kiss a moment, then sat back, growing serious. "Although this bit with the girl is more than madness—it is vile." She arched a brow at him. "I mean to help her, if I can."

"I knew that already."

"I've written to Rachel, at the coffee shop on Adams. She's been looking for a bit of help. She might be willing to assist us."

"It's a good idea. We should hear the girl's story before we decide, though."

It was no short trip, but at last they reached Westmoreland Road in Walworth, south of London. Niall held her hand as she left the carriage and looked up at the Newington Workhouse. As he gave John and the guard some quiet instruction, she stared up at the imposing brick building. Plain, but stretched out long, it stood three stories high. "That is a lot of potential for misery," she whispered with a shiver. "Is it as bad as they say, do you think?"

"I think there are likely degrees of bad," he said quietly. "Let us hope this is a better one."

A porter admitted them into a stark entry hall. "Just a moment, please. I'll fetch the matron."

Kara shivered again. The air was chilly, though this room looked spotlessly clean. The walls and floor were of white stone. The only color in the room came from two wooden doors on either side of the hall and the words etched in black on the forward wall. **God is Good.**

"I thought it would be loud in here," she said in a whisper. "You hear so much of the overcrowding."

"The silence is a little eerie," Niall agreed.

Kara jumped when the door on the right swung open. A plump woman, middle-aged and wearing a veneer of contempt above her dark gown, looked them over.

Niall bowed. "Good morning, ma'am. I am—"

"If you've come for the new babe, you're too late. It's been adopted out already."

"We've come to speak with one of your tenants," Niall began again.

"Tenants?" The woman laughed. "Inmates is what they're called here." She pursed her lips. "And they are hard at work. I cannot be allowing you to interrupt their labors."

"We'll only take a moment."

The woman looked mulish. Kara gave a silent laugh. She hadn't met stubborn until she met her husband. This matron didn't stand a chance.

Niall merely smiled. "I am sure Mr. Cuthbert would not begrudge us a short visit, but I can have him summoned, if you require convincing."

From the report they'd had, Kara recognized the name of the "guardian" who acted as administrator to this particular workhouse.

The woman considered. Finally, she gave a sniff. "I'm sure Mr. Cuthbert has better things to do with his time, successful businessman as he is. Very well. Which inmate do you seek?"

"A recent addition to your institution. Miss Rose Martin."

"Her?" The matron looked surprised. "No better than she ought to be, that one." She set her hands on her hips. "Well, in any case, you cannot go in, sir. I cannot be allowin' a man to come into the women's ward."

"Can you bring the girl out to us?" asked Kara.

"No. She's work to do, hasn't she?" The matron thought she'd got around them. "Of course, you can go and speak to her while she labors, ma'am, but not for long." Clearly, she expected Kara to decline.

"Thank you." Kara nodded. "If you'll show the way?"

The matron blinked. "She's in the kitchens today."

"I will wait right here, Mrs....?" Niall ended on an expectant note.

"Mrs. Ash."

"I will wait here, Mrs. Ash. And I will put my trust in you to be sure that my duchess comes to no harm...or inconvenience."

The woman looked momentarily shocked at hearing Kara's title. Her gaze raked over Kara's gown of green wool and lingered at the embroidered cuffs and hem before she raised her chin. "I run a tight ship, sir. No women are harmed on my watch. There's no coddlin', to be sure. But no harm, neither. To inmate or visitor."

"I am glad to hear it."

"This way, Your Grace." Mrs. Ash opened the door and beckoned Kara through. They walked along a narrow passage before entering a cavernous room, illuminated only by the dim light coming in the high windows. A long table ran down the center of the room. Chairs surrounded it and lined the walls. Women and girls crowded in, some sharing seats or sitting on the floor. Over a hundred of them, Kara would estimate. They all wore the same uniform, and each of them had a bucket full of old rope before them. They were picking apart the ropes, fraying them with a spiked tool. Dust hung in the air, along with the scent of tar and too many bodies packed together. A few of the women glanced at

Kara defiantly. Some shrank into themselves as if avoiding notice. Most ignored her completely as they worked silently, their faces slack or vacant. Just a smattering of whispers faded as they entered.

The matron ushered Kara quickly through. They passed a window through which Kara spotted a courtyard full of men, some pounding staffs into short casks, others using chisels to hammer rocks, before they went into another short passage that turned a corner and led to a series of more brightly lit kitchen rooms.

Women in the same uniforms worked here, sawing chunks of hard bread and stirring large vats of gruel. A younger woman swept the floor beneath a worktable.

"Where's the Martin girl?" the matron asked her.

The young woman jerked her head toward an alcove in the back of the kitchen. "They set her to grindin' barley for the pigs."

"You'll want some privacy, I expect?" asked Mrs. Ash.

"That might be best. Thank you." With a nod, Kara headed toward the bent figure in the shadowed nook.

"I'll wait here, then," the matron said gruffly, before she turned to join the women at the stove.

Drawing closer, Kara could see a thin, young woman bent over a small hand mill. More a girl, really. She could not have been more than sixteen or seventeen. Her focus was on her work as she worked the cast iron wheel with one hand and dipped scoops of grain into the hopper with the other.

"Miss Martin?" Kara said quietly.

The girl jerked upright and turned to face her. So young. So very thin. Her skin shone pale. Great, dark shadows lay under her eyes. She looked Kara over with confusion. "I'm nearly done with this bucket. I'll fetch another in a moment."

"I'm sure you are doing a fine job," Kara said gently. "I've come to speak with you, Miss Martin. Might you pause a moment?"

The girl's confusion deepened. She cast a glance toward the

kitchen. "I don't think I should."

"I see. Well, I'll move over here, and we can talk while you grind."

The girl ducked her head and went back to work.

"For the pigs?" Kara indicated the grain. "I'm surprised they provide you with meat."

"They provide the staff with meat," Miss Martin corrected her. "The inmates get bread and gruel and sometimes a bit of cheese."

Not surprising, as Kara had long heard that the intent of hard work and meager meals was not only to make the workhouse a profit, but to also make it unappealing, so that they might not be overwhelmed with sheer numbers of the poor. She moved slightly closer so that she could lower her voice. "I understand you used to attend a day school for young women. A school run by Mr. Matthew Hanlin?"

The girl flinched when Kara said his name. After a moment, she nodded.

Kara waited. She checked to be sure the other women were occupied. "I heard what happened to you there, Miss Martin."

The girl's knuckles turned white where they gripped the wheel handle. "Who are you?" she whispered.

"My name is Kara. I'd like to be your friend."

"It wasn't like that—not like what they say about me."

"I believe you." Kara lowered her tone. "Mr. Hanlin is no friend of mine."

Miss Martin kept grinding.

"Will you tell me your story?" asked Kara.

"I don't think I should." The girl was whispering again.

Kara considered. "You were a student there for two years or more. I assume you are well able to read and write?"

The girl nodded.

"Can you make change? Add and subtract numbers?"

Miss Martin lifted her head and met Kara's gaze directly for the first time. "I started there as a student, but I became a teacher at that school, ma'am. I wanted to be a governess. I can read and write. I know geography and history. I can speak passable French. I can do accounts."

"I am very glad to hear it. I do not know of a governess position at the moment—"

The girl shook her head. "It doesn't matter. No one will have me now."

"Would you like to leave this place?"

Miss Martin shot her an exasperated look. "Would you want to stay?"

"No. Nor do I believe that you should. I have some rooms available above a coffee shop in the city. My friend runs the shop. She is looking for someone to help serve customers, help in the kitchen, order supplies, things of that nature."

The girl straightened. "Are you offering *me* the position?"

Kara stepped closer. "Mr. Hanlin possesses information that I need. People that I care for are in danger. I need to find someone to prevent them from getting hurt. Hanlin could help me locate them, but has chosen not to."

"That sounds like him."

"I want that information. I want to protect the people I love." Kara paused. "But I also think that Mr. Hanlin did you great harm."

Tears filled the girl's eyes.

"I believe he will do it again, as often as he wishes, as long as he can get away with it. I want to stop him from hurting more girls like you, Miss Martin."

Fear tightened the young woman's face and she began to work the wheel again.

"Did you know that he has found investors to help him start up a new school? A boarding school for girls, all younger than twelve years. He wishes it to become a feeder school for Queen's College, where governesses are taught and certified. He has asked for Queen Victoria's consent and patronage. If he gets it, the school will open. A great many young girls will be put in his charge."

The grinding slowed.

"I don't believe you belong here, Miss Martin. I would like to take you along with us today and introduce you to my friend, to see if you might suit her needs at the shop, at least until you can contrive something better. I will take you either way, if you wish to go, but I do hope you will choose to help me stop Hanlin from harming anyone else."

The girl's shoulders slumped. "What do you want me to do?"

"I need you to tell me your story. Here. Now. Today. That will help me to convince Mr. Hanlin to share the information I need. It will also allow me to send word of his true nature along to channels that will reach the court and prevent the queen's patronage."

"How will you accomplish that?" She sounded incredulous.

Kara lifted a shoulder. "I am a duchess, Miss Martin. It is not a title that I ever expected or sought, but I have it now. I might as well do some good with it."

The wheel stopped. "A duchess?" Miss Martin stared. "You might actually be heard."

"I believe the queen will listen, if I share your story."

"And I must tell it to you now? Here?"

"I'm afraid so. Miss Martin, there is already a new young woman in the house at Pelton Road."

The girl let go of the mill and covered her face with both hands. Long, shuddering breaths shook her thin shoulders. "Yes," she said, the word muffled. "I accept your terms."

"Thank you."

"I think that is long enough." They both jumped at the matron's words, uttered close. "The girl has work to do."

Miss Martin straightened and looked the woman in the eye. "I hereby give my notice, Mrs. Ash. I am leaving this place. I should like to have my own clothes back."

The matron looked taken aback. "The customary notice—"

"I believe the minimum is three hours, yes?" Miss Martin

raised a brow.

"I think we can shorten that, in this case," Kara said firmly. "I doubt the duke will wish to cool his heels in the entry for that long."

"Very good, Your Grace." Miss Martin sounded utterly calm. She turned to the matron. "I will meet you in the dormitory, Mrs. Ash, where I will change and return the uniform."

"Well. That sounds satisfactory, doesn't it? Lead the way, Miss Martin." Kara stepped past the gaping matron and followed the girl down the long passageway to a huge, empty dormitory, lined with many beds. The girl settled on one halfway down the back row. Kara perched beside her.

"I will tell you all, but quickly. Before the matron returns."

Kara merely waited.

Miss Martin let loose a long, slow breath. "My father scrimped and saved to send me to the Hanlins' school. He thought me quick enough to go into service as a governess. A bright future for me. I loved the idea. I worked hard and did very well in my studies. It gained me favor with both the headmaster and the headmistress. They invited me to become a parlor boarder and to help with the younger girls as I finished up my own lessons."

"Did they ever speak of their former pupils? Receive visits from them?" Kara asked.

The girl frowned. "They told us often that they had taught the brightest minds in the realm, but they never had letters or visits." She paused. "Except for one man, but it was always just a guess that the man ever studied with them. He never came to the front, but to the kitchen. The headmistress would go down to meet him there. Always just Mrs. Hanlin, never the headmaster. They would visit and she would send him away with a basket of food and sundries. He looked…odd. Tall and strong. He didn't wear workman's clothes, but his hands looked rough. He was often dusty, with bits collected in his hair. His suit was decent, but not fine, do you know?"

Kara nodded.

"I thought that's why the headmaster didn't meet with him—as if he were a former student who did not live up to his education. A failure the headmaster didn't want to acknowledge."

Kara wondered if that was how Hanlin felt about this young woman. Failure was not the word she would use—but she was going to see to it that he paid for what he'd done to a young girl in his care.

Miss Martin turned her head away when she continued. "He touched me the first time when the school scheduled a trip to the Tower of London. I had a head cold, and Mrs. Hanlin gave me leave to stay behind and work on my own studies. After the rest of them had been gone a while, the headmaster came to my room. He said he came to inquire if I was feeling better, but he locked the door behind him." She bit her lip.

"He kept coming back?" Kara asked gently.

"Many nights. Most nights. I…I didn't know what to do. My father, having settled me, had taken a position in York. I tried to tell the headmistress, but she turned the subject. She didn't want to hear."

"I'm so sorry," Kara whispered.

"I felt trapped. My room and board were considered my pay. I had no money. Nowhere to go." The girl's eyes closed. "When I discovered I was with child, I wrote to my father, asking for help."

Kara dreaded hearing more, given that the girl had ended up here.

"He wrote a scathing response. Called me a whore. Said I'd wasted his money and my own opportunity for a better life. He washed his hands of me."

"What did you do?"

"Nothing. I lived in dread, waiting until the inevitable happened and my secret was discovered. The students began to whisper about my expanding belly, and the headmistress was forced to deal with me then. She shouted at me. She cried. She cast me out." Miss Martin gave Kara an agonized look. "I had nothing. Just the clothes I wore. Not even my books. I just stood there on the pavement, numb. Terrified. Alone. I had just resolved to go and throw myself in the river when one of the footmen came out. He took me several streets away, to a tiny little house on Pelton Road. He had the key. He let me in and told me I would be staying there, then he just…left." She put a hand over her eyes. "I sat down, waiting. The rest of the afternoon, I sat there alone. The headmaster arrived that evening. He carried on as if nothing had changed. All the way up until the baby came."

"But how did you end up here?"

"I think something went wrong with the birth," she said, low. "The headmaster was ready to resume his activities right away, but I was still in pain. Perhaps something hadn't healed? I don't know. There was a servant who came in most mornings, but she wouldn't speak to me. Never. Not once. Not a word. So I had no one to ask. I started to cry every time he came to the house. I fought him, pleading and screaming. I think the neighbors heard. One night, I ran crying into the street."

"What did he do?"

"He left. But he showed up in a carriage the next morning. He hustled me and the babe inside it and brought us here. He left us. That was a month ago."

"Miss Martin, what of your child? Where is it? In the nursery here?"

She shook her head, staring ahead, her face blank. "A couple came to talk to me. They wanted to adopt him. They were barren. The gentleman was a barrister." She shrugged, but tears shone in her eyes. "They could give him a real life. What should I have done? Allowed him to be raised in all this?"

"No. No, of course not."

A door slammed, and the matron hustled toward them, complaining as she came. "This is all very irregular. Very unusual."

Kara stood. "No, Mrs. Ash. It isn't, is it? And that is the problem." She tugged the woman away. "Come, let us give Miss Martin some privacy to change, and then she will be coming away with us."

Kara and Niall would deal with Matthew Hanlin. Afterward, they would see to Petra Scot.

And then…then she would see.

Chapter Seven

THE ENTIRE HANLIN household appeared to be rattled to find a duke and duchess unexpectedly on their doorstep. Niall and Kara had been left in an admittedly impressive hall done up in carved wooden panels, niches with busts of ancient scholars, and several tall-backed benches. The footman who had taken word of their arrival to his employers must have whispered the news along the way, for several giggling maids peeped out from doorways and from the gallery above. Niall straightened as a lady emerged from a passage to the left, while a gentleman clattered down the stairs ahead of them.

Perhaps Hanlin had not recognized Niall's title, for he drew up short, pausing several steps up as he got a good look at them. For a moment, Niall thought it was even odds whether the man would turn and bolt. After a moment, though, he clearly decided to bluster his way through.

"Good afternoon, good afternoon," he said heartily. "I am Mr. Matthew Hanlin, proprietor of the school." Approaching, he gave them a courtly bow. "Your Graces. I bid you welcome."

At Niall's side, Kara regarded the man blandly. Hanlin was not much taller than her. He was slim, with a heavy beard and dark eyes. The man's wife moved closer, stopping just behind and to the side of her husband. Niall bowed, taking note of the downward turn of her mouth and the heavy look of unhappiness in her eyes.

"Thank you for receiving us," Niall said without inflection. "We should like a private word with you, Mr. Hanlin."

"Actually, why don't we ladies withdraw and allow the men to address business?" Kara had fixed her attention on the wife. "We've had a long morning, I fear. I confess, I would welcome a quiet cup of tea, Mrs. Hanlin."

"Of course." The woman stepped back and swept a hand to indicate a parlor to the left. "Let us go and sit a bit. I'll have a tray sent up to the study as well."

"Don't bother," her husband said, smiling at Niall. "It is not every day that a duke comes calling. We shall break out the good brandy."

Kara gave him a look as she followed the wife, and he set off upstairs after Hanlin. The educator led the way, pointing out rooms and features, speaking of the courses they offered as if Niall were a prospective parent. He supposed it was a comfort to fall back on a familiar routine, and hoped that meant he was making the man nervous.

"Come in. Come in." Hanlin led him into a well-appointed study. Again, he pointed out the art on the walls and spoke of first-edition books in his library. Niall found the man as cocky and irritating as a banty rooster.

"So, Your Grace, I can only surmise that you have heard of the investment opportunities available for the new school I am forming." Hanlin poured two brandies and handed one to Niall. "I confess, I can think of no other reason for your visit."

"I have indeed heard of your new venture," Niall confirmed.

Palpable relief flowed off the man. "Oh, good. You must agree, it is important work. Preparing a generation of capable, highly educated governesses can only benefit us all, as a society. After all, they will help mold the new crop of our leaders, noblemen, and businessmen."

"I agree, wholeheartedly," Niall said. He still had not drunk from his glass. "A first-rate education is so important to these women. Valuable knowledge that she can pass on—it seems crucial. As you said, a governess can be such an important influence in a child's life."

Hanlin nodded affably.

"I am very glad we are in accord," Niall said.

"As am I." Hanlin gave a little shrug. "I admit, I was afraid you might be here for another reason altogether."

"But you just said you could not imagine another reason for my visit."

The educator gave an uneasy chuckle. "Well…"

"Petra Scot," said Niall.

"Indeed." Hanlin took a long drink. "I suppose you heard that Scotland Yard was around, asking after her. They said she was making threats against you."

"Yet you chose not to help them locate her," Niall said evenly.

"Well, I don't know where she is, do I? And you must know how it is with her. I don't dare cross her again. Ungrateful chit. We gave her the most superlative education. A brilliant mind, that one. And we provided her with the best tutors. The finest scholars. We gave her access to far more than she might have learned, even had she been a legitimate royal. And what did she do? She used that brilliance to ruin us."

"Only after she discovered you had been siphoning off funds meant for the care and upkeep of her and her fellow students— the children of your great experiment."

Hanlin flushed. "A first-rate education does not come cheap."

"Nor does a place like this. Or the second home you keep in Brighton. It seems you have recovered from the blow she and her League dealt you." Niall raised a brow. "I surmise that you must have squirreled away funds that even William Barnstable, with his superb grasp of finance, did not locate?"

"Now, see here—"

"But of course, there can be no price put on ethics, can there?

On character. Which leads me right back to your original statement on the value of the governesses you mean to train." He directed a level look at the man. "It stands to reason that a steady, stable temperament is equally important for these women, wouldn't you agree? Forming the minds of our children is important work, as you said. It should be undertaken by those who are healthy in mind and spirit, as well as learned."

Hanlin looked confused.

"And given the truth of that, it stands to reason that the man who undertakes the training of these women should nurture them gently, should value them accordingly. He should take the greatest care of the girls he is entrusted with. In fact, I should think he would wish to be an example of how to treasure all women, wouldn't he?" Niall stopped and stared expectantly.

"Ah, of course," said Hanlin.

"Then explain to me, sir, how forcing your attentions on a girl in your care, a girl who has come to you in hopes of fulfilling her dreams, is in any way nurturing or valuing her?"

Hanlin gaped at him.

"No true gentleman would use such a girl in such a way," Niall sneered. "You are no gentleman, Hanlin, but rather a snake. A *worm*. You were entrusted with her care. You were paid to safeguard and teach her—and instead you abused her and made her a vessel for your betrayal and basest weaknesses."

"I don't know what…who—" the man began to sputter.

"Miss Rose Martin, that is who."

Anger and shame flooded the man's features. "I don't know what she has told you—"

"Everything, sir," Niall interrupted. "She has told us every-thing."

"Lies!" Hanlin cried.

"Are they? Peculiar, then, that they should be so similar to Miss Penny Baldwin's, isn't it?" Niall deliberately set his glass down. "And no, Miss Baldwin is no longer in residence at your little nest in Pelton Road, just as Miss Martin is no longer at the workhouse where you abandoned her."

Hanlin paled. "It doesn't matter what those girls say. I am a respected educator. A leader in my field. It is their word against mine."

"Indeed. It is." The look Niall gave him made it clear whose side he would come down on.

"Who will believe them? Girls of low moral character, eager to raise their skirts in exchange for tuition or advancement."

Niall's anger was rising. "I'm sure a look at your books will disprove that defense." He took a step toward the cocksure menace. "And I'm also sure that if I begin to question past students of your school, I will find plenty of similar stories."

"No one will believe them. Or you." The man refused to back down. "And if they do, they won't be troubled about it."

"Oh, I daresay the queen will be troubled. She might find it very interesting information indeed—such disturbing tales about the man seeking her patronage."

"You wouldn't!" Hanlin looked shocked.

"I will," Niall vowed.

"Don't be ridiculous. You would ruin my livelihood over a couple of light-skirted girls of no name or family?"

"Mr. Hanlin, as far as I can tell, you have failed your wife and your students. You have failed to uphold every contract and responsibility you have entered into. I will take pleasure in exposing you."

"If you think this is the way to convince me to give you Petra Scot, then are very much mistaken," Hanlin said, desperate.

"I thought you did not know where she is to be found?"

"I don't, damn you!" He cast his glance about and put a hand to his head. "But the boys—the other two boys…"

He stopped as the study door flew open. His wife stood on the threshold, her eyes wild and her face flushed red. "Truly, Matthew? Another one? What of your promises?"

"Sarah, don't believe them!" Hanlin turned on Niall, his brandy sloshing over as he spun around. "Out, damn you! Get out of my house!"

"Your bluster won't do you any good," his wife said, shedding angry tears. "They have the girl. Both girls, apparently. They know it all. All of your wicked secrets."

"Hush, Sarah," Hanlin commanded.

"Why?" The woman gave a biting laugh as she crossed to the desk and began to write on a slip of paper. "It's too late now. You have ruined us, as I said you would."

Hanlin looked at Niall, his eyes wide. "No. It's not too late, surely. I don't know where Petra is hiding, but I can give you the boys. She might have gone to ground with one of them."

"He doesn't know where to find the boys," Sarah sneered. "He never kept up with them. Why would he? Young men of no fortune or viable connections? They had nothing to offer him."

"Those girls were not offering anything either," Kara said, appearing in the doorway. "Yet they had everything stolen from them. At least one of them came to you, Mrs. Hanlin. She asked for help, and you turned her away. You threw a young girl, heavy with child, into the street."

"I know," Sarah said thickly. "I was already sick with guilt. My guts have grown more and more twisted over the years, but I have scarcely slept since that day. It's haunted me, my own wickedness. I deserve to fall with him." She tore the paper off and crossed to hand it to Kara. "Which is why I am giving you Robert Preston's address."

"Robert Preston?" asked Niall.

"One of the five original children in our experiment. He never excelled enough to suit Matthew, but he was always a sweet boy, and he has grown into a decent man. Robert is an engineer, by trade. He is working with Sir Charles Barry on the rebuilding of the new Houses of Parliament. You should be able to find him at Westminster, but this is his address, in case you miss him."

"How do you know Robert's address?" Hanlin frowned at his wife.

"You are not the only one in this house with secrets, Matthew." With a toss of her head, she moved past Kara. "You will not find Petra with Robert. They always despised each other. But Robert is still close with Tom, and Petra has always run ragged over that one."

"Tom?" Kara asked.

"Tom Hawkins, the last of the five given over for our experiment."

"The child from the streets?" Niall guessed.

"Yes, and he has returned to them," Hanlin snarled. "It's in his blood. As a child he was forever sneaking out, stealing away to fraternize with gin whores, costermongers, and cracksmen. He's still a gadabout and a ne'er-do-well, despite all of our efforts. He's nothing but a card sharp now. He spends his days drinking and gambling and cheating green fools fresh from the country. If it wasn't for Robert, he'd have rotted in debtor's prison long ago."

"Do be quiet, Matthew, and stop speaking of what you don't know." Sarah looked to Kara. "I don't know where Tom is residing now, but Robert will know. Tell him I urge him to cooperate with you." She stilled. "Petra… Associating with Petra is not good for Tom. In the state she's likely in now, she could be a danger to him."

"Petra Scot has proven herself a danger to my family, to the Crown, and to the world order," Niall said scathingly.

Sarah cast a glance back at her husband. "Yet another sin we must atone for. I shall start writing letters to the parents. The girls must be sent home."

"No. Sarah! You cannot!" Hanlin looked panicked, as if the enormity of it all had finally struck him.

"It's over." Ducking her head, she turned and disappeared down the passage.

Nodding, Niall crossed to take Kara's arm. He glanced back over his shoulder. "Atonement is coming for you, Mr. Hanlin." Setting a hand on his wife's, he gave her a tug. "One step closer," he murmured. "Let's go."

Chapter Eight

T HE NOISE WAS impressive.

Kara pressed close to Niall as they made their way through Westminster. The roads were busy, full of pedestrians, cart vendors, and carriages vying for space with supply wagons. A long wooden wall had been built to separate the construction of the new palace from the public thoroughfare. Heavily laden horses and wagons lined up to go through an opening in the barrier. Men waited their turn, each speaking with a porter armed with a thick file before being waved through.

Kara and Niall watched the supplies enter from a little distance. When the last wagon had been admitted, they approached.

The porter eyed them curiously and opened his file. "Names?"

"Niall Kier, Duke of Sedwick." Niall gave the man a friendly smile. "And, of course, this is my wife."

The porter scanned his papers. He looked up once, and Kara gave him an encouraging nod.

It didn't help. The man closed his file and shook his head. "I'm sure I'm sorry, Your Grace. The new House of Lords is in use, and you are welcome there, but this area is still under construction and not open to visitors. It isn't safe."

"We are not visiting," Niall said politely. "We are here to see

Mr. Robert Preston."

The porter made a face. "Mr. Preston is right busy, he is. He's got to get the tower back on schedule."

"Nevertheless," Niall said pleasantly, but firmly.

The porter stared, clearly undecided.

Kara took a step closer. "It is family business for which we need to see Mr. Preston, sir. *Urgent* family business. He won't thank you for delaying us."

At last, the man shrugged and waved them through. "On your head be it, then, if this delays *him*."

They stepped through—and good heavens. The noise ratcheted even louder on this side of the wall. Men's shouts mingled with pounding, sawing, and the creak of ropes and machinery. "It's a hive of industry, isn't it?" she said to Niall. "And it seems to be well run."

She ran an experienced eye over it all. Everywhere men were engaged in moving, building, and crafting. Not a one of them appeared to be slacking. Scaffolding surrounded walls and a tower under construction. It rose up over the trees, and had a crane perched atop it.

The porter saw where her eye had landed. "The King's Tower," he said with pride. "When it is finished, it will be the largest square tower in all the world." He pointed. "And on the other end is the clock tower. It's somewhat closer to the finish."

"It's all very impressive," she told him.

"Where will we find Preston?" asked Niall.

"He'll be at the square tower site. Preston is a skilled man. He was instrumental in getting the Commons opened in time last November. Now Sir Charles has put him on the King's Tower, hoping he can get it back on a decent timeline to be finished." The man narrowed his gaze and surveyed the busy scene. "There!" He pointed toward a pair of men pulling a wagon full of parts. "Follow those men. Those are heading for the place you need. You'll find Preston on site."

They set off. Niall tightened his grip on her arm. "Watch your step," he murmured.

But Kara had toured enough of her own businesses and man-ufactories to know how to stay out of the way. They kept in step behind the porters, following along the long wall of the building, avoiding the swarms of busy men. The tower was the feature at the end of the building, and eventually they followed the men into a stone arch surrounded by scaffolds, with stonemasons swarming over it.

The porters started to unload their wagon, calling for help in hoisting a large gear wheel complete with drum and flange.

"What's this, then?" Kara asked, interested.

Together, the men carried the mechanism inside, and Kara and Niall followed. She peered into the wagon as they passed, noting a crank, a hooked gear, and a spoked handwheel.

The building here was close to finished. Men scrambled over walls, lining them with carved wooden panels. Ahead, though, they could see the large entrance to the tower, a marvel of arched buttresses and incredible stonework.

In the area before the entrance, a large man had made himself a desk of planks over stone plinths. He looked up from it and heaved a sigh of relief as the men entered with their burden. "Well, thank the Almighty, here you are at last. Come on, lads. Get a scramble on and get that upstairs and installed. How are we to finish the storerooms if we cannot get supplies up there?"

"That will be him, then," Kara said brightly.

The man had already returned his attention to the spread of designs and documents on his makeshift desk.

"Good morning!" Kara approached first. "Are you construct-ing a winch, by chance?"

The man looked up. "Repairing one," he answered. "There's an opening in the entrance roof for lifting heavy supplies, but the winch keeps seizing. I'm replacing the largest gears."

"Mr. Robert Preston?" Niall asked.

The gentleman looked back down at his schedules, lists, and plans. "Yes?"

"I am Niall Kier—"

The man's eyes widened as he straightened again. "The newly made duke? Of…" He frowned. "Sorry. I forgot the title."

"Sedwick. And this is my duchess. We would like a word, if you please."

"No time." The man waved a hand. "Apologies, but we've got a long way to go before this tower is finished and we are severely behind schedule."

Kara stepped in. Preston was nearly as large as Niall. He had a long nose with a crook on the end and thick, unruly eyebrows. She thought Miss Martin had given a good description of him. Not a workman, but not quite a gentleman, either. She recognized in him the air of a good foreman—organized, fair, and stern when he needed to be.

"We've just come from Mrs. Sarah Hanlin," she said, getting straight to the point that she suspected would move him.

Preston looked up at once. "Is all right with her?"

"She is fine." She paused. "For now."

The engineer froze. Gripping his pencil tightly, he straightened. "Someone has finally got the headmaster in their crosshairs?" he asked.

"Indeed, they have," Niall said grimly.

Preston shook his head. "I warned her, time and again. This will be the end of the school, then. Well, she can come to me, if she needs to—and she knows it. But *he* can rot in hell."

"Mrs. Hanlin said you might be able to help us," Kara said. "She said you would wish to. We are looking for Tom Hawkins."

The engineer stared. He ran a gaze over them both, clearly perplexed. "What's he done now?"

"He's done nothing, himself," answered Niall. "But we suspect he might be harboring someone. Someone we very much wish to find."

Preston's face went slack. "Not Petra?"

Kara nodded.

This time, the man threw his pencil and let loose a long string of curses. "Forgive me, ma'am. I had wondered why he hadn't been around these last weeks, but I never guessed it would be down to her. Damn it all to hell! The harridan! Why will she never leave Tom be?"

"She's in dire straits this time," Niall told him.

"She always is," Preston said. "Tom gets into enough trouble on his own, but with her at the helm? It's many times worse. She's going to get him killed one day."

"He wouldn't be the first," Niall said darkly.

Preston gave him a sour look. "I grew up with the woman. You don't have to convince me she is a monster." He raised a brow. "Why are you looking for her?"

"Scotland Yard and the Crown are searching for her because she has committed treason." Niall glowered. "I'm looking for her because, while she has eluded them, she has made threats against my family and made an attempt to kill someone in my household."

"That's our Petra, making enemies wherever she goes," Preston said bitterly.

"Will you give us the address so that we may find her?" asked Kara. "We shall happily remove her from Tom's sphere."

"She has a cell awaiting her," Niall added.

Preston began to gather his papers. "I'll take you myself. You'll never get near Tom otherwise."

⤜⤛⤙⤘⤗

THEY STOPPED AT Scotland Yard, as it was so close. Fortune was with them, and Wooten was in his office. He spent a precious few minutes scolding them for investigating on their own, but he came along with them in their carriage—and he organized a wagon full of constables to follow.

Niall and Wooten murmured together as her husband caught the inspector up on everything they had learned, while Kara watched Mr. Preston.

The engineer stared silently out the window. She had the impression that his mind was far away. He startled her, then, when he spoke. "I know you have questions. Everyone does, when they find out about my childhood."

She lifted a shoulder. "I had an unusual upbringing myself. I know it's not always easy to share. But I am interested in learning what I can of Petra."

He nodded, his focus still on the passing streets.

"We were kept separately," he said after a few moments. "There were other children in the school, but the five of us were not meant to interact with them. We had our own living quarters and separate schoolrooms. The rules were strict."

"I imagine Petra was not one for following rules, even back then," Kara said with a snort.

"No. She was not. She snuck out to the other dormitories, on the regular. What a bully she was, even then. A despot. She ran those children with an iron fist."

"Does she run Tom the same way?"

"No." Preston shook his head. "Their relationship is more...interdependent. They fuel each other in the worst ways." His mouth twisted. "Tom used to say that I was the angel perched at one shoulder and Petra was the devil on the other—but he was wrong."

"In what way?"

"It is the headmaster's voice that rings loudest in Tom's head. Always telling him he isn't quick enough, perceptive enough, intelligent enough. When Tom is given a choice, it is always those feelings of inadequacy that spur him down the wrong path."

"Matthew Hanlin has a great deal to answer for," Kara said quietly.

Preston grunted in response.

"And is Hanlin's the voice that drives Petra?" she asked.

"Hell no." The engineer gave a bitter laugh. "She would

never grant him such influence over her."

"What is it, then? What makes her so…warped?"

"Damned if I know." Preston sighed. "Petra craves attention. She doesn't particularly care what sort. Fear and loathing feed her as much as fondness." He shrugged. "They do say her mother was much the same. Being crowned Princess of Wales was not enough for her. She wanted to be adored—but she didn't want to work for it. When she found herself disregarded—by her husband, by the royal family, by England's people—she was happy to become notorious instead. All she had to do was indulge her every craving."

"Petra certainly does not seem lazy," Kara said. "Or ruled by those sorts of passions."

"No. She is not. I believe she deliberately did not wish to be compared to her mother. Certainly, the headmaster understood her craving for attention. He praised her, lifted her above the rest of us. He flattered and cajoled her into becoming one of England's greatest minds."

"But that doesn't explain her cruelty."

"No. Perhaps she was born with it. Or she might have early discovered her taste for the fear in others." He paused. "Honestly, I believe her soul is deficient. She cannot or will not focus on anything beyond herself. She does not care whom she harms or what sort of havoc she wreaks, as long as it brings her the attention she craves. People are only a means to suit her ends. Tom is a prime example. He admires her. He wants to please her. But Tom is weak. He will act against his own best interests to bask in the briefest moments of her approval."

"Then I can understand why you would wish to keep her away from him."

Preston cast her a careful look. "The duke said that Petra has threatened your family. I don't know the story, but I am an engineer, Your Grace. I am putting the pieces together in my head. Were you, by any chance, involved in the destruction of their wretched League?"

Kara hesitated. Not many people were aware of the significant role they had played in destroying the organization. She nodded.

The engineer looked grim. "Be careful, then. The only thing that pushes Petra harder than a bid for attention is a quest for revenge. She is a champion grudge holder. She will go to any lengths to triumph over an enemy."

Kara's mouth thinned. "I'll go to any lengths to protect my family."

"Let's hope we catch her tonight, then. Otherwise, you might have to." He leaned forward to peer out the window again. "It's growing dark. We'll have to stop soon. The carriage won't be able to go much further."

The streets were narrowing, and growing shabbier by the moment. Kara could easily imagine Petra prowling among them, looking like prey but hiding a predator's heart.

True to Preston's prediction, the carriage was forced to slow and come to a halt. The four of them disembarked. Niall stayed close, and Kara was grateful that he never considered the notion to ask her to wait here. Wooten would have liked to, she could tell, but he'd also come to respect her skills. He merely shot her a pointed glance before gathering his constables around Preston so that they could be given the lay of the land and whispered instructions.

The men melted into the night as Wooten returned to them. "We'll give them a few minutes to get into position."

Kara sniffed, catching the sharp tang of turpentine in the air. "There's a gin still nearby," she said, low. "We'd best wait a little further on."

They moved to the next street, where the stench in the air shifted to the scent of urine and rotting garbage.

"Just a few moments. We don't want to give Tom too much time to think," Preston said. He pointed ahead. "We need to turn down that alley."

Soon after, Wooten gave the signal, and they followed Preston to the mouth of the alley. It was a narrow, dark, and noisome maw. "Keep just to the right of the center," he warned them. "It's a bit clearer there and there is less of a chance of traps—or rats. When I stop, you stop—and hold your silence."

Though there was still a bit of light in the sky, it was completely blocked by the surrounding buildings. It was dark as night in the alley. Kara stepped carefully, and they all did an admirable job of not sounding like a regiment threading through a needle. She caught sight of the end, faintly lit by the flicker of nearby firelight. They were halfway to it when Preston stopped.

"Mouse," he said quietly. "Come out of there."

Everyone waited.

"I know you are there."

Silence.

"*Mouse*," the engineer said in a warning tone.

From a darker shadow that Kara had not even realized was a doorway came the sound of a slight, shifting movement.

"Evenin', guv." It was a child's voice, thin and high. "What's all this, then? Bringin' a party to 'is nibs?"

"You might say that," Preston answered wryly. "Run along and tell him it's me coming, will you? There's no need for him to slip out the back."

"Sorry, guv. 'E ain't put me on watch duty tonight."

"Whyever not?" Preston sounded genuinely surprised.

"'Is nibs has been holed up in his rooms, last couple o' days. Stickin' close to home."

"And his visitor too, I suppose? The woman?"

"Aye, I reckon she's why 'e's sticking close, eh?"

Kara winced at the child's worldly tone.

"Well, I'll pay you to go and let him know it's me coming. Go on, now."

"A penny now and another later, eh, guv?"

Preston growled, and the child laughed. Another shifting sound echoed in the dark, then the slap of bare feet moving rapidly away over the cobblestones.

"Let's go," Preston said. "Move quickly, and if there are men gathered around the taverns, put a bit of swagger into it."

Wooten grunted. "He doesn't know you lot well, does he?" he asked. "If he thinks he needs to offer you such advice?"

They emerged onto a slightly wider lane, populated by dark, shuttered shops between well-lit taverns and bawdy houses. The stink of the river moved in, along with a fog that crept about their feet.

They all followed as Preston ducked through an arch that led into a closed courtyard. Several torches burned, illuminating tall townhouses that had once been fine, but had clearly fallen into decay and neglect. Preston marched up the rickety steps that led to a sagging, unlit house.

Naturally.

Kara spied a constable waiting in the shadows. Another lurked in the entry hall, at the foot of a central staircase. One stepped out of the dark and fell in behind them. Preston started up, and they all moved in his wake.

There was no disguising the sound of so many feet on the creaking stairs. Preston climbed to the third floor, where rooms and a spindly railing circled the staircase. He stopped at a door midway down the left passage. A small, filthy boy stood before it.

"'E ain't answering, guv, but I did your bidding, just the same."

"So you did. But did you give it a good pounding?"

"Enough to set the neighbor to screeching."

"And you say you haven't seen Tom for a couple of days?"

"No, but I never saw him leave, either. Thought he was nestin' in there with 'is woman."

Preston glanced back. Kara could see the worry in his face. "All right, lad. Job well done." He tossed the boy a coin.

Mouse caught it. He retreated, but hung at the landing of the stairs, watching. Kara sympathized with him. Her heart was racing. Petra Scot could be on the other side of that door. She squeezed Niall's hand.

"We'll get her," he whispered.

She hoped so. She felt ill at the thought that they might have missed her.

Preston fished out a key.

"Perhaps Constable Berne should go first," Wooten suggested.

"No. He's my brother." Preston shrugged. "For all intents and purposes." He turned the key, swung open the door, and moved inside. "Tom? It's me."

They waited. Kara held her breath.

"What in unholy hell?" Preston said roughly.

Wooten held up a hand to hold Niall and Kara back and waved the constable in. "Check all the rooms."

"Empty," came the call after a moment. "There is no one here, sir."

Kara's shoulders slumped and she covered her mouth as Niall cursed beside her. He reached for her hand. Together they walked in…to chaos.

The rooms had been turned upside down and inside out. Preston prowled around, lifting overturned furniture, looking under drawers tossed in corners, stacking cushions that had been ripped open. Feathers were everywhere, as were ashes from the hearth, newspapers, and broken dishes.

"Would your Tom Hawkins have possessed something valuable?" Wooten asked. "Something that would merit such a search?"

"No." Preston shook his head. "Tom never had two quid to rub together. This is not his doing. This is Petra's work."

Niall stepped further into the room. "You think something provoked one of her rages?"

The engineer abruptly stopped and turned to face them both. "You've seen her? In one of her…fits?"

Kara nodded, shivering as she recalled the gleam of unhinged anger in the woman's eyes and the uncontrolled fury that had accidentally led to a woman's death. "It's how Clémence died," she whispered.

Preston drew a shuddering breath. "I didn't know." His gaze hardened and his hands tightened into fists. "But where is Tom? By God, if she has harmed him, I will wring her neck myself!" He turned back to the mess, poking his way across the room. Suddenly he gave a cry, pouncing to pick up something from the floor. He stood, holding a chain with a small pendant dangling. "Tom's," he said hoarsely. "Something has happened to him. He would never take this off."

Wooten stooped to examine it. "You're sure it belonged to Tom Hawkins?"

Preston nodded. "Clémence gave it to him. He wore it always."

"Would you object to one of the constables doing a quick sketch of it?" the inspector asked.

Preston agreed, but he kept his gaze locked on the pendant as the constable examined it and began to sketch a likeness. "It's St. Simeon Solas, the patron saint of holy fools," he told Kara and Niall quietly. "Tom is such a buffoon. He never stopped trying to make us laugh. He would grease the headmaster's chair, hoping to make him slide off, but he only ever kept ruining the man's coats. Once Tom filled all Hanlin's desk drawers with apples, each with a single bite taken out of it. One spring day, he found a dead pigeon in the garden, strapped it to his shoulder, fashioned an eye patch, and spent the day stamping around, insisting he was a pirate." He snorted. "Clémence gave him the pendant and told him he was going to have to convert and become a holy fool. Dedicate his absurdity to God."

"It sounds as if you did grow up as siblings," Kara said.

"A strange set, but as close to siblings as you can get without blood." Preston frowned. "It's just...something is odd here. Where is Tom? Gone for days, and without telling Mouse? And without his St. Simeon?"

"And where is Petra?" asked Niall.

"Exactly." Preston glanced around again. "Clearly, she has

been here." Straightening, the engineer breathed deeply. "Listen, I will cast about and see if I can find anything about Tom. You continue your search for Petra. You know where to find me. We'll agree to contact each other if we find anything. Yes?"

Kara looked to Niall, who gave the other man a frank look. "We would certainly agree, if we had a notion of where else we might look for her. Have you a suggestion?"

"Have you sought out William?"

"William Barnstable has not been seen since he found a way to release Petra from the custody of the Crown," Kara told him.

"Unless you know where he is?" asked Niall.

"No. We were never close. The last time I saw him was when Tom tricked me into attending one of the recruitment meetings for their League of Dissolution."

Kara raised a brow. "We thought neither of you had any involvement with the League?"

"I certainly did not. Little better than thugs, the lot of them. I am much more interested in building things, rather than tearing them down. But Tom? He flirted with it occasionally. Usually when he was low on funds and the others had some dirty work needing done." He sighed. "If I don't find word of him amongst his gambling cronies, I'll try to track down some of the League men he knew."

The constable, finished sketching the medal, gave it back to Preston, who looked at it a long moment before tucking it away. "I hope to heaven that Tom is merely hiding away somewhere."

"Mr. Preston?" Wooten, his notebook at the ready, beckoned the man. "If I may ask you a few questions about Tom Hawkins? And Your Grace? I know you are a duke now and due all courtesy and whatnot." The inspector grinned. "But would you help Berne turn over that bed? Just so we know what's beneath it?"

Chuckling, Niall went, but Kara was in no laughing mood. She went back out into the passage to see if Mouse was still lingering, but there was no sign of him. As her eyes adjusted, she noted a paned window at the end of the passage, letting in a bit of weak moonlight. She'd just started toward it when she heard a board creak.

She spun around, but there was no one there.

"My apologies, to be sure. It was just me, indulging my curiosity."

She looked up. A thin, untidy man peered down at her over the railing above.

"I say, is he quite all right? Mr. Hawkins?"

"He's not at home. Do you know him well?"

The man grimaced. "Just as neighbors. Passing on the stairs and all of that." He drifted toward the stairs, and she followed, in similar fashion, on her own level.

"Are those *police constables* in there?" he asked.

"Indeed, they are. Won't you come down? They might want to question you."

The man's hands fluttered, but he shot her a grin and headed down. "Good evening to you. I am Sculley. Mr. Douglas Sculley. I live in the north corner rooms at the top of the house."

Kara curtsied. "Kara Kier." She left off her title. She noted the stains on his fingers and cuffs and the distinctive smell of linseed oil. "Are you a painter, Mr. Sculley?"

"I am!" He sounded delighted. "Have you heard of me?"

"I am sorry. I haven't—*yet*. But I am a great art enthusiast. I should love to see your work."

"I should love to show it to you." His glance strayed toward Tom's door. "But do you really think the police will wish to question me?"

She suspected he was in search of a tale to dine out on. "They will, I imagine, since you knew him. They will likely wish to know when you last saw him."

"Saw him? Or heard him?" Sculley tittered. "*Everyone* heard him a couple of nights ago. He had a great row with his guest."

"Did he?"

"Oh, yes. Shouting. Banging. Crashing. All the works. But it has been quiet since."

"Do you know what they were arguing over?"

"A lover's spat, I presume. I could not make out the words."

"Did you meet his guest, sir?"

"Me? No, of course not."

The man was drifting almost imperceptibly toward the door, so she waved him on. "Go on. Inspector Wooten is inside. He will wish to hear about the row."

Aquiver with excitement, the neighbor flitted along and put his head in the doorway. "Good evening, gentlemen," he said before he entered.

With a sigh, Kara moved toward the window again. She stood a moment, gazing into the courtyard below. A movement directly beneath her brought her attention to the constable waiting by the stairs. She could just make out his hat below. The rest of the courtyard looked empty in the flickering torchlight.

Suddenly a shiver went up her spine. She felt certain somebody was watching her.

She spun around, but the passage and the stairs were empty. She could see no one at the railings above. Turning, she looked out the window again and peered into the shadows in the courtyard.

Nothing.

A memory jolted her—a recollection of the last time they had been on the hunt for Petra Scot. She looked up.

There. A figure on the roof opposite. A woman. Her skirts swayed a little as she approached the edge. Very deliberately, she leaned onto the decorative balustrade lining the roof. Kara felt the weight of her stare as if it were tangible.

Déjà vu rippled up her spine. In just this way, she'd once had her first glimpse of Petra—from a distance, in that very same pose.

"Niall," she gasped. "Niall!"

She was running, rounding the corner and starting down the stairs when her husband burst out of Tom Hawkins's rooms.

"She's there! I saw her! Across the courtyard! On the roof!"

Together, they sprinted down the stairs, in pursuit.

Chapter Nine

NIALL HAD SURGED ahead of Kara as he sprinted up the stairs of the house she indicated. He didn't slow, nor would she wish him to. On the second-floor landing, he nearly collided with a young man. He gripped the youngling's arm. "How do I get to the roof?"

"Let *go*, sir!" the young man demanded. "What do you think you are about?"

Niall had no time to deal with a stripling likely here to meet up with his kept woman. "It's urgent." He grabbed the lordling's other arm. "Tell me how to access the roof!"

"On the fourth floor, head right, then take the last passage." A woman with her shift drooping off her shoulder leaned out of a nearby doorway. "There's a door at the end. The stairs beyond it lead up to the roof."

"Thank you!" Niall released the young man and started up the stairs again.

"Come and see me when you are done with your business up there!" she called after him.

"Millie!" Even as he ran on, Niall could hear the youngling's shock—and hurt. He kept going, found the passage and the door, and hurtled out onto the roof—only to find it empty.

Breathing hard, he circled, checking behind chimneys and

peering down over the sides of the building. On the furthest side, he leaned over, straining to see in the dark. Was that a door, standing open into the alley? From the end of the lane he caught a wisp of motion.

Cursing, he turned to run back, and found Kara coming out onto the roof.

"She's not here any longer," he said. "We've got to get back down."

Without comment, she turned and followed. Niall flew down the stairs, passing the still-quarreling couple at full speed and hitting the ground floor at a run. He searched around the back of the house until he found a room that appeared to be used for the collection of rubbish—at the back of it was the open door he'd spotted.

He was swearing in frustration at the empty lane when Kara came up behind him.

"I swear I saw her, Niall."

"I know you did."

"I didn't imagine it," his wife insisted. "She knew we were in Tom Hawkins's rooms. She was watching."

"I don't doubt you, Kara." He gestured into the lane. "Look. Those droppings are fresh. She had someone waiting here. I caught a glimpse of the cart as it turned out of the lane into the street." He struck the door with a hand. "Damn it! It's a maze down here near the docks. She could be anywhere by now."

"We'll never find her," Kara said glumly.

"Not tonight." Reaching for her, he pulled her close. "But we *will* find her. We were close on her tail tonight. I hope it riles her."

"Do we *want* her to be riled up?"

"Yes," he said. "It's when she's angry that she makes mistakes." He draped an arm across her shoulders. "Come along. Let's go home. We'll start fresh tomorrow."

Kara fell asleep against him on the long ride back to Bluefield, but Niall's mind was too busy to let him rest. They needed a new lead, a new thread to follow. The problem was that they didn't know enough about Petra Scot. That meant that they were going to have to start investigating what they didn't know—and Stayme was not going to like it.

"OH, YOU ARE not going to like this," Stayme said.

It was the next afternoon. Niall and Kara had slept late. They had taken breakfast together while they discussed their options in continuing the search for Petra. Niall warned her that Stayme had already discouraged the line of enquiry Niall thought most promising.

"That was meant to be my line," Niall told the old man now.

"We'll go first," Stayme said, indicating Turner as his partner. "Ours is bound to be shorter. And more disappointing."

"Oh, I don't know about that," Kara said sourly.

They had gathered in the guest room, where Turner was still confined by doctor's orders. Kara sat in a chair close to the bed and Niall stood behind her. He watched the viscount and the butler exchange glances.

"Is this about the spy in our household?"

"It is." Turner patted her hand. "The good news is that we don't believe it was any of our usual staff who betrayed us."

"Who was it, then?" Niall asked gruffly. He hated the idea of someone lurking here, in what had always been Kara's safe retreat.

Now Turner looked abashed. "On the day that you returned home, earlier, before you arrived, I interviewed a young man for a footman's position. He didn't have the necessary experience, and frankly, he didn't appear to have the temperament I require in the household. He seemed quite taken aback, however, that I did not hire him on the spot. He protested that he needed a position, a place to live. I sent him down to the stables to see if they might wish to take on a groom. He set off in that direction, but your arrival distracted me. I forgot to follow up with the stable master about him. I didn't recall the interview until yesterday, when Stayme came to me about someone in the household possibly working with Petra Scot."

"We talked to the stable master," Stayme said, taking up the story. "The boy never spoke with him. He was never seen in the stables at all. But he was spotted setting out in that direction from the house."

"In the same direction as the laboratory," said Turner.

"So you think he placed the biscuits in Kara's lab?" asked Niall.

"He's the likeliest suspect," Stayme said. "And I didn't think he would be." He shot Kara a sheepish look. "I'm afraid I put most of your staff to a bit of a grilling yesterday. They are all steadfastly loyal to you, Kara. And to Niall." He ducked his head. "I had to smooth more than a few ruffled feathers, they were so insulted at the idea of any of them betraying you."

Niall saw a bit of tension ease in his wife. Hearing Stayme confirm her staff's loyalty smoothed a few of his own ruffled feathers. "But what of the notes? You think the same young man stuck them to the front door?"

Turner sighed. "We haven't got that part worked out yet."

"But we will," Stayme vowed.

"I admit, it is a huge relief to think that it wasn't one of our people," Kara said. "But sir, I think we are going to need you to focus on helping us find Petra."

"I'm sorry her classmates in that misguided experiment didn't lead you to her, my dear," the viscount said.

"Yes, well, at least we have what we need to prevent Matthew Hanlin from damaging any more children," she said. "But we need to find Miss Scot. She's taunting us."

"Maybe she was taunting you at the last, allowing herself to be seen like that, but I would wager she never expected you to get so close," Stayme said. "I'll bet she's rattled."

"Perhaps. But I'm afraid if she is rattled, she might be prodded to strike again. We need to find her before she does, but we are out of ideas."

"There is still one avenue we might explore." Niall cast a laden glance at Stayme.

The viscount frowned back at him before Niall saw understanding dawn. Stayme hopped out of his chair. "No. I've already told you. That's not a good idea. Surely we'll find another way."

"What isn't a good idea?" demanded Kara.

"Questioning her father," Niall answered.

"Petra Scot's father? But we don't know who he is." She glanced between them. "Do we?"

"We know who he could be."

"*Might* be," Stayme countered. "There is no way to prove it. And right or wrong, if you confront the man and ask, you will likely have made an enemy."

Niall shrugged.

"An enemy? Of whom?" asked Kara.

Niall indicated that Stayme should answer.

"Damn it, Niall!"

"If we had another lead, we'd follow it. Tell her."

Stayme stared stubbornly for a long moment before he let loose an explosive breath. "Very well! But the consequences will fall to you to clean up."

"So be it," Niall said mildly.

"Who is it?" Kara asked again.

"It is *speculation*," the viscount stressed. "But we know several things that make us suspect one man in particular." He held up a finger. "Petra told the pair of you that her father was one of Princess Caroline's trusted advisors. A man of the law. And who amongst her advisors was her greatest champion? The man she eventually appointed her own attorney general?"

"Brougham," Kara said automatically. Her mouth dropped open. "You do not believe it is him?"

"He did champion Caroline repeatedly," Stayme said. "First

when the prince regent tried to prevent her from seeing her daughter, Princess Charlotte. And later when her husband and the Tories tried to dissolve her marriage and strip her of her title."

"But...he was a lord chancellor," Kara breathed. "Surely he wouldn't..."

"He wasn't lord chancellor at the time Petra was conceived. And he was a *Scot*," Stayme reminded them. "He was spending a great deal of time with Caroline then, before she negotiated with Castlereagh to let her go abroad."

"Good heavens," Turner said quietly.

"Brougham also was—and still is—a great proponent of education. A radical, he was called at times, even before he was in office and proposed the Public Education Act."

"Miss Scot said she was sent back to her father as soon as she was born abroad—and that he promptly turned her over to Matthew Hanlin for his educational experiment."

"Exactly what a married statesman with his own family might do with a natural-born daughter, isn't it?" suggested Stayme.

Kara sat, blinking at the possibility. She looked to Niall. "So do you think he knows? What she has become?"

Stayme answered before Niall could speak. "Of course he knows, but he damned well doesn't want anyone else to know it. If he knew you suspected the truth, he'd likely already be moving against you."

"The man hasn't held any political power in years," Niall objected.

"That doesn't make him any less dangerous. Brougham was drummed out of his position *because* he was arrogant and dangerous. He's not afraid to burn bridges. He stood in the House of Lords and threatened to expose George's illegal marriage to Maria Fitzherbert. You and your mother would have been exposed as well, Niall." Stayme shook his head. "Brougham backed them all down. He also made an enemy of Byron and of Wellington, for God's sake. A few years ago, he tried to apply for French citizenship and a seat in the French National Assembly. If he would abandon the country he once led, do you think he would hesitate to ruin a fledgling duke of dubious origins and his slightly scandalous wife? The pair of you are particularly vulnerable to his sort of enmity."

"He's vulnerable, too," Niall insisted. "If it becomes known what Petra has done to undermine the throne and the nation, and his connection to her is exposed…"

"It's a dangerous game," Stayme warned. "And he's a ruthless opponent. Listen, allow me to send out a few feelers. Gauge his current mood. Discover if he is even in the country. He spends much of his time on the French coast. In the meantime, the pair of you think about whether you want to enter a war like this. And try like hell to find another path to Petra Scot."

Niall agreed, and they all stood and started to disperse. He was weighing Stayme's arguments in his mind. His mentor wielded a hidden power that made him a man to be reckoned with, the sort that came from knowing everyone's secrets and where all the bodies were buried. The fact that he urged caution with Brougham meant something.

"Wait." Kara paused in the doorway. "Perhaps we do have another thread to follow. Turner, what was the name of the man you interviewed for footman? If Petra sent him, perhaps he can lead us back to her."

Turner brightened, but it only lasted a moment. "If we can find him."

"His name?"

"Jamie Horton. At least, that was the name he gave me."

"He's not a local, then?"

"No. He said he came in on the early train from London."

"Well, then, perhaps he stopped in the village. Or he might have spoken to someone on the train. We could ask about, discover which locals might have ridden with him."

"It's a long shot," mused Niall.

"It is," Kara said. "But I cannot just sit and wait. It will give me something to *do*. Something to make me feel as if we are getting closer."

Niall understood. "Then let's go."

Chapter Ten

K ARA WOKE EARLY the next morning. Beside her, Niall slept on, so she merely rolled over and eyed the gradually lightening sky. They hadn't found anything to lead them to Jamie Horton yesterday. She racked her brain and watched the clouds moving in, low and heavy. They matched her mood.

"I can hear you thinking," Niall said softly, sometime later.

"I didn't mean to be so loud."

Laughing, he pulled her over onto her back and kissed her. "Good morning, Duchess."

"Good morning, love."

"What gears are turning so relentlessly in your brain?"

Solemnly, she regarded his handsome face for a moment before running a finger along the bristly, hard line of his jaw. "Perhaps we should heed Stayme. Maybe it is not a good idea to take on Brougham."

He sighed. "We will, if we must. You said it yourself. We cannot merely sit and wait for Petra to come at us again."

"Neither do we wish to fight a war on two fronts." She rose up on an elbow. "Nor do I wish for you to suffer the lasting consequences of making an enemy like that."

He scoffed. "What consequences? People being what they are, the commissions for my art have risen along with my notoriety."

She brushed a lock of his dark hair, longer than was fashionable, from his brow. "You know what I mean, Niall. Your title is an opportunity. You could accomplish real good with it. Far-reaching benefits. I don't want anything to keep you from that."

He rolled over onto his back. "Only sixteen representative Scottish peers are elected to sit in the Lords at Westminster. Who knows how long it will be before I am known enough, or reach a level of approval high enough to even stand for election?"

"You know the government and the royals are watching you. If they respect the way you handle yourself, they could grant you another title. An English one. One that comes with *all* the benefits and responsibilities."

"Again, when?" he asked, sounding exasperated. "Petra is a danger *now*. And I would give up a hundred titles to keep you all safe from her."

Scooting closer, she curled up against him. "I know that. I do. I just wish we had some other way."

A quiet knock on the door surprised them both.

"Your Grace?"

"Elsie? Come in." Kara sat up and regarded her dresser with raised brows. "What is it?"

"Oh, Your Grace! We must make you ready. There is a constable downstairs! He's come to fetch you, and he says you both must come to London at once."

Kara rolled out of bed. Niall made to do the same from the other side, but he clearly recalled his state of undress and paused. "Has something happened? Has the constable said anything?"

"Oh, yes, sir!" The maid regarded them both with eager eyes. "He says Petra Scot is dead!"

CONSTABLE BERNE TOOK them straight to Scotland Yard, where

Inspector Wooten awaited them in his office.

"It's true?" Niall asked, moving to shake the man's hand.

"It is."

"What happened?"

"She drowned," Wooten said.

"Drowned?" Kara asked in shock.

"She was found washed up before the first lock in Tedding-ton, late last night. We had sent out a description of her by telegraph, so they knew we were looking for a woman like that. They were quick to bring her straight here."

"We saw her down by the docks the night before last," Niall reminded him. "She must have headed up river right after we saw her."

"Perhaps. The Thames isn't tidal after Teddington, so she could have gone in anywhere past there, even as far as Hampton Court, and been swept back that way."

"I would worry about the particulars if it was anyone else, but I confess, I'm just glad we won't have to worry about her any longer."

"Are you sure it's her?" asked Kara.

"It's her," Wooten said quietly. He crossed the office to bend over her hand. "I thought that, considering everything that has happened, you both might wish to view the body."

Niall certainly did. "I do appreciate your consideration, Wooten. Will you smooth over a visit with the coroner?"

Wooten's mouth tightened. "We have not sent her to the coroner's. After her escape from custody last time, I'm not taking any risks. Imagine the ruckus if the body disappeared, too."

"Where is she?" asked Kara.

"Downstairs." Wooten waved a hand toward the door. "I'll take you if you are sure you wish to see her?"

"You don't have to, Kara," Niall said gently. "I'll look and be sure enough for both of us."

He saw her hesitate a moment, but she shook her head. "No. I think I need to know for myself."

They followed Wooten through the busy main office, filled with detectives, constables, petitioners, and desk after desk piled high with strewn papers and files. At the back of the building, they took a narrow set of stairs down to the basement. The inspector used a key to unlock a small room and ushered them in.

Lamps had been lit. The flickering light only served to showcase the dirty corners of the floor and the dust on the stone buttresses arching overhead. Two tables were centered in the room. One held a form covered in a sheet.

Wooten went to stand at the head of the table. Niall went to the other side. Kara took his arm and stood a half step behind him. The inspector shot him a questioning look, and Niall nodded.

Wooten pulled the sheet back only far enough to expose her face.

Niall let loose a long, relieved sigh.

"Wait. It's her?" Kara was peering past him.

"It's her." Her hair was slicked away from her face. "Look at the nose and chin." Her skin was very pale and bore myriad small marks.

"What's happened to her?" Kara whispered. "What are those cuts and scratches from?"

"The coroner says the abrasions are likely from encountering objects in the currents," Wooten told her. "She would have received them after she drowned."

Kara still peered at her. "Look at her expression. She looks almost…frightened. I never thought to see such a thing."

"If she came to a bad end, then it was no different from the many she brought to others," Niall declared. He refused to feel sorry for the woman.

"I know I should feel relieved, but I can only think of her gifts and the opportunities she was given. It all might have gone so differently."

"All I can remember is the uncontrollable rage which took her over that day. How her loss of control killed her best friend."

Niall's tone grew harsher. "And then I consider the unrest she stirred up, and the chaos and confusion she meant to spread throughout Europe—all in hopes of profiting from it." He shook his head. "She's kept us virtual prisoners with her threats. She harmed Turner! I know I shouldn't say it, but it is a relief that she is gone."

"What will happen to her now?" Kara asked as Wooten covered her face once more.

"Her burial, you mean?" The inspector looked serious. "The Crown took over many assets owned by the League of Dissolution when you brought the organization down. I'll make sure they pay for a proper burial."

"Thank you." Kara gave him a nod.

"It's over," Niall said with relief surging through his chest and making him feel lighter.

She hesitated, still staring at the form on the table. "Yes. You are right, of course."

He took her hands. "Turner is safe. Harold is safe. We no longer have to worry about Gyda going into Town or fires being set on the estate. It's over. Let's go home. And get on with our lives."

And at last, she smiled. "Yes. Thank goodness." She shot Wooten a grateful look. "Thank you, Inspector. Please, send your wife our best wishes."

Niall grinned as she breathed deeply and stepped out of the room. "Yes. Let's go home."

Chapter Eleven

NIALL JUMPED WITH both feet back into a resumption of normal life, but it took Kara nearly a week to truly accept that the threat was over. For days she still found herself watching out windows, scanning the horizon, and listening for a shout of trouble.

She did not understand why the end was so difficult for her to accept. Perhaps it had been the sight of Petra Scot's body. The woman had been as much a force of nature as a storm that blew in, demanded attention, dictated movements, and overthrew the natural order of things. Seeing her so still, quiet, and somehow small—it had not felt real. And that expression, frozen on her face… Kara just could not imagine Petra afraid of *anything*. She would have expected the woman to meet death with defiance and bluster, no matter the form it came in.

She wondered if it was just because the whole thing felt anti-climactic. Their last struggle with the woman had ended in abduction, intrigue, fire, and death. It had brought down an international conspiracy. To find the woman dead with no notion of what happened to her just felt…too easy.

And perhaps that was it, after all. Life had been one adventure after another since she'd met Niall on that fateful day in Mr. Grant's study. Could it be that peace and quiet didn't feel like the normal state of things anymore?

Niall clearly suffered no such doubts. He threw himself happily into constructing his marshland-themed gates. His conversation was full of details about beaver tails, willow, and meadowsweet.

Stayme returned to his own home. Turner went back to work, having received clearance and a warning to take things slowly from Balgate. When Harold wasn't helping Niall or studying, the lad was practicing his lunges on the fencing strip or trying to conquer the rope climb in her gymnasium.

It was Gyda who finally pulled Kara from her haze. Her friend's happiness was brilliant, bubbling, and contagious—as was her enthusiasm for her new beau's project. Gyda convinced Kara to connect Lord Charles with a couple of bright young inventors she funded. In making the introductions, Kara found herself swept up in plans for the new museum. She even agreed to take a week's turn in the living creation spot at the new venture—and thrilled Harold when she asked him to act as her assistant.

Together, the two of them discussed which projects they would work on during their time in the new space. They debated public interest versus what would move Kara forward on her latest commission. They decided to ride into Town one morning with Gyda, to measure the workspace, inspect the light, and finalize plans for their preparation.

It was a pretty, sunny start to the day. Kara could feel the approach of spring in the air as they set out for the train station and see it in the first push of bulbs through the earth. They booked a first-class car, and Gyda spoke of the work already accomplished at the museum during the short ride to London, while Harold worked on a sketch for the sword he meant for his Green Man automaton to carry.

"Charles was so lucky to find Ansel," Gyda was saying. "The building in Soho Square could not be more perfect. Ansel had already begun updating the rooms into gallery space. His connections in the art world have been invaluable. He's had plenty of time to audition artists, while Charles has screened the craftsmen. There are still a few more to be seen, but all is on schedule for the museum to open on time."

"I can scarcely believe everything you have accomplished, and so quickly," Kara marveled.

"Just a few days left before the grand opening gala," Gyda said brightly. "I'm so proud of Charles."

"I'm proud of *you*, too. You've all worked hard."

"But the vision is all Charles's. And his dedication is unmatched."

"And he still finds time to make you happy." Kara grinned at her friend. "In my eyes, that is his greatest accomplishment."

Gyda leaned back against the seat and threw her hands in the air. "In that, he is very accomplished indeed."

Kara laughed, and Harold looked up from his sketch. "Have we reached London?"

"Soon," Kara told him. "Soon."

After the train, they took a hansom cab to Soho Square. They found Lord Charles Osbourne standing outside, waiting to greet them.

"Your Grace," he said, bowing low over Kara's hand. "What a pleasure to welcome you. Gyda can scarcely wait to show you the space." He shook Harold's hand. "Both of you."

"We can scarcely wait to see it." She admired the exterior, her smile growing. "May I presume that Gyda had a hand in choosing the color?" It was the sort of dusky blue that her friend adored.

"You may not!" Gyda protested. "Charles chose it to please me. I had no notion of it beforehand."

"The color is stunning against the white trimmings. And it certainly stands out," Kara noted. The neighboring houses in the row were all russet brick or white.

"That is the idea," Lord Charles said. "We wish to be easy to find and tempting enough to draw people in."

"You have a bowed window," Harold said. "Can I go inside and look out?"

"Of course. Come. Let us show you around."

Kara exclaimed over the inside. It was bright and airy with many windows letting light in. The walls were all done in subtle white paint or patterns instead of the often obligatory scarlet or red.

"We want the art to be the focus," Lord Charles explained. "We'll have the paintings in this front room and the craftsmen set up as you move through the rest of the building."

Servants bustled through the rooms, doing last-minute cleaning and carrying in furniture. In one corner, a chair and an easel were being set up.

"Ansel means to do some painting in here at times," Lord Charles said.

"I'm sure the attendees will find it fascinating," Kara replied.

"Oh, watch behind you," Lord Charles said, and Kara turned in surprise to find a section of the wall, complete with hung artwork, swinging outward. "Apologies. We wanted to maximize the wall space, so made the servants' entrances into hidden doors," he explained.

Kara stepped closer to examine the piece that hung there. A seascape, it showed rugged cliffs over startling blue water and a vivid pink sky. "Oh, how lovely. Is that Cornwall?"

"It is. You have a good eye. It will be joined by other works by Mr. Nicholas Locke, who has traveled all along the coasts of our fair isle. His work highlights the differences along our shores, but also the beauty of them all."

Kara's eyes widened as she moved along the wall and on to the next corner. "Well. This one is different, isn't it?" It was a depiction of Caligula at the Colosseum, feeding his own citizens from the audience to the lions. Catching her breath, she leaned forward. "Good heavens. Is Caligula supposed to be Lord Palmerston?"

Lord Charles bit back a smile. "It is. Mr. Sculley has a series that depicts some of our society's best-known members in tableaus from history and mythology."

"A satirical series, I take it?" she said with a grin.

"Indeed, although his work is vivid and memorable."

"Well, that should draw in a few more attendees." She blinked. "Wait. Did you say Sculley? Not Mr. Douglas Sculley?"

"I do! Do you know his work?"

"No, but I met him very briefly, recently. I look forward to seeing the rest."

"Oh, he had a great many more than we had room to use." Lord Charles's mouth twisted. "And I did have to forbid one piece that depicted our own good queen as the Queen of Sheba—atop a camel." He shuddered. "That sort of attention, we have no need of."

Kara laughed, and he took them on through and stopped to answer questions about a wood and metal frame being set up in one room. "It's to be a bobbinet machine," he told them. "A machine that crafts lace. An amazing invention, one that has stood the test of years, with only a few improvements to change the originally patented machine." He glanced at Gyda. "I am in awe of the craftsmen who create beauty and function with their hands and hearts and the knowledge they hold. I am also a bit enamored of the inventors who create machines to imitate their work."

"Tell them your idea for this display," Gyda urged. "And how it came about."

Her beau smiled at her. "One of the older tenants on my father's home estate makes handmade lace. I've been fascinated by the process for years, and she very obligingly allowed me to watch her as she worked. How her fingers would fly as she would intersect, tie, and knot the threads on her pillow! I was enthralled, seeing her twist and mesh and weave. I was stunned, as a young man, when I heard there were machines that could perform the same functions. I could not imagine coming up with a design to replicate Mrs. Hastings's work. It was one of the first machines I searched out as a young man. When we were talking about the idea behind this museum, I had the idea to place them both in this room, so that people may marvel over both creative processes. Mrs. Hastings has agreed to attend the opening gala and demonstrate her art, next to the machine."

Lord Charles showed Kara and Harold the alcove adjoining the front room, where they would set up their work and interact with attendees when it was their turn to take a week in the space. It was also brightly lit from the square-facing windows. "It's definitely large enough for us to fit two tables in here," Kara told Harold.

"Two projects at once?" Lord Charles asked. "That will be a treat for us all." He beckoned Harold to the windows. "Tell me about the project you'll be working on while you are here? Perhaps passersby will peek in and see you at work—and then come to investigate."

Harold began to tell him all about his Green Man automaton. As he answered Lord Charles's questions, Kara wandered back to the main room and went to stand at the bow window. It looked out onto the square, with its green grass, statuary, and tall trees. A peaceful scene, with couples strolling and children at play under the watchful eyes of their nannies.

As she watched, though, a chill began to swirl around the base of her spine. Kara started to step back from the window, but something made her pause. She moved closer, instead, and scanned the park again.

What was it? Everything looked calm and routine.

There. A woman stood in the shadow of a towering tree. She had one hand on the trunk and her gaze fixed on the window where Kara stood.

Not a woman.

Petra Scot.

The familiar figure stared at her—then flashed a malice-filled grin.

"Gyda," Kara croaked. She needed to know if her friend could see the woman as well. Her tone grew louder as panic set in. "Gyda!"

But her friend had gone to the back rooms to inspect some of the paintings that Ansel had already chosen to mount for their opening. "Kara?" she called. "What is it?"

"Come here, please! Now, Gyda!"

The figure had not moved. The open threat in her stare had not changed. Kara gasped for breath. Fear and shock hit her like a lightning strike to the top of her head, branching all through her body.

"Kara? What is it?" Harold slammed into her, his face full of concern. "What's wrong?"

She looked down into his worried face and clutched him close. "I…I thought…"

She looked back toward the tree, but the woman was gone.

WITH SMALL, CAREFUL strikes, Niall molded delicate petals, one after the other. He would need a great many of them to create a swell of meadowsweet to adorn Blundel's gates.

Pausing a moment, he set down his tools and flexed his arm. He had tired it out earlier, hammering out crossbars that would both form the gate and provide structure to which he would attach the elements of the marshland theme. But these smaller strokes he used now would let him get in a couple of more hours of work, as long as he stretched the arm.

He'd just picked up his hammer again when Kara came rushing into the forge. The surge of pleasure he felt drained away when he saw the strained expression on her face.

"What is it?" He threw the hammer down. "Are you well?"

"I don't know," she moaned, coming straight on until she burrowed in his arms. "I think perhaps I am losing my wits."

He held her tight a moment before leading her over to the small table and chairs in the corner. He settled her, then poured her a glass of water from the pitcher that the maids kept fresh and cool. "Take a drink," he ordered her.

She did as he asked.

"Tell me," he said, taking the glass back.

She hesitated.

"Kara?"

"I don't want you to think less of me," she whispered.

"Not in a hundred years," Niall vowed, kneeling before her. "There is nothing you cannot say to me. I hope you know that, for I have certainly held tight to the belief that I can say anything to you."

She reached out to clutch his hand. "Of course you can. I trust you. I do. I trust *us*. It's just—I've seen something that makes me wonder if I can trust myself."

He nodded, encouraging her to continue.

Haltingly, she began to speak.

He listened carefully as she told him what she had seen, and also about the thoughts and feelings that had been haunting her. She heaved a sigh as she finished, as if relieved, but she still peered anxiously into his face. "What do you think? Have I lost my grip on reality?"

"No," he said firmly.

"But you don't think it was her?"

"No," he repeated, with almost the same force. "We saw her body, Kara. Lying right there on the table in front of us. Petra Scot is dead." He stood and pulled her to her feet. Dropping into her chair, he tugged her into his lap. "Do I think that your mind created something that wasn't there? It's possible. The human brain is an incredible tool—and yours is more powerful than most."

She snorted. "I'll assume that is a compliment."

"It's meant as such," he assured her. "But I think it is equally as likely that someone is trying to upset you."

She looked surprised at the idea. "But…who? And why?"

"Petra had confederates," he reminded her. "Someone was hiding her away. Plenty of others spent years doing her bidding.

Perhaps they are carrying on with her mission. They might not even realize she is dead. There has certainly been no mention of it in the papers. Nor will there be." Shrugging, he asked, "How clearly did you see the woman?"

"Clearly enough." She thought back. "I was convinced. I saw the same height and form. Dark hair. It was the same *attitude*, Niall. The direct stare, challenging me. The posture—all so antagonistic. If it was staged, it was done exactly like when she's attempted to stare me down in the past."

"Probably done purposely," he mused. "The same way she taunted you a few nights ago. We know she is a master of misdirection. She might have put this doppelgänger in play before she left London. Perhaps to make us believe she was still here."

He felt a great deal of the tension melt out of her frame. "I never thought of that. Thank you, Niall." She nestled in against him.

He gripped her tightly. They sat that way for a while. She felt so warm and soft against him, so small in his lap, yet her heart stretched so large and giving and generous. He knew he was the luckiest man in the empire.

Burying his face in her hair, he inhaled her scent—womanly florals cut with just a hint of metal filings and clock oil. So uniquely Kara. As always, it sent desire rolling hard through him.

"My arm could use a rest." It came out nearly a growl. "Why don't we go upstairs, and you can rub it for me?"

She grinned up at him. "Your Grace! Is that an indecent proposal?"

He gave her a look of affront. "I am a duke," he said loftily. "All of my proposals are decent."

"Well, in that case, I accept."

"I am a bit sweaty," he warned.

"Just the way I like you," she murmured, waggling her brows.

He laughed at the echo of the comment she'd made before and let her climb out of his embrace. Taking his hand, she kept a hold of it as they walked leisurely through the grounds to the main house. Niall struggled to maintain a casual mien, but the servants they encountered all noted their clasped hands and turned away, smiling.

"Odin's arse, forget decorum," he said as they started up the stairs. "They all suspect what we are up to, in any case." He bent down and swept her into his arms, taking the stairs two at a time and entering her room, because it was closest.

She was laughing and trying to muffle it in his chest. He kicked the door closed behind him—and then stopped cold.

She started to place kisses along his neck, above the line of the linen shirt he wore to work in.

"Kara."

She raised her head and pulled away, examining his countenance. "What is it?"

He nodded toward her bed.

She turned to look—and gasped.

"Well, now we know." He let her feet slide down the front of him. "Whatever you saw, it was not all in your head."

Chapter Twelve

KARA STARED. ANOTHER bakery box, this one sitting squarely in the center of her bed. Whoever was perpetrating this campaign, they had been in her bedroom. A wave of fury and dismay struck her, but she was forced to admit to a bit of vindication in there, too. She wasn't imagining things. She let herself wallow in her immediate reaction for a moment, then deliberately swept it away as she called up determination instead.

She crept close enough to see the mark that proved it was indeed from Eliassen's Bakery. When she turned, Niall gave her a stern look.

"This was *not* Petra Scot."

"No," she agreed. "It was not."

She moved past him to open the door and call for her maid.

"Yes, ma'am?" Elsie came hurrying down the passage from the guest chamber that she and Gyda had turned into a sewing room as they raced to finish Gyda's Nordic gown. The maid was clearly surprised to be summoned by her mistress at this hour of the day.

Kara stood in the doorway, opening it only a bit. "Elsie, did a parcel arrive for me today?"

"No, indeed." The maid frowned. "Not that I am aware of."

"Did you leave anything in here for me?"

"No, ma'am." Elsie's confusion was clear and genuine. "Were you expecting a delivery?"

"I was not." Kara swung the door wide and beckoned the woman in. "Do you have any idea how that got here?"

Puzzled, Elsie ventured in. She curtsied to Niall, then stilled when she spotted the box. "Oh, no, ma'am," she breathed. "Is that…?"

"It is." Kara drew a deep breath. "Please go and send Turner up here, if you will. And would you ask around amongst the other maids? We need to know if anyone…strange has been spotted in or around the house today."

"Yes, ma'am. Right away."

But Turner's instincts were still finely honed. He turned up in the passage outside just a moment or two after Elsie's departure. As the door was open, he put his head inside. "Is there anything—" He stopped. "That's not…?"

"It is."

Turner entered, and together the three of them approached the bed. Niall gingerly reached out and flipped the box lid open.

"Butter biscuits," Kara said with a sigh. But looking closer, she saw that each biscuit had a single bite taken out of it. "Good heavens. Is that supposed to be a threat?"

"Turner, have you found anything else about that would-be footman?" asked Niall.

"Nothing," the butler said. "I sent one of the lads into the village to ask around again, but no one has spotted him." He tilted his head. "Do you believe it is him, lurking about and leaving these nasty little signs?"

"He might be hanging around the vicinity, carrying out Petra's agenda," Niall mused.

Kara turned at a scratch on the door.

"Ma'am?" Elsie stood there, looking pale and troubled. "I think you had all better come downstairs and have a word with Prudence."

With a shrug in Niall's direction, Kara set off after her. They found the maid in tears. She sat in a parlor at the hearth, a bucket and her duster beside her.

Niall went immediately to soothe her. "There now, lass," he crooned, taking her hand and leading her to a chair. "What has upset you, Prudence?"

"It's my fault, sir." A cascade of fresh sobs emerged. "I'm so sorry!"

Niall looked up at Kara, helpless before her tears.

She gave him a nod and took the seat next to the maid. "Prudence, no one is angry with you. No one is *going* to be angry with you. Just tell us what you think you have done."

"Oh, miss! I mean, ma'am! I mean, Your Grace! I didn't mean to!"

Kara gave the girl a pat and a moment to collect herself. "Prudence, does this, by chance, have to do with that candidate who came to ask for the footman's position?"

Shuddering, the girl nodded.

"Tell us, won't you?"

"I met him the first day he came, hoping for the job," she whispered. "Jamie Horton. He had to wait for Mr. Turner to become available, and they sent him to sit in the servants' hall. I was there, mixing up a batch of wood polish." She looked up into Kara's face. "He didn't seem much like a footman. I thought he sounded so smart and funny. Witty. He made me laugh." She looked down again. "And he flirted with me. I thought he truly admired me."

"That was the day the biscuits were left in the laboratory, to the best of our knowledge," Turner reminded them.

"Did you see him again?" asked Kara.

Shamefaced, Prudence nodded. "I told him that day that I'd heard that there was a footman needed at Wood Rose Abbey. He came back the next day to thank me, as he'd taken the position there. He said he was so grateful and he kissed my hand, just like I was a lady."

"That was the afternoon that the first note was left on the

front door," Niall recalled.

"The next note was left on the day of my unfortunate over-sight, I understand," Turner said.

"The day of your unfortunate *accident*," Niall corrected him.

Kara looked to the maid. "Was Jamie here that day?"

Prudence nodded. "We had Mrs. Canning downstairs after the accident, and when His Grace took her home, she forgot her bag. Jamie turned up later, come to fetch it." She looked indignant. "He tried to kiss me that day, right on the mouth. I didn't let him, ma'am."

Niall shook his head. "The wily little bastard set himself up with a good reason to come back and forth between the estates."

"You mean, I was his excuse to come and make mischief?" Prudence asked. She was starting to sound angry. As she should.

"Was he here today?" asked Kara.

The girl nodded. "This morning. He said he was sent on an errand to the village and couldn't help but stop to see me. It was flattering, Your Grace! But when I heard Elsie asking around, I started to count back, and it was then that I knew what he'd been up to. I cannot believe he had the cheek to go right into your bedroom, Your Grace!" A tear slipped down her cheek. "If he took anything, you can take the cost of it right out of my wages."

"I don't believe he did, so you may rest easy on that score." Kara hadn't even thought to check, but she would have Elsie take a look. She certainly wouldn't tell Prudence if he had.

"I'm sorry I disappointed you," the maid said sorrowfully.

"You have not. You didn't know what he was up to, and when you understood, you came to us." Kara bit her lip. "I'm sorry he used you in that way, and I hate to ask…"

"Oh, ask, please, ma'am!"

"If you could find a way to pretend you didn't know about his perfidy, you might be able to help us nab him."

Niall's eyes widened. "Yes. Brilliant, Kara."

Prudence looked up. "You mean I could help you and also get a piece of my own back?" She leaned forward. "What would you want me to do? Lure him in, like?"

"You won't need to do anything whatsoever, for now," Kara replied. "Just go on as if you know nothing. If he shows up again, however, if you could find a way to notify Turner or the duke…?"

"Of course! I'll do anything to make it up to you!"

Kara stood. The thought that had been wiggling at the back of her mind would not rest. She paced to the window and back. "Niall, when you wrote to inform Robert Preston of Petra's death, did he respond?"

"Yes."

"And did he say whether he had discovered Tom Hawkins's whereabouts?"

"He had not yet found him." Niall's brows suddenly shot high. "You do not think…?"

"You recall what Preston said about Tom's pranks?"

Niall rose to his feet. "The apples! He filled Hanlin's desk with apples, each with one bite out of it! Just like the biscuits upstairs. *Odin's arse!* You think that Jamie Horton might actually be Tom Hawkins?"

"It's not much to go on," Kara admitted.

"But it does make a warped sort of sense." Niall sounded excited. "I think we need to speak to Robert Preston again."

UPON THINKING IT over, Niall persuaded Kara that it would be best for them to go into London to stay.

"We have the rooms above the coffee house in Adams Street. Think about it. If we go, word will spread. Jamie Horton, or whoever he is, will believe he's accomplished his goal and frightened you. It will make him less likely to prance over here and mess about with Prudence."

"Which will make it less likely that she might give the game away," mused Kara.

"Exactly. And it will keep him at Wood Rose Abbey until we can talk to Robert Preston. I hope we can convince him to come down and see if 'Jamie' is truly Tom Hawkins.

"Perhaps we should ask Turner to stop over there and visit Mrs. Canning," said Kara. "If he mentions we've gone to London, no doubt it will be discussed among the servants over there."

"Excellent idea. And if we head up to Town this evening, we can be sure to stop in at Preston's home early tomorrow, before he heads to Westminster," Niall continued. "We might even convince him to come down here after his day is finished."

"The sooner, the better." Kara brightened. "And I can check in on Rose Martin, and see how she's getting along with Rachel in the shop."

They made the trip to the city after leaving instructions with Turner and Elsie, who would travel up to join them the next day. Niall gazed fondly about the apartment when they arrived, recalling the first time he'd been here—when they had been forced to make an unorthodox escape. Throwing Kara a grin, he crossed to the window and peeked behind the curtain.

"The plank should still be there," she said with a laugh. "But I trust we will not be forced to use it."

"You never know." Niall put his hands on his hips and looked around again. "Stayme keeps telling me I should invest in a real townhouse in Mayfair, but I have a fondness for this place and the shenanigans we've got up to in here."

They spent the evening visiting in the set of rooms next door, where Rose Martin was staying. Niall thought the young woman looked both sturdier and happier.

"I am so happy to have the chance to thank you both," the young woman said, pouring tea. "Thank you for finding me a place here. Rachel has been everything welcoming and kind."

"She says you have been a boon to her—a hard worker," Kara replied. "She also says you have revolutionized the storing and ordering of her supplies."

"I have a gift for organization. It's one of the reasons I was asked to help teach the younger girls at school." Her happiness dimming at the mention of her past, Miss Martin looked down at her twisting hands. "I heard that the Hanlins' school has closed."

"Indeed," Kara said reassuringly. "Her Majesty strongly suggested that Matthew Hanlin find a new career. One that does not involve proximity to children or young women."

Miss Martin drew a deep breath. "Thank you. It is easier to focus on my own future, knowing that."

"What of your son?" Niall enquired gently. "Have you considered—"

"No," she interrupted, shaking her head. "He is better off where he is, with a loving family. I will leave them happy. I will concentrate on making my own way in the world. And this is a good place to start."

"I feel sure you will prosper," Kara told her.

Later, after they had returned to their own rooms, she told Niall more.

"Rachel has been looking for someone, a partner with whom she might start another shop, in another part of the city. If Miss Martin continues to impress her, then I will back their enterprise."

"Have I ever told you that you are a marvel?" he asked, pulling her in for a kiss.

"I believe you have," she said, smiling against his lips. "But I wouldn't mind if you took me to bed and told me again."

THE NEXT MORNING, they set out very early to find Preston in his Bridge Street rooms, handily located in Westminster, close to his work.

He looked initially surprised to see them, but surprise turned quickly to gratitude when Niall held up a wrapped box with a covered pot of coffee and a platter of Rachel's pastries.

"Well, then, come in, seeing as you've brought breakfast with you. But I cannot stay long," he warned. "I must prepare for a meeting with Sir Charles Barry this afternoon." He set out cups and dishes on a small table and then sipped the hot coffee. "What is this about, then?"

Niall cleared his throat. "First, Kara is worried that you might feel…conflicted about Petra's death. We wish to offer our condolences, should you need them."

"We understand that you were raised together," said Kara. "That means something, no matter how it all turned out. No one could blame you for mourning her."

Preston heaved a sigh. "I've wondered if I should feel something, but honestly, I only feel relieved. I'm happy she cannot stir up any more trouble. It's a blessing to know that Tom will be free of her. If I can find him, that is."

"We wanted to speak of him as well," Niall admitted.

"Tom is in debt," Preston said bluntly. "I learned that he owes gambling debts that he cannot pay. I hope it means that he is in hiding, and not in worse trouble than even I suspected."

Niall exchanged glances with Kara. "It's possible that we might know where he is hiding." He told the engineer about their suspicions regarding the new footman at Wood Rose Abbey.

Preston just sat staring ahead for a moment before he spoke. "Hard as it is to imagine Tom as a footman, it seems exactly like something he would do—hide himself away from his creditors while doing Petra's bidding." He gave a sharp laugh. "Lord, but I wish I could see him bowing and scraping to some haughty butler! But instead, he's probably sneaking food from the larder, hiding out back to smoke, and crawling up the maids' skirts."

"We were hoping you *would* see him at it, or at least travel down to Wood Rose Abbey to see if Jamie is truly Tom."

The engineer downed the rest of his coffee. "Yes. Yes, so I will. But not today. As I said, I've a meeting with Sir Charles this afternoon and a great deal of work to complete beforehand. But I will make arrangements. I should be able to travel down tomorrow." Standing, he shrugged into his coat. "Should I come to your estate to report, once I've seen him? If it is indeed Tom, I'll drag him over by the ear."

"No, we are staying on in Town," Niall told him. "We have a gala opening to attend tomorrow evening."

Preston shuddered. "Better you than me."

Kara grinned. "Are you sure, Mr. Preston? I know we could procure you an invitation!"

"No, thank you, Duchess. I'm a builder, not a dancer. I'd sooner carry on a conversation with a plaster dauber than a debutante." He shooed them out the door. "I hope you are right and I find Tom down there. I'll send word, then, once I see your mystery footman."

Chapter Thirteen

G YDA WAS A bundle of nerves about the opening of the museum. She had left earlier to help with last-minute preparations. Kara was primping, determined to do her friend credit, and to be as duchess-like as possible.

"This color is a triumph on you, ma'am," Elsie said as she settled the pointed bodice over Kara's middle. "I don't know how they achieved such a lovely shade so perfectly between blue and green."

"They are doing wonders with coal tar and other secondary products for dyes right now." Kara looked over the gown with a satisfied eye. The low shoulders featured a fall of brilliant white lace. At the top edge of the lace, a line of jeweled flowers meandered across her skin. A matching pattern of embroidery adorned the hem and the edges of the split-front skirt.

"Are you sure you won't add another crinoline?" Elsie asked, eyebrows raised. "Wider skirts are all the fashion."

"I need to be able to move, Elsie." It was an old argument.

Niall, entering from his adjoining room, let out a long, low whistle.

Turning, Kara smiled at the sight of him in a frock coat, frilly linen, and his formal Clan Kerr kilt. "I would say the same of you, if only I could whistle."

Elsie quietly withdrew, and Niall came to stand beside her. He grinned at their reflections in her mirror. "Don't we make a fine pair?"

"Yes," she answered seriously. "We do." She didn't mean their appearances.

"Almost ducal." He planted a kiss atop her head.

"Almost," she agreed, tilting her head up for a proper kiss. "But it's the missing part that makes us *us*."

Not long afterward, they arrived at the gala to find carriages lined up to reach Soho Square.

"Should we walk?" Kara asked. "It's a fine evening, and Gyda urged us to come as early as we could. She's to meet the Duke and Duchess of Stratton tonight, and she's quite nervous about it."

Niall handed her down and they made their way slowly to the museum. Footmen kept the gawking crowds back, but the event was obviously going to be a crush. The spacious front room was filled with a sea of well-dressed and well-heeled guests. Lord Charles's family and friends, probably, but also some other, no-doubt-curious members of the aristocracy had turned out. They mixed with members of the artistic community, scientists, inventors, and even a few industrialists.

"Perhaps they are looking for new designs or the latest technology to adapt," Kara whispered to Niall, nodding toward a group of fellow factory owners.

Maids and footmen circulated with glasses of wine and champagne. Kara took one, and she and Niall joined in as everyone raised a glass and toasted Ansel Wells, Lord Charles, and the success of the museum. Afterward, they drifted through the main hall. Kara noted the many attendees admiring the art, and she grinned to herself to see the crowded corner where Mr. Sculley's work hung. People there were whispering, giggling, and peering over each other's shoulders. She thought she spotted the artist, but he was quickly swallowed up in the crowd.

"Kara! Niall!"

They turned to find Gyda beckoning them. She stood near the performance/creative alcove. Tonight it was occupied by a jeweler and looked to be proving a popular draw. Waving, they made their way through the throng to her.

"Oh, Gyda," Kara said. "You are breathtaking!"

Gyda and Elsie had raced to finish the Nordic gown—and Gyda looked like a Viking warrior maiden come to life. Her blonde hair was caught up in elaborate braids that hung down over her traditional dress. She wore a cream-colored underdress with long sleeves ending in substantial cuffs of buff leather. The overdress was in her favorite dusky blue, with a similar cuff-shaped bodice of the same leather. This piece fastened to straps below the shoulder with two carved tortoiseshell brooches. Between them hung the strings of colorful glass and amber beads they had found for her during their travels.

Niall looked his assistant over with approval. "I'll wager you are making many a man here wish he were a Viking right now."

"Let them wish it." Gyda snorted. "I've already informed two fools that Viking women handled the finances, oversaw the land management, and were involved in trading goods. They owned property and could request a divorce and reclaim their dowries if a man failed to live up to their expectations."

"I'll wager that cooled their fantasies," said Kara, laughing.

"Well, it certainly rid me of their company," Gyda replied. She looked around, anxious. "It's going well, isn't it?"

"It looks to be a smashing success," Kara assured her. "You may relax. Look at all of these happy guests." She glanced about. "But where is Lord Charles? We've yet to speak to him."

"He's gone to the back rooms. They've set up a telegraph back there. He is urging guests to send messages from one side of the house to the other. Stayme is back there, explaining how it works and sending naughty messages to ladies."

Kara choked on her drink.

Beside her, Gyda stiffened. "Don't look, but Charles's mother is approaching. She seems baffled by me, but she brightened considerably when I told her I was close to the Duke and Duchess of Sedwick."

Kara made a face. "We will try to behave."

"Will we?" asked Niall.

"Niall!" Gyda jabbed him with an elbow.

"Fine, then. I am entirely too hungry to play nice. I see a tray of veal baskets over there. I'm going to make inroads on it, and then I'm going to go and proposition Stayme over the telegraph and sign it *Victoria Regina*." Laughing, he moved off, but then stopped and looked back. "Gyda, did you order veal baskets tonight just because you know they are my favorite?"

"Yes," she grumped. "Not that you deserve it."

He stepped back, then took her hand and kissed it before backing away. "You are extraordinary. Don't forget it." He looked significantly over her shoulder before turning away and fleeing.

"Coward," Gyda said affectionately as her name was called.

"Miss Winther, there you are." The Duchess of Stratton went around a group of chattering guests to get to them. "Won't you introduce me?"

"Of course, Your Grace."

Kara nodded politely as Gyda made the introductions. Her friend did it with nary a witticism or sassy remark—a sure sign of her anxiousness.

"Your Grace," Kara said smoothly. "What a delight to see you again."

The duchess looked surprised. "Have we met before?" Her entire manner seemed one of puzzlement, as if the event and its purpose was something so outside of her experience that she could find no solid ground.

"Indeed, we have. Several months ago, at one of the queen's receptions."

"Oh, of course." The woman clearly did not recall it, but she struggled on. "Miss Winther tells me that she resides with you at your estate."

"Indeed. We could not do without her, her humor, or her many skills."

"How…how nice. Bluefield Park, is it not? I have heard of its great beauty. It's quite famous for it, isn't it?"

"Thank you. It is quite beautiful, I admit. It has always been grand, but my mother was a great stewardess of the estate and made many improvements. I try to live up to her example."

"I did know your mother, a little," the duchess said. "A lovely woman. She had a sharp wit and varied interests, and yet she was such a lady."

Kara knew a veiled criticism when it was thrown at her. She'd long ago developed the ability to let them slide off. She glanced at Gyda, who rarely let such jabs go and instead returned them in double measure. But her friend merely shifted and smiled wanly—and Kara had *never* seen her care so much about impressing someone. It spoke deeply about how much she must feel for Lord Charles Osbourne.

Well, then. Kara would do what she could to help. She turned a smile on Gyda. "Oh, but you must invite Lord Charles and the duchess to come to tea sometime." She smiled at the woman. "We would love to welcome you."

"I… Thank you."

Clearly, the duchess had expected the invitation to come from Kara, and they had thrown the woman off balance once more. But Kara would show her how much a part of the family her friend was.

The duchess cleared her throat. "I would, of course, be delighted to visit, but if the recent months are any indication, then I suspect my son will be occupied for quite some time in the running of'—her hands fluttered—"the museum," she finished weakly.

"We have been very busy indeed," Gyda replied quickly. "And likely will be for the next few weeks, perhaps a couple of months, as the place gets on its feet and routines are established. But I suspect once that happens, both Ansel and Charles will see the wisdom in hiring a director. Ansel will wish to go back to his painting, and it seems to me that Charles so enjoys his travel, exploring old crafts and art and new industry, that I cannot see him giving it up for very long."

The duchess looked pained to be reminded of her fourth son's odd interests. Among her brood she numbered the very proper heir, spare—currently serving in the Royal Navy—and a third son—studying for the church. Charles, with his fascination with lacemaking, art, and industrial machines, was likely viewed as the broken cog in her well-oiled family. The only one not conforming to expectations.

In this area, Kara could help.

"But how wonderful it must be to have a son with such passionate interests. Not only that, but one with the will and determination to pursue them so boldly—and successfully, as we see tonight. You must be very proud, indeed."

"I… Yes, of course."

Kara leaned in and lowered her voice. "Do you know who I would not be surprised at all to see spending time here?"

"Who?" asked the duchess, clearly worried about the answer.

"Prince Albert. This seems just the sort of enterprise he would approve of," Kara said with a nod. "You know he insists the royal family must have the finest education, including languages, arts, and sciences. And he clearly showed his preference for this sort of event with his work on the Great Exhibition."

"Oh, yes. He did, didn't he?"

"Everything Charles has curated here seems wonderfully suited to Albert's interests. I predict he will become a regular visitor here," Kara said knowingly.

"Do you really think so?" The duchess straightened and looked about. "That would be a fine thing for Charles, would it not?"

"Everyone can see that it took a unique perspective and a great deal of vision to make all of this happen. Not to mention hard work. I don't think there is anything the prince consort would admire more."

"Yes. I think you must be right," the duchess said, growing more enthusiastic. "And so I shall tell his father." She nodded at the crowd around them. "In fact, I think I shall do so right now." She cast a friendlier look upon Gyda. "Do invite me to tea, my dear. I feel sure we have much to talk about."

As she swept away, Gyda clutched Kara's hand. "Odin's arse, but you are diabolical," she whispered. "And brilliant. Thank you!"

Kara waved a hand. "It doesn't take a genius to understand that most mothers wish to be proud of their sons."

"She clearly didn't know what to make of all of this, but you put her on a whole new path."

"She just needed a nudge to look outside traditional notions. It's a small step, but hopefully, it will lead to more."

"Wait until Charles hears! He will be so grateful!" Gyda pressed her hand.

"I do look forward to spending more time with him. But just now, I'm ready to go and squeeze in to see Mr. Sculley's work. I only saw the Lord Palmerston the other day."

"The one depicting Dickens running down a hopelessly twist-ed path, spouting flowers out of his mouth, has some of his fans up in arms," Gyda told her.

"Did you know that Sculley is the artist who lives in the same building as Tom Hawkins? The same one we met that night?"

"What? No." Gyda glanced toward the far corner, where the crowds still gathered around his work. "We knew he would prove to be popular. Ansel says it is sure to get the museum mentioned in the papers."

"Let's hope it draws the public in, then," said Kara. "And let's hope I can find the man and have a word with him. I'd like to ask him if he's noticed any activity around those rooms."

"Come along. He's likely lurking about, listening for reactions to his work and revealing himself as the artist. He seems the sort to enjoy the attention."

They started toward the crowded corner.

"Oh, look! There he is. Mr. Sculley!" Kara called.

But the artist did not respond.

"What's wrong with him? Why is he being so rude?" Gyda said, exasperated.

The man was pushing his way into the crowd toward the wall, shoving people out of his way. Drinks were spilled. Protests rang out. Ladies shrieked in indignation. Sculley ignored them all. He thrust his way through to the wall and began to take down one of the paintings.

"Here, now!" Gyda started toward the commotion. "Stop that! You understood the arrangement, sir! The art stays throughout the length of the contract you signed with the museum!"

Sculley looked over his shoulder at her as disgruntled viewers began to drift away. "No, no." His eyes were wide. "Not this one."

"If you have an offer to purchase it, sir, you can make the sale when your agreement with the museum is over," Gyda declared. "That was the arrangement."

He yanked the painting down. "No. You don't understand. I made a mistake. I should never have—"

"I'm going to get Charles!" Gyda announced, spinning away.

"I've no choice in the matter!" Sculley shouted after her.

"Hold a moment, sir. I don't know what has upset you, but I need a moment of your time." Kara had followed, and now she craned her head to get a look at the painting. She thought it was a depiction of the legend of Osiris and Set. Egyptian lore was not one of her strong points, but she knew enough to recognize the battle between the Egyptian gods. "Oh," she said, surprised. "You've made them both into women, haven't you?"

Osiris's typically mummified legs had been transformed into white skirts. Her elongated crown was slipping off, and she brandished her crook and flail at her opponent. For her part, Set was aiming a staff at her enemy. Her typical jackal-like features had been pushed back, as if they were a mask, revealing the woman's ferocious scowl as she battled...herself. Kara realized both the figures wore the same face.

Wait...

"Mr. Sculley!" Her voice rang with force and authority. "Give me that painting!"

"No! Oh, no," he moaned. He looked utterly panicked. "You mustn't. Just let me go without a fuss or—"

Kara snatched the painting away from him. She knew that face. *Both* of those faces. "I've got to find Niall," she muttered, turning away from the back corner. A few people were still looking at Sculley's paintings, but most had moved off in a huff. Kara, still staring at the painting, began to stride toward the last place she'd seen her husband.

But as she stepped away from the corner, she didn't find Niall. Instead, a maid stopped right in front of her, an empty tray in hand.

Not a maid.

Kara retreated. "Petra Scot," she said quietly.

Chapter Fourteen

"**D**AMN THE MAN and his artist's vanity," Petra said as she raised the forward end of the tray to display the gun she held underneath. "I told him under no circumstances could he show my image." She glared at the painting Kara held. "He'll need punishing."

"You are not dead after all," said Kara.

"Congratulations on your stunning grasp of the obvious."

"Sculley." The man was trying to slide along the wall of seascapes to escape the corner. When Kara said his name, he whimpered. "You were in his rooms when we came looking for Tom Hawkins."

"I was posing," Petra said with a roll of her eyes. "It was the price he demanded for giving me a place to stay. There were too many bailiffs and moneylenders' thugs banging on the door of Tom's place. I slipped out of Sculley's when you lot showed up."

"But you couldn't resist staying to watch."

Petra shrugged. "I do enjoy watching you dance at the end of my string."

Behind her, Sculley slipped away and into the crowd in the main part of the hall, but a gasp came from one of the few people left in the corner. "That maid has a gun," a female voice said in a loud whisper.

"Everyone go," Kara called to the remaining guests in the corner. "Hurry now."

"No." Looking over, Petra brandished the gun in their direction. "You will all just stay there for now. Back up along the other wall and pretend like you are admiring the pretty oceans." She narrowed her eyes at them. "As long as you don't draw attention, I won't have to use this."

There were perhaps eight people left to move and do her bidding. One slid away as soon as Petra turned her attention back to Kara. "I'll bet Robert convinced you all that I tore apart Tom's rooms, didn't he?" she said with a sneer.

"Didn't you?" asked Kara.

"No! It was the moneylender's bully boys, looking for anything of value." Petra rolled her eyes. "Robert always was squeamish about violence." She set aside the tray, and with a tug, she pulled off her apron and tossed it away. "I did enjoy our games for a while." She said it like it was an admission of weakness. "I liked the idea of you unbalanced and frightened."

"As you have felt? Since your League disbanded?" If Kara could keep the woman talking until Niall came... Behind Petra, the party went on. No one seemed to notice the drama playing out in the corner.

"Do not flatter yourself," the woman snarled. "Since I escaped that government prison cell, I have been nothing but focused, angry, and determined."

"And turned away by everyone you approached."

"Not everyone," Petra corrected her with a smirk.

"Sculley knew you have a sister?" Kara looked down at the painting in her hand. "A twin."

"*Had* a sister." She gestured at the artwork. "Loose lips are the perils of drink. Let it be a lesson to you. But posing is such boring work. Especially when you are forced to listen to the droning of a fool like Sculley. I drank to make it through. So many damned sketches he had to make—and that was all before he even began to paint." She glanced at the piece again. "If I had known what he was going to paint, I would have killed him then."

"You told him about her? Your sister?"

"In a moment of weakness, brought on by too much gin. Vile stuff. I must have said too much. But I had been thinking about her lately, you see."

Plotting her death, Kara almost said, but Petra continued to speak.

"I didn't know about her, actually. Not until we broke into the Hanlins' files that first time. We found out about the money they'd been stealing, and I found out that they had stolen my sister." She sneered. "Just another part of the *great experiment*. A comparison. Give her to an ordinary family and see how she fares, measured up next to me with all my opportunities."

"How did she fare?"

"Surprisingly well. Not that I let her know that. She became a teacher herself, you know. I read some of the reports on her. She was respected. Well liked. At least the children were safe with her, unlike with Hanlin." Her mouth twisted. "But then, she had advantages, too. She grew up with a family. Parents, siblings, cousins, all of it. A little house on the river with a tiny garden and a cat." She seemed to be looking inward for a moment, before she shook her head. "But they held her back, in the end. She might have been something, someone of value, had she joined me when I asked her."

"That's what happened? She didn't join you, so you killed her?"

"No. That invitation was extended years ago." Petra shrugged. "She should have taken it. Perhaps I would not have had to kill her now."

"Had to? Is that what you tell yourself?" Kara scoffed. "Nonsense! You took her life just to fake your own death!"

"Yes! To convince the Crown, the Yard, and the government that I was dead. To leave me space, give me freedom to make my plans." Petra snorted. "None of them could find me. They never got close. But you wouldn't stop, would you?" She tilted her head. "You know, perhaps you need to acknowledge your part in my sister's death. If you hadn't been so persistent, she might still be alive."

Kara snorted. "Congratulations on your ability to continually shift blame for your sins on someone else. I will never hold myself responsible for your evil deeds."

Petra smirked. "Well, her death did allow me another chance to torment you, didn't it?" She laughed. "Come now, admit it. You felt your mind was slipping, didn't you? When you spotted me in the square?"

"Do you want to know what I've felt lately, Petra? I've felt actual grief. Sadness, when I saw a woman of your intelligence, with all of your potential, lying dead on a slab—and all anyone else felt was relief."

Darkness flooded the woman's features. "Oh, no. You do *not*. You will not feel pity for me. *You?* You, who have had your own advantages! Intelligence, a pretty face, charm, and money. And you *waste* them all. You might have had a grand alliance. Married into the royal houses of Europe. Or into one of the great banking families. You might have grown your father's empire beyond measure. Instead, you settled for a royal bastard's boy and fiddle around with your clockwork toys." She raised her arm and pointed the pistol at Kara. "I will wield *my* gifts, and I will collect my own fortune and power. I will create my own legacy."

To the side, a couple more of the people trapped along the wall sidled out of range. Kara had to keep Petra's attention on her. "You had your chance," she admitted. "But all of that is over now."

"All due to you and that husband of yours. He's no better than his randy, rotten grandsire. No *vision*. Why cannot any of you *see?* I gave you the opportunity. You might have taken your part in things, secured your spot in the new order." Petra waved the hand with the gun. "But it's your chance that is over now. I have new plans, greater goals. And I'm not alone, whatever you say. There are others who can see the truth, as you refuse to. This country will get what it deserves. I will see to it."

Kara rolled her eyes. "We've heard it before."

"Bitch," Petra spat. "You have become too much of a distraction. All you had to do was to cower away until I set things in motion, but you had to interfere."

Her tone had been growing more strident, and at last someone in the party beyond their corner noticed their tense tableau. A cry went up. In a rush, the people who had been hovering over at the wall ran for the safety of the bigger crowd. As they raced to get away, the people they moved through were picking up on their panic. Someone gave a shout of alarm and the crowd began to surge away from them and toward the doors.

"I tire of this." Petra waved the gun again. "Give me the painting."

Behind her, Kara saw Gyda fighting against the current of fleeing guests. *No.* She stepped backward, away from Petra, and toward the door hidden in the wall.

"I had initially thought to stretch this out a little," the woman said. "I meant to pick off your little band one by one. But between you and that damned Sculley, you've left me no choice." She raised the gun. "I confess, it is no hardship to kill you first. I will enjoy watching Kier suffer your loss before I kill him, too."

Rage surged in Kara's chest, but she was in heavy skirts while Petra wore a maid's uniform, lighter and easier to move in. All she could think to do was to lure the woman away from the crowd, away from Gyda. She moved backward again. She was close, so close to the concealed door. "This is too public, isn't it? Think about it. At this point, no one has seen anything save for a rogue maid who might have objected to Sculley's mockery of Society. You can take the painting and go out the back."

Petra considered it for the briefest of moments. "So I thought, when I ordered Sculley to remove the painting. No one who understood what it revealed had seen it. But now it is too late. He exposed me and then scurried off like a rat. Who knows who he's talking to? You have seen the painting, as has the Winther woman. There will be gossip. He will be questioned about why he removed it. It cannot be stopped now." Her lips pressed thin. "The pair of you have destroyed my ruse. I have lost valuable time because you once again have lobbed a boulder into the smooth flow of my plans." She grinned evilly. "You speak of relief? It will be a relief to kill you."

"No." Gyda stepped in behind the woman, her voice ringing out. "You've had your fun, but there are constables coming in the front. It's over."

Petra threw her head back and sighed. "Once again. *No vision.* Are you people incapable of looking beyond the present moment? Can you not see the steps unfolding out ahead of you? Do you think I came here unprepared?" Abruptly, she shifted her stance and turned to point the gun at Gyda. "I am glad you returned. At least you have afforded me the opportunity to make Levett suffer at the last." She tossed a glance over her shoulder at Kara. "In your last moments, you can watch your friend die before you."

Kara didn't wait. She leapt toward the woman, but beside her, the concealed door flew open. A blur of motion swept past her and Lord Charles collided with Petra, reaching for her gun.

They grappled. Petra's back slammed into the wall, knocking Sculley's art askew. She growled like a dog and cursed Charles as she fought to keep the pistol. They were so close and moving so fast, Kara could not find a way to intervene.

A shot rang out.

"Charles!" Gyda shouted.

Her beau flung out a hand toward her and slumped to the floor.

Still regaining her balance, Petra threw a triumphant glare at Kara—who dived for her feet.

They both went down. Kara heard the gun skitter across the floor. She held on to one of Petra's legs to keep her from going after it.

"Let go of me, damn you!" With her other leg, Petra aimed a

vicious kick at Kara's head.

The blow slammed into her. And then another.

Dazed, blinking hard, she felt the woman's leg slide out of her grasp. Petra climbed to her feet.

Through a fog, Kara saw her glance toward the gun.

Gyda was kneeling over Charles, pleading frantically with him and shouting for help.

"Kara!" It was Niall's voice now, his shout loud in the emptying space.

Cursing, Petra turned to flee, but she paused long enough to kick Kara hard in the stomach.

Oof! Pain exploded.

Another kick. Kara curled up, retching, but through watery eyes she saw Petra disappear through the hidden door.

"Kara! Was that—Oh, hell. Kara?"

She tried to blink the fog away, but it was closing in on her. Niall was trying to help her to sit up. Nausea swamped her. She broke out in a sweat, then bent over again and vomited all over her husband's boots.

She looked up, trying to apologize, but the fog rolled over her and all the shrieking and sobbing retreated, sounding so very far away. The light tunneled around her until she abruptly tumbled into the dark.

Chapter Fifteen

L ORD CHARLES OSBOURNE was dead.

Niall watched Gyda, who bent, sobbing over his still, sprawled form. His heart broke for her, even as he thanked all the deities in every heaven that Kara still lived. She had passed out in his arms, but she breathed. He whispered her name as he tapped her face gently. Looking up into the remaining group of horrified faces, he barked out orders. "Bring me water and cloths!" He glanced over at Gyda once more. "And someone find the Duke and Duchess of Stratton."

A footman came out of the service door that Petra had used to escape.

"Is anyone else back there?" Niall demanded.

"No, sir." The servant stared, dismayed at the scene.

"Where does it go?"

"Down to the kitchen and on this level, out to an alley in the back."

Niall cursed, but the water arrived, and he pulled off his neckcloth. Wetting the end, he used it to bathe his wife's face. "Kara? Darling? Come on, now. Wake up."

She began to stir. Her eyes still closed, she frowned.

"Kara?"

Her eyes opened, but her hand fluttered up to cover them.

"Kara?"

"A moment," she whispered. "Too many of you."

Lying very still, she breathed deeply. He waited. When she took her hand away at last, she looked up at him and nodded. "All right, then. Back to one of you."

She let out a gasp and tried to sit up, but fell back at once. "Oh, saints!" she cried. "Charles?" She rolled to her side—and moaned at the sight of Gyda bent over the man's body. "Oh, no." She started to cough, and alarm shot through Niall when she drew her hand away speckled with blood.

"Kara!"

"Never mind that. Niall, it was Petra! She was here!"

"I know. I saw her." He sighed. "She got away."

"Oh, God. She killed Charles, didn't she?" Tears started to roll down her face. "He's dead."

Suddenly the crowd parted to allow the Duke and Duchess of Stratton through. The duke drew up short. "What's this? What in hell is going on?"

But the duchess knew. "My boy!" she shrieked. "Charles! Charles!" She dropped to her knees, shoving Gyda out of the way as she ran her hands along his face and shoulders. "Charles? No! How did this happen?" She let out a great, racking sob. "My boy!"

The duke knelt behind her, holding her and gazing at his son while silent tears ran down his cheeks.

Gyda moved back and climbed to her feet. She stood there, her head bowed and her hands covered in blood.

Kara moaned again. "Gyda!" She tried to sit up, but began to retch, helpless as her body convulsed.

The sound of it broke through Gyda's grief. Moving slowly, her head still turned toward Charles, she crossed to them.

"I'm so sorry," Kara croaked. "I didn't know he was behind the door. If I had known, I would never have gone near it."

Gyda turned to look at her, and Niall tensed. His assistant's eyes were blank, numb with shock. But slowly, she took in Kara's misery. She fell to her knees. "This was not your fault. Petra took aim at me. Charles charged out of there to stop her." She started to shake. "He died trying to save me—but it's not my fault, either."

Gyda's head dropped. After a moment, she reached out to take both of Kara's hands in her bloodstained grip. When she looked up, the numbness was gone. Fury lived in her gaze instead. "We have to stop her," she said fiercely. "No more."

"Yes." Kara's voice rasped, equally ferocious. "We finish this."

It was a vow made over the blood of a good man. Niall placed his palm over their clasped hands. "We'll find her."

Gyda's eyes glittered. "And when we do, she is mine."

NIALL TRIED TO insist that Kara be taken straight to a doctor, but she refused. "We cannot waste time. We are going hunting, and it must start as soon as possible. Is Sculley still here? We need him."

Niall settled her on a sofa in Ansel Wells's studio and went searching. His artist friend was taking tender care of Gyda, for which Kara was beyond grateful. Ansel was surely facing the demise of the project they'd worked so hard on, but he concentrated on getting Gyda clean, warm, and plied with good brandy.

Ansel did look toward Kara with concern when she suffered through a couple of rough bouts of coughing. He raised a brow when he saw the blood on her handkerchief, but she glared him down. "Do *not* mention it to Niall," she ordered him. "She gave me a couple of good wallops, but I will be fine."

"If you say so." He wrapped Gyda in a blanket and coaxed her into a high-backed chair with her feet up. Kara was glad to see her friend close her eyes. She hoped she could find a few minutes' respite from bleak devastation.

She refused to close her own eyes. She had no wish to relive the horror of the last hour.

Gyda slept on when Niall came back, bringing Stayme, but

not Sculley. "He's long gone," he said.

Kara looked to the viscount. "Send one of your largest, most threatening men to Sculley's rooms, straight away. I want every sketch he drew of Petra Scot. If he resists, tell him Wooten will arrest him for harboring a fugitive wanted by the Crown."

"Sedwick!" They all came alert when the shout echoed from the front of the building. "Damn it! Where's Sedwick? I need to speak to the duke!"

Niall blinked. "Is that…?"

Robert Preston burst into the studio. "Sedwick! Duchess! What in bleeding hell is going on here?" He waved a hand. "Never mind. Listen, you were right! It *was* Tom masquerading as the footman at Wood Rose Abbey."

Kara sat up. "Where is he?"

"I hauled him over to Bluefield and bade your butler to lock him away until I could find you. He had indeed been doing Petra's bidding—and you will scarce credit what he's said!"

"Petra Scot is not dead," Niall said dully. "We are aware."

"What? How—?" Preston stopped. "She was never here?"

"She was," Kara answered.

"Is that why there's a police van outside, discharging an army of constables?" He sounded hopeful. "Have you got her, then?"

"No." Gyda was awake now and getting to her feet. "But we will."

Preston placed a hand on his brow. "Who the hell was it laid out dead on that table, then?" He had been the first person brought in to identify the body. "Tom says he saw Petra just last night!"

Kara stood as well. "It was her sister on that table. Her twin sister. We'll explain more, but we have to go. If Wooten gets a hold of us, it will be hours before we get away. I'm not waiting." She looked around at all of them. "Based on what that woman said tonight, I can think of two paths to follow, to search her out. She spoke of using the time her sister's death bought her. She said she was to use it to lay her plans. Plans that are meant to *give this country what it deserves.*" She looked to Stayme. "Can you look into that? What is going on in the government, in the royal family, or in foreign relations that she might exploit? Where is she going to try to wriggle in and wreak havoc?"

Stayme nodded. She could see the wheels in his head already turning.

"The other thought I had was that her sister's death bought her more than time. It bought her a place to step into. An entire life to hide away in. We need to find out more about this sister." She looked to Preston. "Which is why I want to talk to Tom Hawkins. Right now."

Chapter Sixteen

"**I**'LL GO AND fetch Gyda." Niall held out a hand to his wife, who was pacing in the hall at Bluefield, eager to enter the parlor where Tom Hawkins had been placed.

Preston had gone in first to reassure the man. He could hear the soft murmur of their voices.

"Kara," Niall said softly. Tugging on her hand, he pulled her close. All he wanted to do was to take her upstairs and to bed and spend the night wiping away the realization of what might have happened to her. He needed to reassure himself that she was safe and unharmed. But she was right. They had to finish this.

He sighed and leaned in close to her ear. "If it takes me a while to bring her down, just…wait. Can you do that?"

"Oh." Kara's impatience melted away. "Of course."

After dropping a kiss on the top of her head, he went upstairs to Gyda's rooms. He thought he might have to wait, but she called for him to enter on his first knock.

He found she had changed her clothes, but left her hair in the wild braids. It felt utterly suitable for the journey they meant to embark upon.

"Is Hawkins ready to talk, then?" She was closing the lid of an elaborately carved wooden box. It was covered with Norse runes, knotwork, and depictions of dragons. The top was inlaid with a metal warrior's shield.

"Soon." He nodded toward the box. "I remember when you bought that in the market in Birka."

"I've kept it empty all this time. I was saving it to hold something special."

As he approached, she draped the traditional beads she'd been wearing earlier across the front of the box.

"Please don't be offended," she said quietly. "I love the beads. I will keep them forever, along with the traditional gown, but I don't believe I will ever wear them again."

Niall shook his head. "Do what you must, Gyda. You could never offend us."

She bit her lip. "Charles loved it. I wish you had seen his eyes light up when I walked into the museum tonight."

"I am sure he admired the gown, but it was the woman inside it who made him light up."

Her face crumpled. He opened his arms, and she walked into them and buried her face in his chest. He knew she shed tears, but she conquered them quickly. "I loved him, Niall." Blinking and red-eyed, she looked up at him. "Isn't that a hell of a thing? Who would have predicted it, if they had seen the pair of us competing for the barmaids' attentions in Oslo?"

"Love happens where it will," he said. "And it was very clear that he felt the same way about you."

"It would have been tricky. Difficult. His family would have hated the idea of us together." Her expression hardened. "We might have had only a slim chance at happiness, but that bitch of a woman stole even that." She stepped out of his embrace. "I'm ready to hear what Hawkins has to say, but I want to move quickly. I know you count Wooten as a friend, but we have to stay ahead of him in this."

"Stratton will be calling for justice. Now that she's killed the son of a duke, the quiet part of this investigation will be finished."

"Wooten will wish to keep her, interrogate her about her nefarious plans to harm the nation, but I don't care about any of that. She's a destroyer, Niall. She offers nothing to the world save chaos and destruction. I won't have it. I meant it when I said I mean to finish her."

Niall's jaw tightened. Gyda's heart was broken, and he ached for her. But she had come within seconds of dying tonight, and Kara had been not far behind. "And I meant it when I agreed with you."

"Then let's go."

They found Kara pacing outside the parlor. Turner waited nearby.

She looked up with relief when they arrived. "Oh, good." She took Gyda's hand. "Are you ready?"

"Let's hear what he has to say."

They entered to find Preston seated. The slender man who must be Tom Hawkins stood at the window, staring outside.

"He's agreed to answer your questions," Preston said. "But I fear he doesn't know much of use."

"Let's find out," Niall said. He saw Kara draw a breath, but Hawkins spoke before she could.

"Who is that boy?" Hawkins glanced back. "The pair of you are only just married. He cannot be yours."

Kara crossed to look out. Niall followed. He was surprised to see that the sun was up. Harold was out in the wintry morning. He must have been on his way to the laboratory, but he had stopped to examine the first green shoots of a border of snow drops.

"He *is* ours," Kara countered. "Harold is my ward."

"Your ward? Has he other family?"

"No."

Turning, Hawkins looked intently between them. "The thing is, I think he might. He bears a strong resemblance to a boy I used to know. A small sprig of a street child." He looked out the window again. "An uncanny resemblance, it is. I think there must be a sibling out there, somehow."

Niall exchanged glances with Kara. "Was the urchin you

knew called Pip?"

Hawkins's brows rose in surprise. "Yes! You know him, then?"

"That *is* him. Harold was called Pip in those days."

"Those days? But…that's the same boy?" Hawkins seemed to struggle to believe them.

Kara nodded.

"And you've taken him in? Why?"

Niall was growing impatient. "Because Harold has a good heart and a quick mind. Because he told the truth when he didn't have to—and when it would have been safer for him not to. Because he helped to clear my wife's name of a misguided accusation—"

"Because he needed us and we needed him," Kara interrupted.

Hawkins stared, as if trying to judge the truth of her words. "Well. Well, then."

He turned around completely, to face the room—and noted Turner standing near the door. He flushed red. Ducking his head, he went to sit next to Preston.

At least he had the grace to feel ashamed.

Hawkins glanced quickly around the room, then hung his head again. "I suppose I owe you all an apology."

"You owe Prudence an apology," Kara said darkly. "You owe Turner a pound of flesh."

"True enough." Breathing deeply, Hawkins raised his head. "I do apologize, Mr. Turner. Not to excuse myself, but I was meant to shoot you. But you were kind to me when I came for that interview, and I heard many good things about you at Wood Rose Abbey. I couldn't bring myself to do it."

"I suppose I must thank you for your restraint," Turner said wryly.

"I decided to spook the horse instead. Let me tell you, I was on pins and needles while you were so ill. I worried it might have had the same effect, in any case. If it makes you feel any better,

Petra knocked me about the head when I told her I'd missed you."

"She did far worse tonight," Gyda said coldly. "She meant to kill Kara. She succeeded in murdering my…" She stopped and swallowed. When she spoke again, both her rage and her grief sounded clear. "She killed a man that meant very much to me. She shot him in cold blood."

Hawkins paled. "I'm sorry to hear it, miss." Clearing his throat, he looked up and met each of their gazes directly, one by one. "She won't stop there. I spent days with her, and she did go on about you all. She means to see each of you dead. And that won't be the end of it. She means to bring down the royal family, half of Parliament, and England itself, should she find a way to manage it."

Preston made a distressed sound. "And with you as her accomplice, Tom? You *know* what she is. I don't understand how you could have gone along with her."

"Well, I didn't know at first, did I? She first come 'round just asking for a place to stay while she looked for William."

"William Barnstaple? Did she find him?" asked Niall. Stayme would be interested. As would Wooten.

"Nary a hint of him. And that lit a fuse to her temper, didn't it? Then she heard the fuss about your homecoming. And that dredged up the news of your wedding beforehand. Didn't that enrage her?" Hawkins sighed. "I believed it also worried her. You'd mucked up her works once before, hadn't you? She started to plot against the lot of you. In the way of passing time between drafting her bigger plans."

"And you just came down here to do her bidding? To frighten and harm these people, who had never lifted a finger against you?" Preston asked, incredulous.

"I did," Hawkins admitted quietly. "It got me away from her."

"And your creditors," Preston said savagely.

"Well, yes. They were getting insistent. But I thought I had better remove myself from her vicinity, mostly. You know how she is when her temper is riled, Rob! And it just seemed never to pull back from a boil. Do you know, she even tore off my St. Simeon medal? You know what it meant to me. So did Petra. But she ripped it off, raging over Clémence's death. She flung it somewhere and I never did find it."

"I found it in the wreck of your rooms. I have it back at my place." Preston's tone grew rough. "Petra killed her, Tom. She killed Clémence in the midst of one of her fits."

"I feared as much. There was something in the way she spoke of it. I could hear it in her voice. And she saw that I suspected. I know it." Hawkins hung his head. "We've all seen it. The look in her eye when someone ceases to be of use to her and she starts to turn on them. To be honest, I feared I might go the same way as Clémence. I figured I had better do something to get back in her good graces. So I came down here and left her to stay in my rooms. At first, it was just pranks. The biscuits. The notes. But then she bade me to kill Mr. Turner. Well, I figured I could bumble my way through a couple of her orders without suffering too much. It would be no more than she expected of me. I thought I would stretch it out, this time here, while I worked out a place to run to."

"And Petra showed up here at times?" asked Niall. "To give you orders? To hear reports?"

"Yes. She would come to the village on the train."

"Did she mention anything more about her bigger plans?"

"Not much. I got the sense that she was making progress. I know she had others involved. But she didn't want me near them."

"And did she ever say anything about her sister?" Kara asked.

Hawkins frowned. "Nothing more than I already told you, raging about Clémence dying—and sometimes remembering to blame it on you."

"Not Clémence. Her real sister. Her *twin* sister."

Hawkins looked horrified. "Never say there are two of them!"

"We won't, as only one is left," Niall said dryly. "Come, man. Preston says you were with Petra last night—" Stopping, he looked at the light growing outside the window. "The night before last, I should say. She'd only just recently killed her own sister, and she said nothing of it to you? Nothing at all?"

"Not a word!" Seeing the doubt in their faces, Hawkins held up a hand. "I swear it! The other night, she railed at me again for ruining her plans for Turner. She said as she had to go into Town again for a meeting with her fellows. That's what she calls them." He looked troubled. "She never would take me along, but I did trail after her a time or two, just to see what she might be tangling me up in. I glimpsed her with more than one of them. I tell you, I didn't like the look of them."

"In what way?" asked Niall.

"They weren't flashy, not loud like some of those League men used to be. Nor did they seem to be at her beck and call. She always has a few of those sorts around, ready to do her bidding."

Niall did not remind Hawkins that he was one of *those sort*.

"These men…they are different. When they were together, it looked like a meeting of professionals. Simple. Direct." His brow furrowed. "Not one of them looked like anything out of the ordinary. Nobody you would notice in a crowd. Plain. Someone your eye would slide right past." He shivered. "Until you looked in their faces. Then it struck my nerves, I tell you."

Niall didn't like the sound of that. "You say she never mentioned a sister. What about a woman's name? Any name at all?"

Hawkins shook his head. "No. I would have remembered. Petra don't like most women. She don't find no use for them." He shot Kara and Gyda an apologetic glance.

"Is there nothing else at all?" Gyda asked, impatient. "Anything we might use?"

"Nothing…except she did say as she had her sights on a new hole to hide in, but that it was too far. She thought she might have to change locations."

"Where?" Gyda demanded. "Where was it that was too far

away?"

"I don't… Wait! She did say something, once. Something about the river. Let me think. Prince, something? No. King. Kings."

"Kingston?" asked Niall.

Kara shot out of her chair. "Kingston on Thames! Niall, it is upriver from Teddington Lock! The sister's body floated down to Teddington Lock."

"But she said she must move to a new spot," Gyda objected. She glared at Hawkins. "Where?"

"She never said. I swear it!"

"It gives us a place to start." Kara was already moving toward the door.

"Wait! Please?" Hawkins was on his feet too, shifting in place, his color rising. "I was wondering…hoping…"

"What?" asked Niall.

"It's much to ask. I know it," he said miserably. "I'm ashamed to ask it. But do you think…might I stay here? Until this is wrapped up and Petra is in custody? If she finds I'm gone from the abbey, she will look first for me at Preston's." He frowned. "I don't want to put him in her sights."

"I'm not sure that is a good idea," Preston interjected.

Kara hesitated. "I'm not sure I can ask such a thing of Turner."

Her butler stepped forward, eyeing the man who had injured him. "In the normal state of things, I'd be traveling with you, Your Grace. But I concede, my ribs are not yet healed. I won't be a hindrance to you all. So, then." He tilted his head toward Hawkins. "As I'll be here to watch him, I won't object to Mr. Hawkins's staying. Not as long as he will pledge to make himself useful."

"I would appreciate the chance to make amends," said Hawkins.

"If you think to warn Petra, or in any way inform her of our doings…" Gyda stopped, but the threat was left, clearly dangling.

"No. I only wish to avoid her. Completely," Hawkins said earnestly. "She will never think to look for me here."

"Are you sure about that?" Preston asked.

"She'll think I've scarpered off after failing to complete her task." Hawkins gave them all a bitter grin. "It's what I usually would have done."

"Turner, are you sure?" asked Kara.

"Perhaps Mr. Hawkins merely needs some time to think about how he means to go on," Turner ventured. "We will keep his hands busy and free his mind to ponder the question."

"Yes. That is it, exactly. Thank you." Hawkins sounded genuinely grateful.

Turner nodded. "He'll stay here with us, then." The butler turned to look at Niall, then raised his brows at Kara. "As long as you promise to keep us informed. I will do the same. We can use the old network, if messengers cannot be easily had or will be too easily detected."

"Of course," Kara agreed. She glared at Hawkins. "You will stay away from Prudence," she warned. "And the rest of the maids, too." The threat was clear in her tone.

Turner cleared his throat. "It might be best if I put a cot in the laboratory. He can stay out there with no one the wiser. No one goes in there, save for Harold and me. And the boy will enjoy being in on the secret."

"You are being far kinder than we deserve," Preston said. "Perhaps I will come out, when I can find the time, to check on things here?"

"Of course," Niall said. "I'll tell Stayme he might use you as a courier."

"Let's go," Gyda called from the threshold.

Kara was right behind her.

Niall set out after his wife and his best friend, sending up a silent prayer for their safety. "Yes. Let's go."

Chapter Seventeen

"O H, YES. I know her." Mr. Norrey of Kingston Larder and Goods managed to infuse quite a large amount of disdain in so few words. "Or, at least, I thought I knew her. I had thought her to be a well-bred lady of morals and decency."

Kara, Niall, and Gyda had arrived in Kingston Upon Thames just after noon. They had taken the measure of the high street and decided to start their search for information on Petra at the general store. A wise choice, it seemed.

Kara raised a brow at the shopkeeper. "Would you share the lady's name, sir?"

"Of course. That is Miss Katherine Prentice." He returned her expectant look. "May I ask why you are looking for her?"

Kara shared looks with Niall and Gyda, but didn't answer right away.

"Some trouble, I take it?" The shopkeeper leaned in, as if inviting her to share the secret.

"You might say so."

Norrey sniffed. "I will take the liberty of warning you away from any idea of doing business with her."

"Is that what changed your opinion of the lady?" asked Kara. "A disagreement in business?"

"That's not what I would call it," he replied, surly.

"What would you call it, then, man?" Gyda asked sharply. As an attempt to blend into the traditional village, she had tried to tame her fierce braids by sweeping them up into a knot, but the effect was still a little…unruly.

"Outright thievery," he said indignantly. "It can be named naught else. Though I would never have thought her capable of such a thing, not so long ago."

"What, exactly, was her offense?" asked Niall.

"None at all, for near on to three years. I counted her a good, if infrequent, customer. Her parents took a cottage hereabouts and she visited them—that's when we would see her about. After the parents died, she continued to come and stay for a few weeks at a time, during school holidays."

"Is the cottage here in the village?" asked Gyda.

"Just outside. A pretty spot, right on the river. She would come in once a week when she was here. Her orders were always modest, but she always paid in full." His lip curled. "Until recently."

"Miss Prentice made an order without paying for it?"

"Two, in fact, and both deuced odd, if you ask me. The first appeared normal enough. She made her selections, but didn't carry them away or pay me right then, as was her custom. It was market day, and I was busy, so I didn't press her. But didn't she come in a few hours later, acting as if the first visit had never happened? I gave her the chance to pay for the earlier order, but she refused and practically ran out of the shop." He heaved a sigh of disapproval.

"And the second?" Niall prompted him.

"Well. That one was odd. She wanted canned salmon and tinned vegetables. Oh, yes, and dried meat." Norrey straightened. "I ask you, is this the sort of product a village general store would carry, in the normal course of things? No, indeed. I told her I was not in the way of outfitting jungle expeditions or filling the galleys of the ships in the Royal Navy. But she insisted. I had to make special orders to get everything she requested. She wanted enough of them to fill a trunk. I know, because that's how I sent it out to her."

Kara frowned at the others. "What could she have intended to do with it?"

"She didn't intend to pay for it, that much I can tell you," said Norrey. "When I arranged delivery, she told my man she would be in early the next morning to make payment for it."

"But she did not?"

"No, she did not. In the afternoon, I sent the man back and told him not to return without her payment. And what do you think he found? The cottage left open, with Miss Prentice gone, along with her supplies and everything of value in the place!"

Kara was still stuck on the strange order. "Canned, tinned, and dried foodstuffs?" she mused.

"She did tell Tom she meant to change hiding spots," Gyda reminded her. "Perhaps the new spot is remote?"

"No, she told him she wanted to move closer to Town," Niall said.

"Perhaps she didn't want to be seen?" Kara guessed. "With those sorts of supplies, she could hide away for a good while without venturing out."

"Or she might be planning to feed more than just herself," Niall offered.

"Did anything she said give you an idea of where she meant to go with all those supplies?" Gyda asked the shopkeeper.

"No. I just assumed she returned to her teaching position. In the usual way."

"Petra did say her sister was a teacher," Kara said.

"Do you know where she taught?" asked Niall.

The man stilled. Kara thought he must have noticed Niall's use of the past tense.

"I... Well, now that you ask, I suppose I do not."

"Come, man, surely you can recall something?" Gyda was growing impatient. "Listen, we need to find this woman. If you tell us something to help us find her, we'll settle her accounts."

She glanced askance at Niall, who nodded.

"I can't recall… Well, she once did remark upon the quieter nature of the village," Norrey said. "I took that to mean she normally resided somewhere closer to London."

"We cannot stop in to enquire at every school between here and London," Niall said, exasperated.

"We will, if we must," Gyda declared.

"Perhaps her uncle will know the name of the particular school, if you can locate him?" Norrey suggested.

"Uncle?" they all said in unison, staring at the shopkeeper.

"Yes, well, I've never met the man, to be sure. But I am not the only merchant Miss Prentice left with unpaid bills. Mr. Hartford, the tailor, has been engaged to make something for Miss Prentice's uncle. I don't believe he has finished yet. I told him to stop and give it up for a lost cause, but he believes Miss Prentice will honor her order. He told me himself that he expects he will be paid."

"Why does he think so?" Gyda asked. "Has he reason to?"

"I very much doubt it." Norrey leaned in as if making a confession. "Mr. Hartford, I fear, is an *optimist*."

"OH, YES. I am sure that you have heard an earful from Mr. Norrey." Mr. Hartford, the tailor, kept a small shop a little further down the main street of Kingston Upon Thames. He stood over his worktable and continued his careful cutting as he spoke. "Mr. Norrey, I am afraid, is a *pessimist*."

"I never would have known," Gyda said under her breath.

"He is forever convinced that someone is stealing from his cask of boiled sweets or his barrel of tenpenny nails. I ask you, who is going to build something one or two stolen nails at a time?"

"Surely he might have a point?" Kara lifted a shoulder. "With a large order delivered, received, and gone unpaid for?"

"Perhaps."

"Can you tell us anything about this uncle that Miss Prentice placed an order for? What was the order? A suit of clothes?"

"Indeed. A very elegant set this time, too."

"This time?" Kara sent Niall a puzzled look before turning back to the tailor. "Miss Prentice has placed an order from you before, Mr. Hartford?"

"Oh dear." Hartford finished his cut and looked up, dismayed. "It was supposed to be secret, that first order. And I've kept quiet about it, until now." He thought about it. "Oh well. No harm done, I suppose. She did not ask me to refrain from discussing the new order. It is indeed for a new suit of clothes. Very fashiona-ble." He gestured to a waistcoat upon a nearby form. "I've only just finished the last piece." It was of gray woven silk and wool in a checked pattern, and sewed to fit generous proportions.

"And Miss Prentice made these orders for her uncle?" asked Kara. "Very unusual, isn't it? For a woman to order clothes for an older male relative? I would have thought it would be the other way around."

"That was exactly my own comment, at her first request. But Miss Prentice explained that her uncle is a scholar and an eccentric. He would wear sackcloth, she said, as long as it didn't distract him from his work. That's why the first set had to be plain, loose, and comfortable, she said."

"And the new, fashionable set is meant for the same uncle?"

"I assume so, as I was to use the same measurements."

"Did Miss Prentice pay you in advance for these elegant clothes?" asked Gyda.

"No, indeed." Hartford looked amused at the very idea. Niall didn't doubt he found it droll. Tradesmen were never paid in advance, and often had to invoice for their goods and services several times to receive payment, even when their customers were of wealth and standing.

Niall snorted. *Especially* then.

"Did she pay you promptly for the first set?" he asked.

"Oh, yes. She insisted on coming in after business hours to pick them up herself, but she paid that very evening."

"Then it was definitely Petra doing the ordering, not Katherine," Kara whispered to Niall.

"She must have come here while her sister was still alive," he answered. "Perhaps she was watching Katherine, learning her ways and the particulars of her circumstances and behaviors."

But Gyda's attention had not wavered from the tailor. "Are you expecting Miss Prentice to come again and fetch these clothes for her uncle, as well?"

"Oh, no." Hartford had already begun to cut another sleeve.

"You've heard the woman has departed the village?" Gyda asked. "Were you planning on waiting until she returned on another school break?"

"Goodness, no. Now that I am finished, I am to send the suit on to the address she left me. To the school where she teaches, in Chiswick."

Gyda let out a whoop of relief and triumph. "At last! Now we are getting somewhere!"

The tailor stared, dazzled at her transformation from dour impatience.

"My dear Mr. Hartford," Gyda said expansively, "we desperately need to see this woman, and quickly. We will be happy to pay in full for her order, in exchange for that address."

"Oh, I don't know…"

"We will deliver it ourselves and save you the cost of delivery as well."

Full payment and a savings on delivery? The tailor was no fool.

"Oh. Very well, then. Seeing as you are traveling that way, and mean to see the lady, I suppose there would be no harm." Hartford nodded. "I'll just pack it up for you, then." He gave them a crook of a smile. "And then I think I shall just stroll down to Mr. Norrey's shop and tell him that everything worked out, just as I predicted."

Chapter Eighteen

N IALL HANDED THE ladies into the carriage before spending a few moments speaking with John Coachman. He nodded to the guard they had brought along, who was riding along at the back in ill-fitted livery, playing the role of footman. He tossed Hartford's bundle under the seat as he climbed in.

"Whom do you think she's bought those clothes for?" Gyda asked. "One of her associates?"

"I think she's bought them for herself," Niall answered grimly. "Recall what Stayme said, when we first arrived home—he had a watcher keeping an eye on his home from the garden square. He was convinced that both the woman and the 'aging clerk' were Petra Scot."

"What a busy little bee that bitch has been," grumbled Gyda.

"Chiswick." Kara looked worried. "It has a train line and easy roads into London proper. It's not far from Kingston Upon Thames." She cast Niall a worried look. "And it's not far from Bluefield, either. She's been going between all of them."

"It makes sense as a location for her viper's nest, but I wonder if she is in it alone?" Somehow, Niall doubted it. Petra always did have a taste for lackeys.

"But we don't truly expect to find her at this school?" Kara glanced down at the address the tailor had given them. "She might be able to convince a couple of merchants that she is Katherine Prentice, but surely she couldn't keep up such a masquerade at her sister's place of work? With people who have spent so much time with her sister, day in and day out?"

"If nothing else, the children would know," said Gyda. "They always know. Children can spot a sham from fifty paces. And they wouldn't have been likely to keep quiet about it, either."

Kara frowned. "By all accounts, Katherine was a normal sort of woman. She was a teacher, which must mean she would have possessed the ability to empathize and commune with others." She shook her head. "Petra couldn't manage to act normal for longer than ten minutes, if that. She's a self-centered blowhard who wouldn't recognize an empathetic thought if it smacked her right between the brows."

"She must be maintaining some sort of contact within the school, if she meant to have her elegant men's clothes delivered there," Gyda mused.

"All we can do is ask," Niall said. "It does worry me, though. What could she have planned, in which she would have to pass as a finely dressed gentleman?"

"Nothing good," Gyda said darkly. "Which is why we must get to her quickly."

It wasn't quite two hours before they pulled up before the Clifford School for Girls in Chiswick. John Coachman asked for directions and found his way around the village green and to the south before he drove through the gates and onto the school grounds.

"Good heavens," Kara said as they descended into the drive. Set in a large park of its own, it was a vast expanse of pale stone stretching up three stories, with long wings on either side of the formal entrance. The façade was beautiful, broken up with pointed gables and octagonal turrets. A many-windowed addition that looked newer graced the far right end of the school. Green lawns spread out before and behind the building. A stack of croquet equipment lay on the front lawn, as if waiting. From somewhere in the back rang the laughter and excited shrieks of children taking advantage of the afternoon sun.

The guard had leapt down and rang at the door to announce them. As they moved away from the carriage, the door opened wide and a somber woman in gray skirts stepped out, her hands folded.

"Behold, the dragon," Gyda said, low.

The woman sank into a very correct curtsy as they reached her. "Your Grace. Your Grace." Standing, she cast a questioning glance at Gyda. "And...?"

"May I present our very good friend, Miss Gyda Winther," Niall said.

"Miss Winther." The woman gave Gyda a nod. "I am Mrs. Brennan, the director of the Clifford School. I am delighted to welcome you all." She stepped aside and waved a hand. "May I invite you inside?"

Niall followed the ladies into an impressive marbled hall. He noticed Kara's attention was captured by the two main portraits that dominated the far wall. "The fifth Duke of Devonshire and his second wife," she said.

"Oh, yes. You might be aware of the influence the Devonshires have had on Chiswick, what with Chiswick House being so popular with the family and their friends."

"The street names alone betray the association," Kara replied.

"Indeed." Mrs. Brennan noticed Gyda admiring a wall of mounted swords and bayonets and went to stand at her side. "This particular sword belonged to one of our founders," she began.

Kara drew Niall down to whisper in his ear. "Clifford is the surname of the illegitimate son of the fifth duke and his then-mistress, Lady Elizabeth Foster."

"Oh, yes." He recalled the story now. "The infamous *ménage à trois*." He glanced at the portrait. "That's her? The mistress?"

Kara nodded, but Mrs. Brennan had turned back to them. "Would you care to join me in my office?"

"Yes, thank you." Niall nodded. "We would like a private word."

The director led them to a large, sun-filled room done up in blues and featuring another portrait of the late Elizabeth Cavendish.

"I have not yet noticed a portrait of the duke's first duchess, Georgina," Kara remarked.

"Nor will you," Mrs. Brennan answered. "Our founder was a close connection and admirer of Elizabeth Cavendish. She revered her spirit, her determination, and her willingness to go far to protect her children. Those qualities inspire our own mission— to educate and guide our girls so that they might fulfill their richest potential and grow into the best version of themselves."

Niall hoped they were not training the girls to be schemers, which was his general impression of Lady Elizabeth, or Bess, as she had been best known. Everyone knew the story of how she had moved in with her bosom friend, the duchess, and promptly become a mistress to her husband. He knew the duke had sired children on the woman and seen them raised with his legitimate brood. He'd rather thought Bess had used her children as weapons in her quest for advancement. And it had worked. After living with the couple for years, when Georgiana died, Bess became the new duchess.

He thought Kara looked as if she was thinking much along the same lines, but she merely nodded. "A noble goal."

He noticed Gyda was wearing a smirk, and it struck him suddenly that Mrs. Brennan might be wondering if her three visitors were living out a similar scenario.

He worked to suppress a groan. *Odin's arse.*

"Now, what may we at Clifford's do for you?" Mrs. Brennan asked. "If I recall the stories in the papers correctly, you and the duchess are newly married, Your Grace. You will have no daughters of an appropriate age for our school." She turned an expectant look on Gyda.

"Oh, no! Not me." Gyda raised her hands in protest.

"Perhaps you have heard of our good work, then?" the director asked. "We do have several patrons who support us in expectation of a place for their own daughters, when they are ready."

Kara's eyes widened. "That does indeed speak well of your efforts. But I am afraid we are here on a different sort of business. We need to speak with one of your teachers. Miss Katherine Prentice."

Mrs. Brennan's pleasantly fixed expression abruptly shuttered. "I'm sorry to disappoint you, Your Grace, but Miss Prentice is no longer employed at our school."

Niall gave the woman a sympathetic smile. "We did wonder if that might be the case. Can you, then, give us her new address or the name of her current place of employment?"

"I cannot. It is our policy to keep private such information for our instructors, past or present."

Kara arched a brow at the woman. "Mrs. Brennan, we are here on business regarding Miss Katherine Prentice's family."

Not a lie, Niall reflected.

The woman maintained her dignity. "Your Grace, I know that some feel that teachers are little better than servants, but they do deserve the same consideration of privacy as anyone else."

"Of course they do," Kara said gently. "But I assure you, ma'am, we are here to help."

The director merely shook her head. "Nevertheless."

Niall leaned in toward the desk. "Mrs. Brennan, our business is quite urgent." He tilted his head. "You might have noticed that Miss Prentice might not have been acting herself when she returned from her holiday."

The woman's lips thinned.

"Well, there's your answer," Gyda said.

Relenting a little, the woman nodded. "I did notice. We all did."

"Do you expect her back?" asked Kara. "To collect her possessions, perhaps?"

"No." The woman closed her eyes. "I'm sorry. The truth is, I don't know where Miss Prentice has gone. She took everything she wanted and bade the maids to keep or burn the rest. It was quite disturbing, the way she acted. I could never have imagined such a thing."

"Might she return, perhaps, to pick up the last of her salary? Or her post?"

"Miss Prentice will not be returning," the director said coldly. "She made that very clear when she demanded what was due her. And frankly, after her antics, she will not be permitted back on school grounds."

Kara tossed Niall a questioning look. They had agreed not to tell the truth about Petra masquerading as her sister, for fear of putting those who knew at risk. But it did sound as if Petra had burned her bridges here.

"You are quite sure she won't be allowed back?" he asked. "To visit her colleagues or students, perhaps?"

"Absolutely not. All the staff and security have been informed."

Niall nodded to Kara.

His wife drew a breath. "You have a good eye, Mrs. Brennan, and we spoke more truly than you could guess. It was not Miss Prentice who returned here after the holiday. It was her sister, pretending to be her."

The director blinked. "I… What was that?" She looked to Niall for confirmation.

He nodded.

Kara told her the whole tale. When she had finished, Mrs. Brennan sat very still. "Good heavens. I never guessed. They were so exactly alike. At least in appearance."

"Twins," Kara said.

"What an incredible story. It's like something out of a novel. I would never have believed such a thing, had I not seen the differences in behavior for myself. I was in shock, truly, to see

Katherine acting so brash, so harsh and insulting. And some of the things she said to the students!" She glanced at Niall. "You are sure?"

"Positive."

Suddenly, the woman covered her mouth. "Oh, poor Katherine."

"You cannot share this truth with anyone," Kara warned. "Not with your teachers or students. Not until the sister has been caught. The woman is dangerous."

"Oh, but—"

"She won't hesitate to kill again if she thinks she's been found out."

Alarm replaced the sorrow in the director's face. "Oh, but then you must tell Joshua! Even if no one else is to know!"

"Joshua?" asked Niall.

"Mr. Joshua Dalton. He is one of our instructors. He teaches history and geography." Her brow furrowed. "We do not encourage fraternization among our teachers, but he and Katherine are—were—close. Very close." Her hand went to her mouth again. "That woman! She broke his heart! She cut him loose in a most cruel fashion. But he refused to believe it. Joshua won't give up on Katherine. He's vowed to get her back. I know he's been spending all of his free time looking for her." She suddenly looked frightened. "You must tell him the truth. There are whispers among the teachers that he's seen Katherine with another man. If he confronts them, what might happen?"

"He might end up dead," Gyda said flatly.

"Please," the director whispered. "You must tell him."

Niall nodded. "You are right. It sounds as if he needs to know. He might be able to help us find her, as well." He gave Mrs. Brennan an expectant look. "Does he reside here at the school? Can you send for him?"

"We have two male instructors. They have rooms in a separate building out past the stables." Mrs. Brennan shook her head. "But you won't find him there now. Any time he is not in class, he is out in search of Katherine. Or drowning his sorrows at the Fox and Hare."

He glanced out the window at the fading light. "The Fox and Hare, you say? Is it a respectable place to stay the night?"

The director gave a shake of her head. "Chiswick scarcely has an undesirable set, but if they are to be found, that would be the place. I would instead stay at the Meryton Inn. It is just down the high street from the corner where the Fox and Hare sits, but it is of a more elevated setting. Many of our parents stay there when they attend to school matters and functions."

Kara stood. "Thank you, Mrs. Brennan."

Niall joined her. "If I were you, I would take every precaution against allowing the fraudulent Miss Prentice back in."

"We will. Thank you for sharing the truth." Mrs. Brennan cast them both a candid look. "And please, someday, when you have daughters of your own, think of us again."

Niall thanked the woman, but he had no room for such thoughts right now. Until Petra was stopped, all their plans for the future were in jeopardy.

Kara looked like she were sharing the same grim thought.

Gyda, however, looked about her with satisfaction as they emerged into the approaching evening. "We are catching her up," she said with fierce delight. "Let's go see if we can snare her at the Fox and Hare."

THEY SENT JOHN Coachman and the guard to reserve them rooms at the hotel before they went in search of the tavern. They found it at the end of the high street, sitting back from the road a little, at the corner. Kara examined the narrow building and the crudely carved sign above the scarred door before they stepped through into the tavern.

The place had good bones, but Mrs. Brennan had been correct—the Fox and Hare was not an entirely respectable spot. It was thick with shadows and dark corners. The floors were sticky, the tables dirty, and the smell of spoiling meat and stale ale hung in the air.

As usual, when she entered a business that needed a guiding hand, Kara's fingers itched to get to work. A thorough scrubbing, a bit more light, a good menu and a touch of care... That was all it would take to turn this place around. It was almost like it was *trying* to be dissolute.

The patrons didn't seem to mind the shabby surroundings. They looked to be a mix of laborers, clerks, country folk, and lower servants. A step above the kind one might find in London's low spots, at least. But here and there a more questionable sort stood out, and there were more bosom-flaunting serving wenches than such a small taproom called for. Indeed, just as they paused on the threshold of the room, she saw a laughing barmaid take a grizzled man's hand and lead him toward a narrow stair at the far side of the room.

Ah. Now they knew what they were dealing with.

It became obvious when the three of them were spotted. All the raucous conversation and coarse laughter abruptly died away, only to start again, louder than before.

"Well, then," Gyda said. "They know we are here. We might as well see what we can see."

The closer they came to finding Petra, the more predatory Gyda's manner became. Kara watched her reach up and remove the pins anchoring her hair. She shook out her mane of braids and blonde locks and cast a feral grin around the taproom. Stalking over to the bar, she leaned in to speak with the woman manning the taps.

Kara followed, with Niall on her heels.

The woman behind the bar shook her head at Gyda. "We don't tell tales on our customers."

"A good business practice, in general." Gyda cast an amused glance around the taproom. "But in this case, we are here to warn

Mr. Dalton. He won't continue as your customer, or anyone else's either, if he keeps on as he's going now."

The woman ran her gaze over by Gyda, then looked past her to eye Kara and Niall.

Kara returned her look of frank assessment, then stepped forward. "Is this your establishment?"

The woman raised her chin. Older than Kara, she looked thin and worn, but pride still shone from her. "It is."

Nodding, Kara looked around. "As a business owner myself, I commend your loyalty to your customer. But in this case, loyalty would demand that you help us locate Mr. Dalton. I fear he is in some danger."

"This is about the woman, isn't it?"

Gyda nodded. "Oh, it most certainly is."

Kara pulled one of Sculley's sketches from her bag. "Is this the woman you meant?"

"Aye. That's her." The tavern keeper shook her head. "A teacher over at the girl's school, they say she is, but she's the last sort I'd think you'd want around innocent young ladies. She's only been here a time or two, and that's only lately, but I picked her out for a hard one." She looked with approval at Gyda. "But I wouldn't give her long odds against you." She thrust her chin toward an empty table along the back wall. "Sit there. Order something. Dalton's not here now, but he'll be along, if his pattern holds. I'll give you the nod when he arrives." She shrugged. "But I warn you, the wait might be long."

Behind Kara, Niall cleared his throat. "Thank you. Ales all around, please."

"Nothing to eat?" The woman's disapproval shone clear.

Kara had no desire to discover what was giving off the gamey smell hanging in the air. "Bread and cheese, then."

The tavern keeper nodded, and a certain tension fell away from the room as they turned to take the table. Kara paused, though, before taking her seat. "If we'll have to wait, perhaps I should take the chance to send word to Turner. I can send a messenger to tell him what we've found so far, and he could send word back to the Meryton if he or Stayme have learned anything of significance."

Niall stood. "I'll go and see about it."

"No. You should stay. I wondered if Mr. Dalton might be more likely to talk freely with you. Masculine sympathies, and all that."

"She might be right," Gyda said.

"Whom will you send, though?" asked Niall. "I did see a livery, and they might have someone to hire, and a mount as well. But I don't want you out on the streets here alone."

"I'll ask," she said, nodding toward the tavernkeeper. "She'll likely have paper and pen, and if she doesn't have a messenger I can hire, I'll ask her to send out to the livery for someone to come here."

Niall reluctantly agreed, and Kara went back to the bar to broach the subject.

"Aye, you can use my office to write out your message. I'd let you hire out my groom, but he's broke his foot, and the doctor has him on crutches. The livery is a good idea, though, and the boy is well enough to hobble down the street to have them send a lad to you."

"Thank you. I do appreciate your help," said Kara.

"A moment, though, eh? Let me pour these lads another round and then I'll take you upstairs to the office."

Kara nodded and thanked the woman again. Leaning against the bar, she waited. Trying to be discreet about it, she turned her attention to the serving girls.

They appeared to be a lighthearted lot. They laughed and flirted, but Kara could not see that any of them looked skittish or forced. She could see no bruises on any of them. None looked haunted or frightened. A few of the men teased them, but no one grabbed or groped at them. Kara didn't see any of the women touched at all until she spotted one crooking her finger at a strapping young man in invitation. A few of his mates gave hooting encouragement as he wrapped an arm around her and they started for the stairs.

"Follow me, then, aye?" The tavern keeper came out from behind the bar and jerked her head. Kara trailed her out of the taproom, into the entryway, and up the main staircase to the next floor, where the woman deposited her in a small, untidy office.

"There's paper and nibs in the top drawer," she said, pointing to the desk. "Ink's on top there, somewhere. Help yourself. I'll send Hamish down to the livery. They'll likely send one of their younger lads, seeing as you said it's not a far journey. When he gets here, I'll send him up here to you."

"Thank you. You have been most helpful, and I am grateful." Kara started to move toward the desk, but the tavern keeper leaned against the doorframe and cast a wry glance at her.

"I saw you watching the girls. Perhaps it will ease you to know no one forces them to be here, or to do aught they've no wish to."

"That's the conclusion I was coming to myself."

The woman lifted her chin. "It's easy to look down your nose from a great height, but most of these girls have other occupations. Shop girl. Flower maker. Laundress. But those jobs don't often pay enough to cover rent, food, and the needs of families." She shrugged. "Some of these girls only come in here for a little extra, when they need to. Some are regulars. I let them use the rooms upstairs, as they will. I take my cut, but I don't hold with anyone mistreating them." She jerked her head down toward the taproom. "This lot knows to treat them with a bit of respect. I won't tolerate anything else."

Kara met the woman's gaze directly. "I do not object to anyone doing what they must to make their way in the world, as long as they are not hurting others."

The woman snorted. "Most of them aren't' hurtin' no one. A few are only harmin' themselves, if you know what I mean. But they do what's needed, for them and theirs."

"I do know what you mean," Kara said with a sigh. "I only

wish it *wasn't* necessary."

The tavern keeper looked surprised. She nodded begrudgingly. "Maybe there will come a day when it won't be, but it won't be in our lifetimes." She straightened. "Stay as long as you need to. Come down when you finish with the messenger. In the meantime, I'll fetch ale and bread and cheese for you and your friends."

When the woman had gone, Kara sat down, cleared a space on the desk, and outlined all that they had learned for Turner. She told him to send word back with the messenger if he had need to. She hoped they would not still be here past the next morning.

She'd just found the sealing wax and had lit a candle to melt it when the livery's boy arrived. She gave him detailed instructions on how to find Bluefield Park before handing over the message and coins so that he could take the train as far as Hammersmith. "You can hire a mount there, and if you hurry, now, you might make the last train back to Chiswick and save yourself the longer ride back."

The boy nodded, eager to go. Once he was gone, Kara sat a moment at the messy desk and drank in the quiet. They'd been caught in a whirlwind since last evening, and it was likely to get worse tonight. She only hoped they would find Petra here in Chiswick. She was beyond ready to put the woman, and all the grief and trouble she brought, behind them.

After blowing out the candle, Kara left the office and paused in the narrow, dark hall. Based on the squeak of a mattress emanating from the next room, this was where the serving maids brought their customers. That meant—yes, there, at the far end of the hall, was the landing of the narrow stairs that led to the taproom. She went to it and started down, but paused in the shadows at the top.

Someone had taken her spot at the table. A dark-haired young man, sitting with his shoulders hunched and his head hanging low. He spoke to Niall, who bent over, listening intently. Gyda listened as well, but she sat back in the shadows, her gaze roaming the taproom, watching for trouble.

Kara waited until Gyda had seen her. With a nod, she started moving again, but she'd only made it a couple of additional steps before, across the room, the taproom door began to slowly open.

She stilled.

A man took up most of the doorway, his broad frame draped in a long, dark coat. But someone lurked behind him. A woman. Her skirts brushed the man's legs as she leaned in beside him.

Petra Scot.

Kara's eyes widened. Gyda had looked away, but she glanced back and noticed the expression on Kara's face. Kara widened her eyes again, then darted them toward the door, frantically trying to transmit the message. Gyda, bless her, merely nodded and did not look over in that direction.

Kara backed up the stairs again, moving slowly. Petra and the man peered around at the tables and stopped, their attention caught as they spotted Niall at the table with the young man. Petra whispered something and the man inched back, closing the door again.

Kara backed up the last couple of stairs, whirled, and raced quickly down the hall toward the main stairs, at the other end of the passage. She kept to the edge, trying not to make any noise. When she reached the main staircase, she stood at the top, clutching the rail and listening.

Petra and the large man stood below in the entryway, whispering intently.

The noise from the taproom had grown loud. Even with the door closed, it interfered. Kara couldn't make out their words. Kneeling down, she strained to hear.

They were arguing. Petra cursed and stepped back from the man. "You heard me. That teacher is a loose end. Someone's been lurking about the farm. It must have been him. Who knows what he's seen? And what might he be sharing with Kier now? And what of Kier? If he is telling that sniveler the truth about who I am, then he is sealing the man's fate."

The woman stepped in a circle, her hand at her brow. "Damnation," she cursed bitterly, before turning back. "How did Kier find me? And where the hell is his bitch of a wife?"

Kara shrank back as the woman below circled again.

Suddenly Petra stopped. "Finish him. Finish them both. We are going to have to move more quickly than we planned. I'll go back and collect the cases and head straight into Town. If you are quick about it, meet me at the livery and you can travel back with me to fetch them. If you dawdle, then make your own way into London. You know where we will be. Just be sure to care of those two."

The large man clearly did not enjoy taking orders from her. He started to object, but Petra stepped close and leaned in. Staring upward, she hissed something close to his face.

The man stiffened and nodded. Turning, he yanked off his long coat with angry, jerky movements. After hanging it on a nearby rack, he headed back for the taproom. Petra watched him go, then spun on her heel and went out the front door.

Kara slipped down the stairs. A large, drab shawl hung on the coat rack as well. She snatched it up, wrapped it around her head, and followed the woman into the darkened street.

Chapter Nineteen

T HE CROWD IN the taproom had grown rowdy. High spirits reigned. At the table beside them, a man laughed uproariously as he waved a hunk of sausage at the end of his knife. The rest of the sausage was clearly visible, half chewed in his wide-open mouth. Grimacing, Niall turned away to the man he'd convinced to sit and talk with them.

"You won't understand. No one does." Joshua Dalton's voice was ragged, his spirits obviously low. "The other instructors, even the director at the school when I teach, they think I am just a brokenhearted fool. I am, of course, but it's so much more than that." The teacher looked up. "Katherine is not herself. I don't know how else to explain it. It's as if someone else lives inside her."

"You are not a fool," Niall reassured him. "And you are not far off the mark, either."

He explained about Katherine's twin taking her place.

Dalton sat straighter, his breath coming faster as he listened. "I knew it," he said in a whisper. "I knew I was not losing my wits."

"You are not," Niall agreed.

The teacher frowned. "But she knew things. Things I had only discussed with Katherine."

"It appears she has been watching her sister for some time."

"Did Katherine keep a journal?" asked Gyda.

Dalton nodded. "She did. Her dream book, she called it. She filled it with little drawings, with stories, with her wishes and plans." His face fell. "The sister read it."

"The sister imitated her in Kingston Upon Thames. Perhaps she was testing the masquerade."

"I never liked her going there alone, but I could not accompany her. Not until we married." His expression was unfocused, as if he were casting back, recalling their interactions. "I was right. I knew she could not speak to me so. Katherine and I had so many plans for our future. Plans we dreamed up together. I knew she could never disparage our hopes and ideas in such a cruel fashion." He put both hands on the table, as if he meant to push off and run. "But where is she? Where is *my* Katherine? What has this sister done with her?"

Niall was forced to tell him the truth.

Dalton crumbled in on himself. "No," he whispered.

Gyda spoke from the shadows. "She is a criminal, the woman you have been following here in Chiswick. She is a murderer. A traitor to the Crown."

The man was still caught in the shock of Niall's news. "She's dead?" he asked quietly. "You are sure?"

"I am very sorry," Niall told him.

Dalton was clearly in the grip of very real grief. A shudder went through him. He swallowed several times, but fought back tears. He closed his eyes and breathed deeply. But when they opened, his expression had hardened. "A traitor, you said?"

Gyda nodded.

"Yes. I knew it. I knew something wasn't right. I just did not want to believe my Katherine could be involved in something like that."

"Something like what?" asked Niall sharply.

"I don't know. That other bitch is up to something nefarious."

Out of the corner of his eye, Niall saw Gyda stiffen, her attention caught on something else.

He kept his focus on Dalton. "Tell us what you have seen."

The other man covered his face with his hands. "I'm not sure. She has been spending time with a gunsmith. I've seen them in his shop. They were going over plans, diagrams. Gibson is his name. He owns land, a farm out on the road toward Ealing, although he doesn't stay there. He keeps rooms above his shop. But he's been going out there with her. I followed them, more than once. Something is going on out there."

"What? What do you think is going on?" asked Niall.

"I don't know. There are other men staying there. Some of them are foreign, I think. They very obviously do not want anyone getting close to the place. Someone is always on watch. I have been chased off several times."

"Niall." Warning rang in Gyda's tone. She sprang out of her seat and surged past him.

He looked up to see a large man stalking toward their table. Planting herself in his path, Gyda snarled up at him. "Where is she?"

"Out of my way," the behemoth growled.

Was that a *Russian* accent?

"That's one of them," Dalton said. He stood. "He's one of the men from the farm."

"Tell me where to find Petra Scot," Gyda hissed at the man. She barely came up to his shoulder, but she faced him without a qualm. "Tell me now and we'll allow you to leave. You won't have to go down with her."

Niall stood, but the man growled at Gyda again and roughly pushed her aside, shoving her into the next table. Shouts of protest arose, but the brute ignored them. Without preamble, he stepped forward and swung a meaty fist at Dalton.

The teacher, caught by surprise, stumbled back and fell into his chair.

Stepping around him, the assailant pulled out a blade. Wordless, his expression fierce, he aimed a slicing swing at Niall's throat.

Startled by the swift escalation, Niall dodged, but it was a close call. Crouching, he pulled his own knife from his boot and came up, thrusting for the assailant's kidney.

The man jumped aside, more agile than Niall had expected, given his size. He struck the table where they'd been seated, gripping it with both hands for stability as he knocked into the back of the chair Dalton had landed in.

The teacher looked back, grabbed his tankard, and slammed it into the brute's knife hand, loosening his grip on the blade.

The big man roared. Knocking the tankard aside, he spun, grabbed Dalton by the scruff of the neck, and lifted him into the air like a kitten. Kicking the chair away, he slammed Dalton's face down onto the table.

The other patrons were becoming aware of the situation. Some slipped out of the taproom. The tavern keeper came out from behind the bar holding a cudgel. She stood back several paces, and a few others spread out on either side of her. The men at the next table were hooting and cheering and pawing at Gyda.

The brute had left his back exposed. But even as Niall lunged, the man lifted Dalton again and flung him at Niall.

With a gasp, Niall twisted to avoid skewering Dalton. The teacher hit him hard, and they both went down in a tangle of limbs. Trying to suck in a breath while pushing Dalton away, Niall glared up as the assailant stepped toward them. He had regained his blade. Menace written in his face, he raised it high.

Metal flashed over his shoulder. The behemoth stopped, his arms suddenly flung wide. He gave a shout and turned as Gyda skipped backward—and Niall saw the neighboring table's sausage knife buried high in his back.

Shockingly, it didn't stop him. Niall scrambled to his feet as the brute went after Gyda. The man swung a long arm and clipped her, his knife leaving a thin slice of crimson across her arm.

The men from the other table were finally scrambling out of the way. Gyda tripped over one of them and stumbled to one knee.

The brute reached for her, but he suddenly stopped, frozen in place.

Niall, finally back on his feet, stumbled over to see Gyda's own blade, etched in Nordic runes, pressing into the fabric between the man's legs.

"Give over the knife or I will cut off your prick," she snarled. "Then I will buy a round of ale for the room and we will all watch and laugh while you bleed to death."

Niall snatched the blade from the man's hand. The behemoth did not move or resist. "Damn you to hell, *cyka*," he growled at Gyda.

Definitely Russian. And judging by Gyda's expression, she understood the insult.

Some of the men circled around them were shouting encouragement at Gyda, while others moaned in sympathy for the brute.

They were at a stalemate. Niall didn't know how—
Thunk.

Dalton struck the man on the head with the pewter ale pitcher. Hard. The assailant's eyes rolled back, and he slumped to the floor.

Gyda glared at the teacher.

"What?" Dalton asked. "You can emasculate him later. We might need him for information."

Niall pointed at the tavern keeper. "Rope," he ordered her. "Now."

He turned to Dalton. "Roll him over. Tie his hands and feet behind him, and call the constables." Reaching down, he helped Gyda to her feet. "Are you all right?"

She peered at the cut on her arm. "Yes. It's just a scratch. The bleeding is already slowing."

"Good. Now, tell me one thing."

"Yes," she answered. "I would have done it."

"I know. That's not what I meant." He looked around the taproom, his unease growing. "Where the hell is Kara?"

PETRA MOVED QUICKLY down Chiswick's high street. Kara hurried in her wake, trying not to make a noise, and trying to stick to the darkness and avoid the bright circles left by the street lights. She was grateful she had worn her altered skirts. It was cold, and she might have been warmer in thicker petticoats, but there was more comfort for her in knowing she had potentially useful weapons and gadgets tucked away in her pockets, linings, and hidden compartments.

Petra ducked into the livery. Sticking to the shadows outside, Kara moved closer until she could hear the woman berating the grooms.

"Did I not leave instructions for the horses to be left in their traces? Get them out of those stalls. At once! This very minute!" The volume of Petra's voice was rising. "Dullards! Idiots!"

"Beggin' your pardon, ma'am, but you did say as you was to be quick, and that was this morning." One of the livery men was brave enough to stand up to the woman's ranting. "One of our lads took a delivery at the station, and he saw you boarding the train for London. We knew you'd be some time then. The beasts were—"

"The beasts are mine and I will do with them as I please! If I tell you to leave them standing for a fortnight, then you do so! Get them back in their rigging and get that cart—" She stopped and let out a screech of fury. "You don't even have the hay loaded yet?"

"Nearly done, ma'am! Nearly done!"

"Where the hell is my driver?"

"He's just gone for a pint across the way. No one had any

idea when you—"

"Fetch him!" she ordered the man. "I want to leave before ten minutes are up. Do you understand me?"

Cart? Had Petra said *cart* instead of carriage? Kara crept close enough to peer around and into the livery courtyard.

It *was* a cart the grooms were swarming around, a long, narrow farm cart with a grid of slatted boards inserted to extend the sides higher and contain a load of hay. Petra was stomping about, still ranting, and making the horses dance as they were led out of their stalls.

Kara ducked back into the shadows. A farm cart? What was the woman up to? And how was Kara going to follow her to find out?

She shrank back as a man came running from the pub across the street. As Petra turned her rage on him, Kara risked another glance. The cart had been turned so that the last of the hay could be added. Kara saw that a grid of boards had been added to the back, too. Attached at the bottom, it tilted back, the top secured with chains to allow it to fan out. It left an open, triangular space at the back of the wagon. Staring at it, Kara knew it was her only chance of discovering Petra's hideaway.

She waited. The men hurried to get the cart ready—and Petra gone, no doubt.

When they had finished, and Petra and her driver had mounted the narrow plank that served as a seat, Kara watched, poised and ready.

The cart rattled out of the courtyard at a clip. It turned right onto the high street. Kara followed it out onto the street, not wanting to be glimpsed crossing the light that shone from the livery. Hurrying, she moved to the back of the vehicle, keeping pace with it. It was a complicated maneuver. Keeping her feet moving, she braced her hands on the side of the cart and on the slatted grid, and managed to hoist herself into the inverted triangle of open space.

Unfortunately, the cart shifted with her added weight.

"What was that?" Petra's sharp question drifted back.

"Something in the road, most like," the driver answered.

"Get this crate moving," Petra returned. "We have to get it unloaded and filled again with the supplies for London."

"Vehicles are meant to take it slow on the high street," the driver replied.

"I don't care! We are leaving tonight. There is work to be done. We have to move!"

Kara pulled herself further into the space and hung on as the driver whipped the horses into a faster trot. At least the hay was warm at her back, and she had the shawl she'd taken from the tavern.

She settled in as they left the main street and the road grew bumpy. As the lights of the village were left behind, she hoped she was up to the task ahead of her.

Chapter Twenty

I T WAS A long, chilly ride in an uncomfortable position, but Kara gritted her teeth and hung on. She guessed they had traveled several miles before the cart turned off the road and into a rutted lane.

She started to maneuver herself backward and partly out of the triangular space. She did not wish to still be there when Petra reached her destination, or to be spotted by her confederates as they drove in.

Saints alive, she cursed inwardly. A button had caught on the frame of the slatted grid. Kara had to wriggle to get it loose. The cart was slowing when she finally worked free. Scooting backward again, she braced herself and dropped off the cart, rolling onto the cold ground just before the cart entered the square light coming from the opened doors of a tall, timbered barn.

She lay there, not moving as the cart entered the barn. Several outbuildings stood nearby, and off to the left she could see a two-storied brick farmhouse, with a lantern hanging outside the door. Several lights showed in the ground-floor windows. Ducking her head, Kara covered her face with the shawl as Petra came striding out of the barn. "Get that hay out of the back." Petra clapped her hands. "And get the powder loaded. All of it. All the way to the back of the cart. We'll load the cases inside, and you can help carry them out when you are done." She threw open the door and then stopped. "Damn it all! We'll have to leave all the dried and tinned goods I ordered." She cursed again. "We'll have to send you lot with the wagon back again to pick it all up. I don't want to listen to those ninnies whining about being hungry again." She strode off toward the farmhouse, blowing on her hands.

Kara's heart had sunk at hearing her mention *powder*. After their experiences with Petra and her League of Dissolution in London, she feared she knew what it meant. Climbing to her feet, stepping carefully, she crept to the barn and made her way along the front so she could peer inside.

Her chest tightened. The driver and another man stood in the cart, pitching hay into a pile on the right. Waiting on the left was a stack of small, familiar casks. Gunpowder. She crept away and dropped her head back against the barn. *Not again.* Why was that woman's solution to her own misery always to murder someone or blow things up?

Kara had to discover what they meant to do with it. But there were two men out here, and how many more inside? She would need more weapons than the paltry few she had hidden in her garments.

Perhaps she could find some tools in the outbuildings? She edged her way around the corner of the barn, but paused to listen. She caught the low murmur of voices. Someone was approaching from the direction of the house. If they went in to help with the loading and unloading, she would be safe enough. But if they came further…

Her hand encountered a door latch. A man-sized door stood toward the back of the barn. The tack room?

The voices drew nearer. She opened the latch and stepped inside.

Pitch black.

She pressed her ear to the door and heard the voices pass by.

On their way to one of the outbuildings? She held her position while her mind raced.

Information. She needed to find what she could about their plans, and then do what she could to delay or stop them. It wouldn't be easy, working alone. She would do her best.

After only a few moments, the voices came by again, on their way back.

She kept still for several minutes more. *Light.* There might be something useful here, but she needed to see. Feeling her way around the door, she found a hanging lamp. Matches were one of the things she carried in her altered skirts. It took a moment to get the lamp lit, but she managed it, and turned the flame low.

It was indeed the tack room. Surely she could find something useful. She pocketed a hoof pick. Took up a coil of rope and slung it crossways over her shoulder. Tucked several horseshoes into her belt, widely separated so that they wouldn't clang together. At the very least, she could fling them at an adversary.

She drifted past another shelf, then paused before bringing the lamp back. Reaching up, she pulled down a large glass bottle.

Dr. Acker's Spavin Cure
Cures spavins, ring bones, and splints

A spavin was a swelling or bony enlargement in a horse's hock joint. As far as she knew, there was no cure for it. Her stable manager scoffed at such products as nothing more than quackery, of the same sort that desperate people bought off predatory salesmen.

Kara knew that most of those quack products were laced with opium. And this…this would contain a dose fit for a horse.

Well, now.

Tucking the bottle beneath her arm, she shoved the shawl into a drawer, blew out the lantern, and slipped out the door. She moved to the back of the barn and listened carefully. She could hear the two men still working inside, but nothing else moved or made a sound. Moving quickly, she struck out for the back of the house.

❯❯❯❯❮❮❮❮

KARA WAS NOT in the office where the tavern keeper had left her.

"She's not in any of the bedrooms, either," the woman reported.

"She wouldn't be, would she?" asked Gyda. "I saw her starting down those stairs at the far end of the taproom. She was the one who spotted that giant arse coming in. If she hadn't given me the signal, he might have caught us by surprise."

"Where the hell did she go after that, then?" Niall was growing more frantic by the minute.

"What if our bloody big brute didn't come alone?" asked Gyda. "What if Kara caught a glimpse of Petra?"

"She wouldn't chase off after her alone," Niall protested.

"She would if the alternative was to lose the woman again." Gyda turned and strode down the main stairs. The others followed, with the tavern keeper scurrying after them at the rear.

"Would there have been anyone posted here? Anyone who might have seen what happened?" asked Niall.

"No." The tavern keeper paused, frowning at a coat rack in the corner. "But my market shawl is not where I left it."

"The farm," Dalton said tightly. "If that woman spotted us together, she would likely run, right? But whatever is happening at that farm, she would go back to hide or remove it, wouldn't she?"

"Let's go," said Niall.

"Wait!" the tavern keeper protested. "What about that mountain of trash you left tied up in the taproom?"

Niall glanced at his companions.

"Forget it," Gyda scoffed. "You know better. There is no way I'm staying here while you go off after her."

"You need me to find the farm," Dalton reminded them.

Niall turned to the tavern keeper. "Keep him quiet until the constable arrives, then tell the officer that the man assaulted the Duke of Sedwick. That should convince the law to hold him until we are ready to deal with him."

"But who is the Duke of Sedwick?" the woman asked, looking confused.

"I am," said Niall as he strode out the door.

"He is," Gyda confirmed as she followed. "And you don't want him as an enemy."

Niall paused as Dalton spilled out of the tavern after them. "How far?"

"A little over three miles, I would say. We take the road to the north west, toward Ealing."

"Our horses will be tired," Niall mused. "Fresh mounts will be faster." He looked to Dalton. "Lead us to the livery."

The teacher nodded. "This way."

⇥⟫⟪⇤

THE FARMHOUSE HAD a large and robust garden planted behind it, reaching right up to the back of the house. Winter crops still flourished near the shelter of the walls, which meant that Kara now crept between a row of cabbage and another of leeks. She kept close, trailing a hand against the rough bricks as she moved.

She'd been obliged to remove two of the horseshoes from her belt, as they would not stop slipping about. She left one tucked in, discarded another, and held the third in her other hand as she made her way toward the little courtyard outside the kitchen door.

A lighted window lay between her and the kitchen. Kara crouched down and crept low. She thought she could hear Petra's strident tones from inside as she passed.

Gripping tight to the bottle of horse tonic, she moved on, stepping carefully over a row of herb boxes and onto the paved stones. She pressed up against the kitchen door, listening. She could hear nothing. No chatter. No chopping. No clang of pots or pans. It was late. The odds were that the kitchen was empty.

She hoped.

Twisting the latch, she eased the door open a bit, then listened again. Nothing. She pulled it open just enough to slip inside.

A short, narrow passage led directly into the brick-floored kitchen. The room was empty and dimly lit. A single lamp stood on the center table, next to a tall bronze samovar. The tang of citrus hung in the air.

Kara stepped in, peering into the dark corners to be sure no one lurked there. There was no one, yet the samovar bubbled, and a teapot sat atop it, warming and exuding the lovely, fresh scent of Russian tea. She paused. Petra would be urging her minions to get ready to leave. Would they pause long enough to take a last cup of tea? She doubted the woman would allow it. But perhaps someone would prepare hot flasks to carry with them into the cold night?

She had to take the chance.

She could hear voices. Not in the next room. Perhaps a couple of rooms away. Quickly, then. And quietly.

She set the horse tonic and the horseshoe on the table. The samovar was hot. Grabbing a kitchen towel, she lifted away the teapot, removing the lid and pouring a healthy dose of the opium-rich tonic into the concentrated tea. Carefully, she used the towel to lift the top off the larger bronze section and poured more tonic into the heated water. She thought about adding a little extra, but hesitated. She didn't know how strong this tonic might be. She put the pieces all back together and breathed a sigh of relief.

A door at the back of the kitchen led to a pantry. She left the horse tonic on a shelf inside, took up her horseshoe once more, then went to see what she could hear.

The next room was a dining area, containing only a long, empty table and a great hutch, its many shelves bare, save for a lone, cracked bowl. She moved past them toward the open arch that led to the room beyond. She kept well back, for the voices came from there. She detected Petra's, giving orders in a sharp, high tone. And another. A man's voice, trying to soothe her.

"Pack the straw in tight around each one," Petra said. "This batch is definitely sturdier, but we cannot afford to lose any to cracks."

"We will not lose any. These are perfection. Your smith has done himself proud, at last."

The tone was smooth, the words accented. Austrian? Russian, it sounded more like, which made sense, given the samovar. And he did not address Petra like a lackey. He spoke in the urbane voice of a gentleman. A confederate, then?

Kara recalled that a Russian had been among the top conspirators in the League of Dissolution.

"The tests this morning proved these will perform just as we require," the gentleman continued. "Still, they are packed as gently as if they were hen's eggs. There is no need to fret."

"There is every need to fret," Petra argued. "I thought all we had to do was to tie up loose ends here. I sent your man in to deal with that mewling history teacher—but it turned out he had to confront Kier as well. It's entirely possible it didn't go well. Your man didn't make it to the livery in time to head back here, despite their ridiculous delays."

"I have every faith in Rybakov."

"Then where is he?" Petra demanded. "You don't understand how damnably slippery Kier is. If that teacher is the one who has been lurking about here, then Kier could be hot on our tail. *Damn* him! He should never have been able to track me here."

"Ah, but should you not give him his title and call him Sedwick?" The Russian sounded amused. "The man certainly scrambled hard enough to get it."

Petra's filthy response was enough to make Kara blush, but the gentleman merely laughed.

"Calm your nerves, my dear. I was only poking at you. If the duke does come knocking, my prickly little bear, we are more than prepared." Pausing, the gentleman gave a little hum. "In fact, might it not be best if we await him here? Conquer him now so that we may proceed without worry that he will interfere with us later?"

"No," Petra said flatly.

"Interesting. He frightens you."

Kara flinched as something crashed.

"He does *not* frighten me." Petra's tone had lowered, and she gave a deep, scornful laugh. "I would have thought you intelligent enough to understand that there is no man alive who can frighten me."

"Don't be ridiculous," the gentleman scoffed, but in a light tone. "Have you met every man alive? How could you know such a thing?"

"I know," Petra assured him.

Were they *flirting*? Kara's mouth dropped open.

"Nevertheless, I become more intrigued with this Duke of Sedwick with each passing day. I admit, I am almost tempted to test myself against him."

"No," Petra said again. "The man is mine to dispatch."

"Then why not—"

"Enough about Niall Kier! You know the timing is critical on this mission. And I tell you again, we will only get one chance at our real target."

"And I say again, you give these English too much credit."

"You do not give this particular Englishman enough estimation," Petra countered. "We must get to London and deal with him before we move further. You asked me about the obstacles in your path and I told you—he is the largest. This one is smart. Wily. Ruthless, too. He has vision, I tell you, and that is a quality that is severely lacking in nearly everyone."

"Not everyone," the Russian said. He sounded deliberately sulky, as if fishing for a compliment.

Petra did not give it. "It is rare enough. One attempt. That is all we will get. Right now, he is distracted."

"Not distracted enough, or none of this would be necessary."

"Still. He is unsuspecting at the moment. If we fail, however…" Petra sighed. "He will put the pieces together. He will be on alert. If anyone could track it back to us, it would be him. He will come after us."

Who? Kara wondered. Whom were they talking about?

"So. We will make sure he dies."

Kara put a hand to her mouth. An assassination. They meant to kill someone? But whom? Whose death were they plotting?

"Everything you say makes me think we would be wiser to deal with Sedwick now," the gentleman said. "Remove the distraction he represents while we have the chance."

"No. We can brook no delay. We must go before he arrives. We must remove every trace of what we have been up to. There is no way Kier can have any idea of our plans—and we must not give him the chance to learn a thing. He has the sort of connections that could ruin everything."

"But—"

"We go," Petra insisted. "We accomplish our aim. We clear your path."

"And yours."

"And mine. Afterward, I will have time. I will have focus. And I can concentrate on filling Kier with misery before I finally kill him."

The Russian laughed. "I find you admirably bloodthirsty, Petra Scot."

"I have many other admirable qualities that I may allow you to explore, but not now. We must go."

He laughed again. "So single minded. Here—this is the last of them. All are tucked in, safe and snug." The Russian paused. "But what of the last piece? Now that your gunsmith has proved the concept of those pins, we know we need a good deal more of the explosive to fill them. I sent out a man to investigate the manufacturer that supplies the British military. If he reports back here and finds no one—"

"No. His report matters naught. I told you, we cannot raid a military supplier. Suspicions would be aroused. And in any case, there is no need. I have found a way to get what we require. I took care of it just today." She gave a nasty laugh. "And I was able to punish an old adversary at the same time."

"Fascinating," the Russian breathed. "Very well. We will proceed as you say. Now. Go and call your men to come in and nail these crates and carry them out. Then you must sit down and breathe for a moment and enjoy a cup of proper tea. I put the bellows to the samovar just before you came in. It must surely be ready by now."

"Are you not listening? We have no—"

"Stop there," the Russian interrupted. "First, Rybakov is extremely formidable. I believe the odds are high that we will not see Sedwick at all tonight." Petra made a sound, but he did not allow her to interrupt him. "Yes. I do believe we should prepare, in case he prevails, but I assure you, he will not have an easy time besting my man."

Petra grumbled something that Kara could not hear.

"Second, while you wear interchangeable gowns and no doubt live right out of your trunk, I have an actual wardrobe."

"It is only sensible to be ready to leave at a moment's notice," Petra said.

The Russian sighed. "My very fashionable wardrobe is currently spread out across the abominable quarters I occupy here, and I assure you I will not be leaving without my waistcoats. Bad enough that I will be forced to leave a very decent samovar behind, but it will be entirely too hot now to think of packing. At the very least, I will enjoy a last decent cup of tea. So, go and summon your men, then you may enjoy one too, while I pack my things."

"Fine," Petra grumped. "But pack quickly, will you?"

Kara scurried to plaster herself against the wall on the far side of the hutch. She held her breath as the Russian passed through on his way to the kitchen. All she could make out was that he was short in stature, and slender. He did indeed appear to wear a fancifully embroidered waistcoat and linen with billowing sleeves. She could not see the color of his hair, but it appeared to be a mass of curls, slicked back and tamed with pomade.

He did not spot her. He went through to the kitchen, where she heard a brisk and efficient clatter as he prepared the tea tray.

Kara crept back to the other side of the room to stand so that she would be hidden behind the door when he came back through. She cringed, though, when she heard the front door open and Petra return. If the woman decided to head to the kitchen, Kara was caught.

"Sit down, my prickly little bear," the Russian called. He came through the door, trailing the scent of lemon and orange behind him.

Kara tucked herself further behind the open door.

"Here you are. Enjoy the warm spices. Let them calm your nerves."

Kara heard the rattle of cups as the tea was poured.

"A toast," the Russian said. "To our success. And to removing roadblocks. Now, relax for just a minute or two, I implore you. Then gather up all your plans here. I shall be done in a trice."

Nerves fluttering, Kara went back to her spot behind the hutch. Petra urged her accomplice to hurry once more. The Russian departed for the upper floor.

Sinking down, Kara waited and listened.

The rustle of papers sounded clear. Drawers opened and closed. Was that the stutter of a missed step? How long would it take for the opium to take effect?

It was an agonizing wait. She worried that the dose might have been too strong. What if she killed them? Yes, she wanted to put a stop to Petra's reign of terror, but she didn't want the woman's death on her conscience. Nor the Russian gentleman's, though he was clearly an enemy of England.

Besides, Gyda would be furious with her.

She was distracted by a loud curse from Petra. And then another. Her words sounded slurred. Then came a loud *thump*.

Silence.

Kara got to her feet. She crept to the arched doorway and waited.

Nothing.

She peeked around the arch. Petra was stretched out on the floor.

Kara crept closer. The woman lay on her back, frowning at the ceiling. Her gaze shifted. Kara saw the moment Petra recognized her. The woman scowled. Her mouth opened. Then her eyelids fell, and her head rolled to the side.

With a gasp, Kara knelt beside her and felt for a pulse. She breathed a sigh of relief. Petra's heartbeat felt slow, but strong and steady.

Something upstairs thudded, as if an object had been dropped to the floor. Then came another loud *thump*.

Kara stood. Her heart was pounding, but she rushed to one of the crates resting on side tables and pushed the lid aside. She stared down, wondering what she was looking at.

Reaching out, she lifted one of the objects free. It was oblong, fashioned of hammered metal and slightly too big to be truly comfortable in her hand. Hollow, it featured a large cap that had been screwed in at one end. Nine smaller holes had been drilled into it, in seemingly random spots. Glancing into the crate, she realized that some of the objects were slightly different. Square nuts had been attached over the holes, ready for something to be screwed in? But what?

What in blazes *were* these things?

She froze at the sound of the front door opening again. Dropping the object, she whirled to run. As she burst through the dining room door into the kitchen, a man came in from the back of the house, carrying two heads of cabbage.

"There was not much out there, but I grabbed a couple of—" Spotting her, he stopped. "What's this, then?" he asked in surprise.

Another huge specimen of a man. Where did Petra find them all? He stood in the narrow passage, blocking it completely.

Kara spun around again and fled back the way she'd come, only to bump into the farm cart driver just inside the dining room. She leapt back and dodged, heading around the other side of the dining room table.

But he turned and lunged when she headed for the arched doorway. Getting a hand on her, he dragged her back, grabbed her by an arm, and held her tight with one hand and took the horseshoe from her grip with the other. "What were you going to do with this, eh?"

Kara did not feel the need to state the obvious.

"The boss lady is laid out on the carpet," her captor told the larger man when he dashed in, without his cabbages.

The other man's eyes widened. "Where's the foreign nob?"

The driver shrugged. He gave Kara a shake. "Where is he?"

Her mind was racing. "Upstairs."

"Go look," the driver ordered the other man. He yanked Kara aside so that the man could pass, then pulled her back to the parlor, where he stared at Petra in fascination. "I ain't never seen her quiet afore now," he marveled.

The other man came racing back. "The foreign gent—he's in the same condition. Stretched out on the floor."

The driver cast a glance over the tea tray. "Poisoned?" he asked her.

Kara shook her head. "No!" she said in surprise.

"What is it, then? What'd you give 'em?"

He gave her a shake to make her answer.

"It's just opium. They are only asleep."

"Oh, she ain't gonna like that," the other man breathed.

"She'll be spittin' mad," the driver agreed. "But for once, she won't be aiming it in our direction."

"But what do we do?" The big man was looking decidedly nervous. "She wanted everything loaded up and out of here. You heard her." He gave a grimace. "Someone's coming. The police? The government? We cannot let them find us here with all of this." He waved a hand toward the crates. "If they don't hang us, then she'll strangle us with her bare hands."

The driver rubbed his chin. "Well, I suppose we just do as we were told. We'll load everything up and take it into Town."

"But what about the boss lady? And him?" The other man gestured toward the ceiling.

"Ah. Well." The driver hesitated. "I know—get these crates loaded, then throw some of that hay back in the cart. We'll lay them out in the straw and cover them with their cloaks and deliver them, along with the goods."

"All right, then. I s'pose it's the best we can do, considerin'." He looked at Kara. "But what about her?"

The driver drew a deep breath. "She's got a length of rope on her. Use it. Tie her to the chair, while I think about it." Pulling the rope from around her shoulders, he shoved them both over.

The big man sat her in a chair and set about restraining her. He knew what he was about, unfortunately, thwarting her efforts to keep the knots loose. The last horseshoe, tucked into the small of her back, pressed against her. She didn't mention it.

The driver nailed the crates shut. When they had both finished, they lifted a crate together and maneuvered it out and toward the front door.

Kara immediately went to work, trying to get free. It wasn't easy, but at least he had tied her hands to each side of the chair instead of together, behind her back. She was able to use her fingers to grab her skirts and bunch them up until she could slip her fingers into a pocket. It took several tries before she managed to get a grip on the tiny, folded razor tucked inside, and several more before she got it flipped open.

Turner had gifted her the small blade for her birthday. Sending up silent thanks, she had to do some very careful maneuvering, but managed to aim the blade toward the length of rope attached to the chair—without slicing her fingers. Working carefully, she started sawing at the rope.

It didn't take long before the men came back for the second crate. She hid the blade beneath a fold of her skirt and tried to look innocent.

The driver paused a moment, looking between the box, Petra, and her. "It's not all going to fit," he said to himself.

"Let's load it and see," his partner said.

They departed again, and Kara sawed frantically, but it was slow going. She could not add any pressure to her cuts and had to rely on the sharpness of the blade.

"This is all your fault," she said to Petra, still asleep on the floor near the sofa. "Why could you not use all of your gifts in ways to improve the world instead of trying to destroy it?"

At last she made it through. Frantically, she cut her other hand free and started on her feet.

She wasn't fast enough. The men came back through the kitchen before she managed even to cut loose her first foot.

"Well, damn it to hell." The driver strode in and snatched away the razor.

With a silent curse, she swung at him and tried to stand, but with her feet still held fast to the chair, she was out of balance and unable to move. The driver merely gave her a push to knock her back into it.

"What are we going to do with her?" the other man asked. "We can't trust her. She's wily."

"She won't fit in the back with the others unless we stack them like sardines."

"The boss lady won't like that."

"She'll like it less if she finds out that we had her and let her get away." The driver rubbed a hand across his brow. "You've heard the boss ranting. This one must be one of those nobs she holds such a grudge against."

"So let's not tell her. She don't ever need to know we even seen the woman."

"We cannot just leave her here. When the government shows

up, she'll tell them everything." The driver snapped his fingers. "They will be on us like that."

"We cannot kill her!" The other man was starting to sound anxious. "She's a bleedin' lady of the realm. They'll hang us for sure."

"I've got it." A crafty grin spread across the driver's face. "We'll give her a taste of her own medicine." He appeared to be relieved by this solution.

"No," said Kara.

"Yes. By the time you wake up, we'll be long gone."

The big man considered it. "Fine, but I still say we don't need to mention her to the boss lady."

"Agreed." The driver laughed. "Fetch the lady a cup of tea."

Kara wanted no part of that opium-laced tea. She reached down to try to pull the rope from her foot, but the driver pushed her back upright and held her there with a hand on her shoulder.

With her other hand she reached behind her and grabbed the horseshoe from her belt. She brought it down hard onto the hand where he held her, then threw it at the other man, aiming for the cup he was bringing her. Her aim was true. It hit and the cup shattered.

Both men cursed her soundly.

"Hell and damnation. This one is a pain in the arse. Wait until I tie her hands again, will you?"

"Hold her head back," the big man said grimly as he poured another cup of tea.

Kara fought, but she was soon bound again. They held her tight, tilted her head back, and pinched her nose. She spat and tried to bite, but eventually, they won.

Staring down at her, the driver frowned. "I think we'd better give her another."

She fought again, but it was a lesson in humiliation. She glared at them when they finally let her go. "You would do better to take your loaded wagon straight to the authorities and turn yourselves in before she wakes up." She glanced down at Petra, still fast asleep and sprawled across the floor. "If they succeed in their plans, do you think there is a chance you won't hang for murder?"

"If they succeed, then we will be paid well, set for life, and far away before the confusion dies down," the driver answered smartly.

The pair of them conferred for a moment before the driver sent the other man to fetch cloaks for Petra and the Russian. When he came back, they stood before her, watching her closely.

She wanted to snarl at them, but she could already feel the opium affecting her. A haze was settling over her vision. She tried to blink it away.

"There it is, then," the driver said with satisfaction. He gestured. "I'll take the boss out to the wagon, then come back to help you with the nob."

Kate watched him bend down to lift Petra in his arms. She couldn't look away. His motions were so slow. Was he moving at half speed?

The other man said something, but she couldn't make out the words. Everything was distant and muted.

Wait. Was she underwater? She looked up at the man beside her, and her head kept going back. It rested on the chair and she could not seem to lift it. She tried blinking again, but her eyelids were so heavy. Perhaps she would close them. Just for a…

Chapter Twenty-One

A HEAD, DALTON REINED in next to a thick copse of bare trees. Niall pulled his mount to a halt beside him. The moon had risen above the trees so that they could decently see the road, but in the shadow of the wood, forms all blended together.

"The farm is just around the next turn. Every time I've approached, I've been stopped by a sentry posted at the lane. I'll engage him." Dalton patted the pocket where he'd stashed Kara's pistol. Niall had taken it from her bag in the carriage and loaned it to him for this mission. "Once I have him in hand, we'll go up. The wood remains thick enough for cover a good part of the way up. We can leave the horses in there and get a good look at the place before we move in. We should be able to duck in and hide behind the barn or one of the outbuildings."

"Let me handle the sentry." Niall's nerves were stretched thin. He ached to do *something*. He could scarcely tolerate the idea of Kara in Petra Scot's clutches. He kept reminding himself that Kara knew what she was about. He couldn't blame her for taking a chance if it had been presented. She knew enough to stay hidden if she was outnumbered. But he was sure she would take every chance to discover what these fiends were up to. He knew because it was exactly what he would do. But then, what might go wrong?

Urging his mount forward, he rounded the curve and approached the lane. No one stepped out to confront him. He took the turn as if he meant to approach the farm.

Still no one.

He circled on the horse and waited a moment, but there was no sign of a sentry.

Gyda and Dalton had been watching. They rode out to join him.

"I haven't been here without encountering a watchman," Dalton said. "What does it mean?"

"It means we'd better hurry," Gyda said grimly.

They left the horses where Dalton had suggested and hunched together in the wood to survey the place.

"No movement at all," Gyda whispered. "Barely any lights. Is that barn door partway open?"

"Enough of this." Niall could take no more. Pulling out his own pistol, he pushed out of the covering wood. "The livery said that Petra left in a farm cart. Check the barn. I'm heading for the house."

A single room was lit, off to the left of the front door. No smoke from any of the chimneys. No other signs of life at all. What if they had gone and taken Kara with them? What if…

He blocked the thought and started to run.

The front door was unlocked. Slipping inside, he stood in the dark to listen. He could hear nothing. He did detect a faint, spicy citrus scent in the air.

As his eyes adjusted to the dimmer light, he could see a small sort of office to the left, a room with a desk, a shelf of books, and stacks of files piled about. Faint light came from the arched door at the back wall. Stepping quietly, he crossed to it. Slowly, silently, he shifted so that he could see into the next room.

"Kara!" Panic was a knife blow to his chest. From the strike emanated a sharp, consuming fear.

She had been tied to a chair. She slumped in it, her head lolling to one side.

"Kara!" Her name ripped out of his throat, rough and jagged. He crossed the room in an instant, shaking her. He didn't breathe, couldn't breathe, until he saw the rise and fall of her chest.

"*Thank you. Thank you.*" It was a whisper to the heavens, to every god, angel, or being that might have had a hand in ensuring she lived.

He pressed his fingers to her neck. Slow. Her heart beat slowly, but steadily. Ignoring the tears that had welled in his eyes, he patted her cheek gently. "Kara? Sweeting, wake up."

She slept on.

What had been done to her?

He took a moment to look around, spotted a tea service, then the shattered cup on the ground…and a horseshoe?

He squeezed her hand, sure that she would have quite a story to tell. If she would only wake.

He went to take up the teapot. Lifting the lid, he sniffed, but if something had been added, the smell of orange and spice masked it. Going back to her, he lifted her eyelid. Her pupils were constricted. They must have dosed her with laudanum, if he had to guess.

He patted her cheek again, smoothed her hair, gave her shoulders a shake. She did not stir or show any sign of consciousness. How much had they given her?

"Sedwick!" The call came from the front of the house.

"Here!"

Dalton came in. He froze when he spotted Kara. "Is she…?"

"Alive. Drugged."

The teacher sighed in relief. "The cart is gone. It looks like they have deserted the place, but they left two mounts behind. Why would they do that?"

"I don't know. Where is Gyda?"

Dalton looked sober. "She found traces of gunpowder. Casks of it. She went to look around in the other outbuildings."

"I don't think anyone else is in the house, but will you go through and have a look?"

Nodding, Dalton raised Kara's pistol. "I'll look upstairs."

Niall knelt before Kara to untie her. When he had freed his wife of her bonds, he lifted her and settled her gently on the sofa.

"No one upstairs," Dalton reported when he returned. "But I found women's clothes. And men's. Some finely tailored. Fancy. At least one toff has been staying here."

Niall nodded, staring down at Kara. "Could you go to the kitchens and check for any sign of what they might have given her? I don't want to leave her." He harbored a terror that she might stop breathing. "And check to see if there is any coffee?" Perhaps she would wake faster if they could give her a stimulant?

Dalton went through. Niall could hear him rummaging.

"There's a great, fancy tea warmer in here!" he shouted. "What are they called?" A pause. "A samovar!"

"Don't drink anything!" Niall called back. A Russian accent from the man who had attacked them. A samovar. He glanced again at the tea service and the citrusy, spiced tea.

"Niall?" Gyda stood in the doorway that led to the office and the front door. Her gaze fell on Kara, and she rushed over. "Odin's arse! Is she all right?"

"She's been drugged."

Dalton came back, carrying a large bottle. "There are slim pickings in the larder, but I found this."

Niall took it. "Horse medicine? Likely it is opium, then." He looked at Gyda. "Russian tea. A Russian assailant. What would Petra be getting up to with Russians?"

"I don't know, but I think you had better come outside."

"I don't want to leave her." Niall looked again at the bottle. "What if she's had too much? It could kill her. We need to get her awake." He turned to Dalton. "Was there coffee?"

"No. I'm sorry."

"Let Dalton stay with her, for just a moment," Gyda said. "You need to see this. Then we'll get her back to Chiswick and call a doctor."

Niall looked at his friend. Gyda's expression was solemn.

More worried than angry, for the first time in two days.

"Watch her carefully," he told Dalton. "Make sure she is breathing."

The man paled. "What if she stops?"

"Shout." Niall stood, pushing the thought away. "Show me. Then we go."

"Bring a lamp," Gyda ordered him.

He followed her out past the barn and the semicircle of out-buildings, to a field that lay bare in the moonlight.

But not exactly bare. Gyda stepped through several feet of scattered dirt and rock and set her lantern on the ground.

He gave a grunt of surprise. "Is that—"

"Yes."

A crater. A massive hole blown in the field. "How far?"

"Give me your lamp." Taking it, Gyda walked around the circumference of the thing, stepping carefully. When she reached the other side, she set the lamp down.

"It's big," Niall said. "What is Petra doing? Hauling around a cannon and explosive shells?"

"And if so, what does she mean to do with it?"

Niall closed his eyes. "We'll figure it out."

"We don't know where she's gone," Gyda said bitterly.

"We will find her," Niall vowed. "But first, Kara."

⟫⟫⟫⟪⟪⟪

IT WASN'T EASY, but he managed to get Kara back to Chiswick, riding double on his rented mount. Not easy at all, in fact, but the alternative was to wait for the carriage to be fetched, and he could not countenance the delay. His wife was still out cold. Not even the difficult ride in the chilly night air roused her. By the time they reached the village, he was starting to feel frantic.

Gyda and Dalton had ridden ahead to secure rooms at the Meryton Hotel. Niall was able to carry Kara straight upstairs and lay her out on the bed in their room.

Dalton saw them settled, then ran downstairs to ask for coffee. Looking worried, Gyda sat next to Kara on the bed and took her hand. "Niall, do you remember Eval?"

"I've been thinking of nothing but him during this entire, miserable ride." Eval had been a friend they had shared during their time in Oslo. The unfortunate man had had a severe problem with opium.

"One time when he indulged in too much—"

"One time?" Niall interrupted bitterly.

"One time," Gyda said patiently, "not too long before the last time… He took too much and a chemist friend of his used a hollow metal needle to inject him with a stimulant to bring him around."

"I knew something like that had happened. I was trying to recall the particulars." He couldn't look away from Kara. "I'm starting to get truly worried. But where would we find someone like that here?"

"I'd wager that lady tavern keeper might know someone," Gyda said wryly.

"No need to consult the local opium users," Dalton said from the doorway. "We have a decent, knowledgeable physician in the village. He's a friend of mine. He's used to dealing with excess of all kinds, with the sort of parties that go on at Chiswick House. I'll go and see if he's at home." He approached, carrying a tray with coffee and tea. "And then I'll go and tell the director that I'll be taking a brief leave from the school."

"Are you sure?" Niall asked.

Dalton glanced at Gyda. "That woman killed my…" He choked. "My Katherine. Do you think I feel it any less than you?"

"No." Gyda lifted her chin. "You deserve your part in this, too. And we'll appreciate the help."

"Thank you," Niall said, taking the tray from him. "And please, do fetch the doctor. And Dalton?"

"Yes?" The teacher had already started for the door.

"Please, hurry."

Chapter Twenty-Two

"Bring the light a little closer, please?"

An unfamiliar voice sounded close as Kara shied away from a bright, insistent light.

"Ah, there. You see, she's coming around."

"We did manage to rouse her enough to get a couple of cups of coffee in her while we waited."

Niall. That was Niall's voice. She tried to reach him, to pull herself out of the darkness that held her.

"I offer my apologies for the wait, but the local midwife needed assistance with a difficult birth. You did just as you ought, though. The duchess is breathing at an acceptable rate. Her heart sounds steady. Since you have been able to rouse her…"

The voice went on. It sounded kind, but she couldn't follow it all. Something made her frown, though. *The duchess,* he'd said. *Me.* "It's me," she said out loud, but the sound of her voice made her cringe. Why did she sound like a croaking frog? "I'm the duchess."

"Kara."

The bed sank as Niall settled on the edge.

Bed? She looked around. "Where are we?"

"Back in Chiswick. Can you open your eyes, Kara?"

She hadn't realized she'd closed them. She opened them with

difficulty, and smiled at Niall, hovering close. He looked both worried and relieved at the same time.

"We took rooms at the hotel. Here." He wrapped her fingers around a warm cup, but kept his hands around hers. "Drink. We need to get a little more coffee into you."

It was warm and strong. She breathed in the steam, trying to chase the fog from her brain.

Fog. Fog in her brain.

She nearly choked as it all came rushing back. "Petra!" she gasped. "She has a Russian!" Why wasn't she making sense? Why did her mouth feel like it was thick with cotton? "She's working with a Russian!"

"We surmised that much," Niall said. "Take another drink. They drugged you. You need the stimulant."

"I drugged *them*!" she corrected him. "Petra and the Russian both. But her henchmen caught me, and they made me drink the tea, too."

"Hallucinations are not unusual in a patient that has ingested that much opium," the unfamiliar voice said. "But I can see her pupils are improving. Give her a little more coffee and then allow her to sleep it out. She'll be fine in the morning."

Kara looked over to see a handsome gentleman of middle age packing tools back into a leather bag.

"Thank you, Dr Lewis." Niall still sounded worried. "Are you sure there are no other measures we need to take?"

"Positive. Just a little rest and she'll be fine."

Kara stared as Gyda walked with the man to the door. "How did I get back here?" She tried to remember, but had only a fuzzy recollection of the parlor in the farmhouse. Of being tied up… She reached further—and it all came rushing back. The tavern, Petra…

"That man!" she cried. "Petra sent him after you. She sent him to finish you and Dalton. I tried to warn Gyda."

"You did. We handled him. He's in the constable's cell now. I'll send word to Wooten so that he can send a man to pick him up."

"But how did you find me?" She sat up straighter, recalling that strange ride. "I had to take the chance, Niall. I couldn't let her disappear. We couldn't lose her again."

"Dalton knew about the farm. He'd followed Petra there a few times." Niall shook his head. "Without him, we might not have found you. You scared me witless, Kara."

"I'm sorry. But you know I had to follow her. Gyda—"

"Gyda is right here." Her friend grinned at her and sat on the other side of the bed. She looked as exhausted as Kara felt. "Don't let Niall scold you. You did exactly as either of us would have done in your place."

Kara knew it was true, but Niall did look shaken. She cringed, thinking how she would have felt had their roles been reversed. Panicked. Deathly frightened. Furious.

She gasped suddenly. "Niall, she is planning an assassination! Petra and her Russian!"

"An assassination? Who?"

"I don't know. Someone in the government. They both knew whom they were discussing and never said the name."

"Think, Kara," Gyda urged. "Surely they must have said something about their target. Something we can use?"

Kara put both hands on her brow. "I don't think so? It's all so fuzzy. Oh! Yes! He was an obstacle to the Russians, in some way. She said he was wily. Resourceful. I...I don't think there is anything else."

Niall and Gyda exchanged glances.

"Stayme," Niall said. "We need to get word to him. He might know who any likely targets could be."

"I'll go." Gyda stood.

"No. It's late," Niall objected. Kara could tell he was reluctant to dissuade her. "The last train will have left. It's been two very long days. None of us has slept beyond a few snatched minutes in the carriage."

"Except me," Kara interjected.

They all laughed a little. Niall reached for her hand, then Gyda's. "Let's sleep tonight and head out in the morning."

"I cannot." Gyda swallowed. "I wouldn't be able to rest, in any case, knowing there was something to be done and I wasn't doing it." Kara felt for her as her friend gave Niall a pleading look. "Let me take the carriage and go to Berkeley Square. I'll sleep on the way into London. It will be easier to rest knowing that I am accomplishing something. Leaving no stone unturned. No chance to catch her untaken."

Kara squeezed Niall's hand.

"I'll fill Stayme in and set him to work," Gyda continued. "Then I will rest there until morning. You two can take the first train in. We'll see what Stayme can dig up and start planning accordingly."

Kara began to feel guilty. "Perhaps I can—"

"No," Niall interrupted, his tone resolute. "You will do as the doctor said and rest right there until morning." He nodded at Gyda. "Very well. It is a good plan as any."

It was probably just as well. Kara could feel the pull of exhaustion. Tugging Gyda closer, she gave her a long hug and whispered her thanks. When her friend pulled away, she blinked tearfully. "Be careful," she whispered.

"You be careful," Gyda returned indignantly. "No more horse tonic for you."

Kara laughed and shook her head. "I only hope Petra is feeling worse than I am. They hauled her off in that farm cart, stretched out in the straw." The words triggered a memory. "Oh, how could I have forgotten? They are hauling some sort of devices. Hollow, oblong, made of metal. There were holes all about them. I had no idea what they were, but there was gunpowder in the barn and they meant to take it with them."

Niall told her about the craters blown in the fields. "They mean to destroy something, and make a big splash about it."

"They were missing a piece," Kara said, trying to remember. "The Russian mentioned it." She looked helplessly between them.

"I hope Stayme will know something, otherwise I don't know how we are going to find them. Maybe Petra will sleep long enough to delay their plans."

"I hope she sleeps for days," Gyda said harshly. "And then wakes up to find us upon her." She raised a brow. "But as for you, I expect you to be up and pushing on in the morning. Sleep it off," she said gently. "I'll see you tomorrow."

Kara nodded and lay back while Niall walked with Gyda to the door. Nestling in, she watched them speak, flooded with the warmth of love she felt for them both.

She blinked, fighting the sleep that pulled at her. Down, down. She struggled, but it was too strong. Her eyelids drooped, and she fell.

Her dreams were vivid. Some of them frightened her. She thought her drugged mind had taken pity on her at last when she dreamed a knock on the hotel door. Niall rose to answer it, and she knew it for a dream when he opened it to reveal Turner standing outside.

Her butler and longest close friend entered, looking grim. "Tom Hawkins is gone. He left sometime during the night."

A shiver went through her in the wake of the cold air that had come in with him. Surely she hadn't dreamed that.

Was she awake?

Turner's gaze lowered. "I'm sorry. So sorry. Harold is gone, too. I came to tell you straightaway."

Kara gasped and sat up. It wasn't a dream. But Turner's words made her feel as if she were still trapped in a nightmare.

NIALL PULLED TURNER inside. He steered the older man to a seat by the fire before kneeling to poke it back to life.

Kara, still fully clothed after all her adventures yesterday, climbed out of the bed. She was still a bit wobbly on her feet, but she made it across the room and dropped into a heap at Turner's feet. "Tell us, Turner."

"I am so—" the butler began again, but his gaze ran over her and he stopped, clearly startled by the picture she presented. Niall looked, too. The rumpled gown, the bare feet, the bits of straw throughout her ebony hair—none of it meant a jot to him. She could still put any *tonnish* debutante to shame. It was the fright in her eyes that moved him.

"Your Grace? Are you well?" A similar scare showed in Turner's face as he stared at the woman he'd cared for since she was a girl. "What's happened?"

"Petra's henchmen poured opium down her throat," Niall said bitterly. Those men would pay for that before all of this was over.

"To be fair, I dosed Petra and one of her accomplices first," Kara said. "But never mind that. Where is Harold? What's happened?" She stared up at the older man. "Turner, you look positively gray." She glanced toward the window, which was just starting to brighten with morning light. "You must have left in the middle of the night to get here so early."

"Your message said you hoped to leave here this morning, if all went well. I wanted to catch you before you left." He looked between them. "I am forced to imagine it didn't go well?"

"It went…" Niall paused. "The entire escapade was…unusual."

"As our typical matter of course, then," Turner said wryly.

"Yes, yes. But what's happened to Harold?" Kara demanded.

"I do not know for sure," Turner answered miserably.

"He's not hurt?" Niall could see Kara holding her breath, waiting for the answer.

"I have no reason to think so, but I cannot say." Turner drew in a breath. "Your message reached us late last evening. I went upstairs, thinking to share the news with Harold. I knew that he would have been relieved to learn that we had heard from you. But he wasn't in his room. Nor could I find him in the schoolroom or the gymnasium. I thought he must have gone out to visit with Mr. Hawkins."

"He knew Hawkins was in the laboratory," Niall said, remembering the discussion.

"Yes. After you departed, I took Mr. Hawkins out there to settle him in, making sure none of the staff realized he hadn't gone with you. The lad was out there working when we arrived. They had quite a reunion."

"Yes, Tom said he knew Harold," Kara recalled.

"Harold remembered him, too. They had a grand time, reminiscing over old adventures and mutual acquaintances. They talked and talked, all the while I was setting up Mr. Hawkins's cot. I asked the man if he needed to rest or if he wanted to go to work right away, as he had agreed to do. He was quite ready to dedicate himself to some useful task, he insisted. The duller the better, as he needed time to think. I set him to sorting the new shipment of gears and then pulled Harold aside and explained how we needed to keep Mr. Hawkins's presence a secret. As I suspected, the lad was proud to be a part of it all."

Niall could well picture it.

"I explained that Mr. Hawkins needed some time to himself. That he needed quiet to contemplate the choices that lay before him. Harold agreed to leave him to his work while he concentrated on his own. I left them to it, but several hours later, the lad came to report that he was done in the lab and that Hawkins had not even noticed his leaving, so engrossed was he." Turner sighed. "That was before dinner, and it was the last I saw of the boy. He was eager to report to me and felt sure he could be a help, because the kitchens were used to him stopping in to get snacks to take with him before heading out to the forge or the lab."

"That sounds like Harold," said Niall. "All stomach and focus on his projects."

"When I failed to find him, I thought that must surely be what happened, and I would find him out in the laboratory, sharing Cook's ginger snaps. It took me a few minutes to arrange to go out there without any of the staff knowing and wondering. But when I made it out to the lab, neither of them was there."

"Was there a note?" asked Kara.

"Any sign of a struggle?" Niall asked at the same time.

"Neither," Turner said. "I questioned the staff. Harold had indeed stopped to raid the larder earlier, but no one had seen him since. It wasn't until I spoke with the men posted at the gate that I learned that Mr. Preston had come back."

"Preston?" Niall repeated sharply. "And he didn't come to the house?"

"No. No one else had any notion of his visit. He must have gone straight to the laboratory."

"Preston did not seem enamored of Tom's request to stay at Bluefield," Kara said.

"Would he have convinced him to leave? And taken Harold with him?" asked Turner.

"It's just as likely that he might have convinced Hawkins to leave and Harold followed after them," said Niall. "The lad has been itching to prove himself. If he heard something he thought valuable or found suspicious, then he would act." He raised a brow at Kara. "Much like someone else I know."

"Yes, it does sound like you," she returned pertly before dropping her head into her hands. "Oh, saints," she breathed. "What if he's out there on his own?"

"He's a capable lad," Niall said.

"Yes. I *know* he's lived in the streets. I know he has good instincts. I know he's learned much since he came to us. But does any of that make him capable of taking on Petra Scot and her ilk?" Kara demanded. "We have to find him. What if she gets him in her clutches?" Her voice lowered to a whisper. "But where? When do we start?"

"With Preston," Niall said darkly. "What in blazes is the man up to?"

"Gyda is going to want to strangle us for the delay, but we

need to find Harold." Kara hopped to her feet and promptly swayed.

"Hold on there." Niall was at her side in an instant. "You need breakfast."

"I need to find Harold."

He raised a hand. "I'll send for train tickets and have the kitchens prepare a basket. We'll take it with us." He waved a hand before her. "While I am doing that, you have a wash and a change of clothes."

"And a brush through her hair," Turner murmured.

"All right," Kara grumped. "Message received."

Niall clapped a hand to his brow. "Odin's arse, I nearly forgot Dalton. I'll wake him."

"I'm coming, too," Turner stated.

No one argued.

"I am sure we can use you. We are going to need all the help we can get," Niall said grimly.

Chapter Twenty-Three

WORRY ATE AT her all during the short train ride, but Kara pulled in a deep breath as they disembarked. *Think. Focus. Find Harold. Then find Petra.* They could do this.

She felt nearly fully recovered from her dose of opium. Perhaps the chill in the air helped. She hadn't drifted off, even with the sway of the train. Turner, however, had begun to fade, and he whitened a little more with each step along the platform.

Nudging Niall, she nodded toward her oldest friend. He followed her hint. He ran an assessing gaze over the older man, then gave her a return nod.

"Let's head straight out for the line of hacks," she said, taking Turner's arm and moving off at a slower pace than she normally would have used. "Niall and Dalton can bring our bits of luggage and meet us there."

Once they made their way outside, she allowed Turner to hail a hackney. They stood next to it as the others caught up to them.

"All right now," Niall began with authority. "Here is when we split up. Turner, you go straight to Stayme's. Inform him of Harold's disappearance."

"And Gyda," Kara interjected.

"And Gyda," Niall repeated. "The viscount's network should

be familiar with the boy. They can check in at all of Harold's usual London haunts. Make sure they know we are covering Preston's work and home."

"If Stayme has found any information on who Petra might be targeting, then I imagine Gyda will leave Harold to us and waste no time setting out in pursuit," Kara said.

"If she hasn't gone out already," Niall said dryly.

"It's a lot of pieces to juggle." Kara turned to Turner. "It will help if you stay at Stayme's for now and act as coordinator. We will all report in to you. You can send out vital information to the right parties as needed."

Turner knew what she was doing. She could see it in his eyes. But he merely nodded, which told her he felt as bad as she suspected, which made her worry more.

"Don't take too long to send word of what you find," the butler cautioned before he climbed in the hack.

"We'll join you at Berkeley Square as soon as we can."

The cab started off, and Niall waved for another to move up. "Dalton, Preston's rooms are at—"

"No," Kara interrupted. "You and I have to split up, Niall." He started to object, but she raised a hand. "Dalton doesn't know Preston from the prince. We need someone who knows the man at each site. Dalton can come with me to Westminster. You head over to his rooms." She paused, thinking. "If Preston is not there, stay and keep watch. We will do the same. If you do find him or Harold, then come to find us once you've figured out what is going on."

"I don't like separating from you," Niall said with a frown. "You've had two close calls with that woman in as many days."

"I'll watch over her," Dalton assured him. "If that Scot woman shows her face, she will be too busy dealing with me to worry over the duchess."

Niall started to speak, but then shook his head. "Fine. If anything goes wrong, head straight to Stayme's. I'll find you there."

"Agreed." She read the concern in his face and burrowed into his arms.

He held her tight. She never wanted to leave the warmth and love he wrapped around her, but Harold was out there, likely trying to prove his bravery and worth. She needed to find him and convince him that they already knew both. That he proved himself every day with his contagious laugh, his kind heart, his willing work ethic, and his eagerness to learn. "We will find him, won't we?" she whispered. "She doesn't have him?"

"Unlikely. Not yet. It's Preston that worries me now."

"He wouldn't hurt him, surely," she protested. She could not have read the man so wrong.

"No. Not in the normal course of things. But if he is forced to weigh Harold's safety against Tom's?" Niall shrugged.

Hearing it said out loud made it easier to step away. "Let's go, then. We need to find Preston before he has to make such a choice."

She kissed Niall fiercely and climbed in the cab. Dalton followed, and the hack set out for Westminster. It was not a long trip. Kara directed the driver to let them down right near the construction entrance they had used before. As Dalton paid the driver, she approached the gated entrance.

"Good morning," she said brightly, relieved to find the same porter stationed there. "I see you are having a bit of a slower day today."

The porter blinked. "Duchess!" he said after a moment. "Yes. Not so many deliveries today. But have you come to visit with Mr. Preston again, ma'am? Or have you another appointment?"

"I'm afraid I'm here to see Mr. Preston, please. It seems our business is not quite finished." She smiled at the man. "But I promise not to take up too much of his time."

He frowned. "Stars above, but the man has had a stream of visitors, hasn't he? I'm sorry to disappoint you, Your Grace, but Mr. Preston is not here at the moment. He got word from one of the quarries and had to go straight out." He shook his head. "It seems as if there is trouble with the type of stone they are using in the royal entrance hall of the tower. I hope it doesn't put them too far behind schedule."

"Oh dear. How distressing for Mr. Preston." Tilting her head at the man, she gave him a smile. "Did he happen to mention what time he would be back?"

"Oh, no. He wouldn't keep me informed of his comings and goings, ma'am."

Kara allowed herself to look dismayed. "I beg your pardon if I misspoke."

"No, ma'am. Not at all. Not at all." The porter blinked. "Oh, but I did hear Mr. Preston tell one of the masons that it would be late this evening before he made it back, if at all. The mason had concerns about the calculations for the stone needed for the storage room floors. There will be ever so many of them, ma'am, for the King's Tower will eventually house all of the Parliamentary records, stretching all the way back for years and years."

"How interesting," Kara told him. "Oh well. I suppose I will have to come back, if Mr. Preston does not mean to return until late."

"If at all, miss. We might not see him until morning."

"I suppose it cannot be helped." Kara started to turn away, but stopped to face the porter again. "You said that Mr. Preston has had several visitors recently?"

"Aye, miss. You and the duke were the first, but there has been a steady stream of them since. Sir Charles Barry himself come around to speak to him, ma'am. I admitted him myself and heard him complimenting our progress."

"How gratifying," Kara said with approval. "If I might ask..." She pulled Sculley's sketch of Petra from her bag. "Was this lady one of Mr. Preston's visitors?"

The porter's eyes narrowed. "She was, at that."

"When did she visit, if you can recall?"

"Oh, I won't soon forget her. She came yesterday, and let me tell you, she had no encouraging words for any of us. Insistent, she was, and more than a bit nasty with it."

"Sounds right," Dalton muttered.

"Thank you. You've been so helpful," Kara said warmly to the porter. "I'll be sure to mention it to Mr. Preston."

The man brightened. "Thank you, ma'am! I would like to get a better assignment. Assistant foreman, or something like. I'm sure I could do a decent job of it, and a good word can't hurt."

"Good day to you."

Dalton offered his arm. Kara took it, her mind whirling while they walked away. "So Petra leaves Chiswick for London yesterday morning. She stops in here to see Preston, then goes back to 'tie up loose ends.'"

Dalton snorted. "A nice way of saying she meant to kill me."

"Last evening, she told the Russian that she took care of obtaining the missing piece to their device and—punished an old enemy at the same time." She stopped walking. "She must have tasked Preston with obtaining whatever they are missing. It makes sense, doesn't it?"

Dalton gestured to the massive construction going on behind the wall. "An engineer, in charge of a project like that? He could likely obtain all manner of odd or dangerous things."

Kara started walking again. "But one of the first things Preston does is visit Tom Hawkins, who promptly leaves his hiding spot."

"Scared away?" Dalton asked. "Or forced away?"

"Niall was right. Petra must have threatened Tom." She started striding faster. "Come, we have to tell him. There's no use hanging around here waiting for Preston if he doesn't mean to return until late."

"We are going to the duke, then?"

"It's not far," Kara told him. "It will be faster to walk. Let's go."

NO ONE ANSWERED when Niall knocked on the door of Preston's rooms. He waited a moment and knocked again. "Preston?" he called.

All lay quiet.

"Tom Hawkins?" he said even louder. "It's Sedwick. I'm looking for Harold."

No answer.

Giving in to frustration, Niall gave the door a thundering pounding, to no avail. With a sigh, he turned and left the building. He would find a vantage point nearby where he could wait and watch.

He hoped Kara was having better luck.

"Niall?"

Joy and relief flooded through him. "Harold!"

The boy was crossing the street, running toward him. With a whoop, Niall scooped the lad up into a crushing embrace.

He felt Harold stiffen a moment in surprise, before the lad squeezed him back.

Letting out a whoosh of relief, Niall released him, not wanting to overly compromise the growing boy's dignity. "Thanks be to all of the gods. You scared us witless, lad."

"How did you even know I was gone?" the boy asked, baffled.

"Turner."

"Oh." Harold seemed to take it for granted that Turner could be responsible for all things difficult or miraculous.

Because it was so often true.

"What happened?" Niall asked. "What are you doing here? Did Preston force you to come?" For the first time, he really looked at the boy. "And what in blazes are you wearing?"

Harold curled his hands proudly around the tattered edges of his bedraggled coat. "Beggar's clothes," he answered proudly. "I'm in disguise."

"So I see. Where did you get such an…authentic disguise?"

"Off an old mate of mine. I gave him enough coin for a couple of nights in a dosshouse, and in exchange, he let me borrow his coat, hat, and blanket." The boy looked up and down the street. "Come on," he urged Niall. "I'll show you the spot I've been watching from."

Niall followed him back to the other side of the street. "Well, if you are watching Preston, then I must surmise that he didn't force you to leave Bluefield."

"Oh, no!" The boy sounded proud and excited. "He don't even know I saw him there, but I came upon him in the grounds, stickin' to the shadows, sneakin' his way to the lab." Harold stopped and ducked into a narrow alley between two homes. He took a deep breath and made an effort to drop the street slant to his words. "I'm watching from here. It's got a good view of the front of the house." He raised a hand. "And before you ask, there is a gate in the back garden that leads into an alley, but only the landlady has a key. She doesn't want her boarders going in or out that way. She likes to keep track of them." He grinned. "I've been thorough. Just the way you taught me."

Niall knew he had never given Harold lessons in surveillance, but he hadn't had to. If the lad applied the lessons he learned from them to the skills he'd learned in his early life, well, he would likely become a force to be reckoned with as he grew. "And how did you discover the landlady's preferences?"

Harold shrugged. "People like to talk. Especially about their neighbors."

Hiding a grin, Niall glanced back toward Preston's lodging house. "Well, tell me all, then. What happened after you found Preston skulking toward the lab?"

"I listened when he went in to talk with Tom." Harold raised a defensive hand. "He was definitely skulking, and he had not gone to the house to announce himself, so I didn't feel guilty about it."

"And what did you hear?"

"He didn't want Tom to stay at Bluefield. He said Petra must surely be having the place watched. Preston told him that the woman had come to him, making threats against Tom."

"What was Tom's response?"

"Tom didn't want to hear it. He had no wish to leave. Least-ways, not until Preston told him he might be putting everyone at Bluefield in danger. Then he agreed to go, but he didn't like a bit of it. Preston said he knew a place to hide him."

"So they went, and you followed?"

"I wanted to know where Tom would be." Harold hesitated. "And there was something else."

Niall waited while the lad gathered his thoughts.

"There was something about the way Preston spoke about Petra Scot. Something in his voice. He sounded…upset. Tom heard it, too. He asked about it, more than once, but Preston put him off. I needed to make sure Preston wasn't going to turn Tom over."

"He didn't, did he?" Niall asked, alarmed.

"No. They took the train back to London. I followed. Preston took him all the way to Greenwich, to a little house there. Tom must have kept on at him, asking about Petra, 'cause they were having a row over it when they left their hack to go in." Harold shrugged. "At least it made it easy to jump off the back and hide."

"A row?" Niall asked, thinking.

"A big one. Preston was that worked up about it. *I have no choice,* he was shouting. *If I fail, you die. Do you understand?*"

Niall sighed. "I was afraid it would be something like that."

"They were still arguing when they went in the house, but Preston must have convinced Tom, 'cause only he came out later."

"You followed him again?"

"Yes, but he only came back here. I knew Slanted Nick had a spot pretty close, so I went and traded him for his night rig and came back to watch."

Niall cringed at the thought of Slanted Nick being eager to seize the opportunity for a couple of nights at a dosshouse—usually a run-down place where men, women, and children paid for the cost of sleeping packed in together, out of the weather but most often on wafer-thin mats, or the floor. "We'll see what we can do for Nick once we've dealt with Petra, but did Preston leave home again?"

"Not until this morning, when he went to Westminster. He didn't stay long, though. He took a mount from the stables there and rode out." Harold's shoulders drooped. "There was no way for me to keep up with him then, so I came back here to wait."

"You did a fine—" Niall stopped and gestured across the street. "Look there."

Kara was striding down the pavement. Beside her, Dalton looked like he was struggling to keep up.

"Go and meet her, lad. She's been worried about you."

With a grin, Harold ran across to intercept her.

Kara gave a cry of joy at the sight of him and snatched him up for a long hug—and, by the sounds of it, a bit of a scolding.

"But I am fine," Harold protested.

Chuckling, Niall went to rescue the lad and greet his wife. They all spent a moment exchanging news, and they introduced Dalton to Harold.

"I've been a bundle of nerves," Kara told Harold afterward, squeezing his shoulders. "But you did well. Now listen, we need to send word of all of this back to Turner, Stayme, and Gyda. You have had a night out in the cold, so you will take the report back. Tell them everything. Get warm for a bit. Get fed. Get rested."

Before he could protest, she took both of his hands. "We will watch for Preston's return, but be sure to replenish yourself. Things are going to come to a head, and we will need all hands on deck."

Harold straightened. "I'll be ready."

"I know you will. Now, hurry back to Berkeley Square."

Kara leaned into Niall as they watched him go. She glanced up, looking both sad and proud. "He's scarcely a boy anymore," she said.

"No. We need to adjust. We cannot stifle him, but for today, Stayme will find a way to occupy him."

"As he did for you?"

"Hopefully, he'll have better luck with Harold. But in the meantime"—he gestured toward the lodging house—"we wait."

"Yes, but not in the cold. I have my tools. I'm sure I can get us into Preston's rooms."

Dalton rubbed his hands together. "That's the best news I've heard all day."

Niall was just reaching for the small gate when Kara spoke. "Niall, look."

It was Preston, walking toward them. His attention appeared to be focused on the tall box he carried. He didn't seem to notice them until he had grown quite close, but when he looked up and spotted them, he gave a moan.

"Damn you all for meddling fools. Stay there," he cried when Niall took a step toward him. "Don't come closer. Don't touch me at all. I cannot drop this box, do you understand? It would ruin everything."

Chapter Twenty-Four

KARA TOOK A slow, careful step toward the man. "What is in the box, Mr. Preston?"

"Never you mind. Just get out of the way." There was a desperate edge to his tone.

"It's the last piece. The missing piece to the device Petra is constructing, isn't it?"

Preston stared at her, incredulous.

"We know Petra is forcing you to do her bidding. That she has threatened to harm Tom if you don't cooperate," Niall said.

The engineer gave a sharp laugh. "I am beginning to see why she despises the pair of you. How could you possibly know that?" He shook his head. "Never mind. Just *move*. I very badly wish to find a safe place to set this down."

"Very well. But we are coming in with you."

As Kara and Niall stepped aside, Preston passed them, muttering and still stepping carefully.

They all trooped inside after him. Preston went through the main room and on to the bedroom, where he placed the box in the middle of the bed. Straightening, he heaved a sigh of relief, then looked around.

"Who the hell are you?" he asked Dalton, staring at him in surprise.

"This is Mr. Dalton," Kara said sharply. "He intended to marry Katherine Prentice. Petra's sister. The one she murdered," she reminded him.

"Which makes clear his motivation for helping us to stop Petra's machinations." Niall raised a brow at Preston. "What we don't understand is why *you* are helping her. You cannot actually imagine she will follow through on her end of any bargain you strike with her."

Preston rolled his shoulder, as if he'd gone stiff carrying that box so carefully. "Listen, you have had your own dealings with Petra. I understand that. But I *know* her. Bone deep, I understand her. I know the *only* chance I have of keeping Tom alive is to do as she says. I don't know the odds of her keeping her word if I follow through, but I know with certainty that if I do not, she will go to extreme measures to follow through on her threat. She will kill Tom. She will bide her time if she has to. She will travel to the ends of the earth to find him, wherever I hide him. She would gnaw her own foot off to get to him. She is that tenacious."

"I don't know what you have in that box, Mr. Preston, but I know she means to use it to assassinate someone," Kara said.

"Likely more than one person," Niall added.

"Do you think I don't know that?" Preston sank into a chair by the hearth and dropped his head into his hands. "Tom is my brother. I've always had the keeping of him. I was the only one who looked out for him. I cannot just..." He looked up at Niall. "Don't tell me you don't understand. Would you sacrifice your wife?"

He and Niall stared at each other for a long moment.

It took less than that amount of time for Kara to realize that she would never trade Niall's life. Not even with what they knew.

Niall cleared his throat. "Maybe there is another way. Show me what is in the box."

Preston straightened. "Why?"

"She had a gunsmith designing her devices. Forging is what I do," Niall reminded him. "Let me look at it."

Preston blinked. Kara could see his mind starting to whirl. He stood and crossed to the bed. "Be careful, for God's sake." He lifted the lid gently.

They all gathered around to peer inside.

Kara frowned. An insert had been placed in the box. Nine holes had been hollowed out of it, each one lined with thick padding. Resting in each soft hollow was a small metal object.

"May I?" asked Niall.

"Lift one out, if you must, but do not put any pressure on it," Preston said.

Brow furrowed, Kara stared. The object was cylindrical, and featured a screw fitting on the bottom. The rest of the cylinder looked like it had been fashioned of thin metal. Her mind pulled up a recollection of the objects in the crates at the farm. "Some of Petra's devices had square nuts attached at the holes. These screw into them? But what is the cylinder?"

Niall looked at Preston. "It is a percussion cap, isn't it?"

Shamefaced, Preston nodded.

"I don't understand," said Kara.

"It's larger and adapted, but it's like the piece used in a rifle or pistol to make a spark and ignite the powder." Niall gave Dalton a wry look. "Suddenly the gunsmith makes sense." He glanced again at Preston. "What is inside?"

"Mercury fulminate," Preston answered.

Niall's eyebrows rose. "A much larger amount than would normally be used in any sort of arms," he breathed. "You really did go to a quarry, then?"

"Yes. They keep larger amounts about because they use it in detonators on their explosives."

Kara was putting it all together in her mind's eye—and growing horrified. "So, you screw one of these into each of those holes on the devices. And what sets them off?"

"Contact," Preston said quietly. "They are made to be easily crushable, which is why I beg you to be careful," he said to Niall. "You set it off prematurely and it will be useless to Petra. And if one goes off in the box, they might all catch and be ruined—and Tom will be as good as dead."

But Kara was still talking it through. "Contact. All the saints in heaven," she breathed. "The screw top. The gun powder. She fills those devices full of gunpowder, attaches these protruding caps all over it—and what was it? If any of the caps are struck, they cause a spark, all that gunpowder ignites…" It was a horrific thought. "An explosive shell that you don't need a cannon to shoot."

"Someone could carry it in a pocket," said Niall.

"And what, just toss it into the crowd?"

"Or at someone specific," Niall reminded her.

"The damage it could do," Kara said, her horror growing. "That much explosive? Dozens could be killed with just one device." Her gut clenched. "And she had two crates full of them." She turned to Preston. "How many caps are in that box?"

"Five layers of nine. Petra said she needed five bombs for the first attack."

"First attack?" Niall said, appalled.

"And we still don't know who she means to go after."

"It's Palmerston."

Kara gasped, and they all turned toward the bedroom door.

"Gyda!" Her friend looked like she had indeed rested. She looked fierce, ready, and…dangerous.

"Stayme figured it out. It's Palmerston. He's been chafing over his loss of control over foreign policy. The prime minister is irritated, but with the Russians concentrating troops on the Ottoman border, Palmerston won't stay out of it. He means to speak out, to urge that the Royal Navy should join the French in the Dardanelles, as a solid warning to Russia."

"Palmerston has always worked to preserve the balance of power in Europe. He won't stand for Russia expanding into Ottoman territories," said Niall.

"They said their target was standing in Russia's way," Kara said. "Petra and her Russian crony. Stayme is right, then. It's

Palmerston whom they mean to assassinate."

"We are not going to allow it," Gyda stated flatly. "Petra Scot is not going to harm anyone else, and certainly not the home secretary. Stayme has already gone to warn him. We are not going to allow it." She directed a glare at Preston. "Are we, Mr. Preston?"

NIALL SAW THE dismay on Preston's face start to turn to defiance. He took a step forward before tensions could escalate. "We are not going to allow it," he agreed with Gyda. "But neither are we going to let her harm Tom. We are going to put an end to her machinations once and for all." He held up the percussion cap. "And I know how we are going to do it."

"I asked at the quarry," Preston said with a shake of his head. "We cannot break the seal to remove the mercury fulminate without setting it off. It will be obvious that they have been rendered useless."

"We don't have to alter them. I can replicate them. When are you supposed to deliver these to Petra?"

"Tonight. At the King's Tower. Long enough after the workers are done for the day, so we will not be observed." Preston's gaze dropped away. "I knew she must be targeting someone in Parliament. The House of Lords is meeting tonight."

"With five of those devices, she could destroy half of them in one go," Gyda said angrily.

"Not if we give her alternate caps," said Niall.

"Do you have enough time to accomplish it?" asked Kara. "Just getting to your forge at Bluefield and back will take time."

"I know half the smiths in London," Niall replied. "I can find a spot to work on them in Town. And the design is simple enough. I'll have Harold help me, and we can turn them out quickly."

"We have already pulled a trick like that on her once before,"

Kara reminded him. "With the locket portraits."

"Yes. *We* have. But these are coming from Preston. She must know he could never replicate them."

"That's true enough."

"Go and get started," Gyda urged him. "Kara and I will get all the details about the meeting point from Preston. We will begin to formulate a strategy for the meeting."

Preston hesitated. Niall could see the man weighing his decision. At last, he nodded.

"I named the sovereign's entrance as the place to meet," he said. "And I did it for a reason. Let me show you." The engineer pulled out paper and began to sketch.

Niall waited until they were all absorbed before he wrapped the percussion cap carefully in his handkerchief. Tucking it into his pocket, he hoped like hell that tonight would be the end of it. He wasn't above a bit of extra skullduggery to make sure it was.

Chapter Twenty-Five

"STOP FRETTING," GYDA said.

"How can I?" Kara asked. "I thought he'd be done by now."

"He will be back soon," Gyda said with confidence. "That is not a job to challenge someone with Niall's skills." She had settled in a chair next to the fire and proceeded to sharpen several blades that she then tucked away about her person. She held the last one up to the light and examined the edge. "All will be well," she said with quiet reassurance. "Tonight, we end this."

"How can you be so calm?" Kara felt like her every nerve ending was fizzing—much like the bubbly water that had been so popular at the Great Exhibition.

"Because we have a plan. Because we can count on each other. Because nature abhors imbalance, and Petra has had her way for too long. It is our time to shift this contest of wills out of the murky dark."

Kara wished she could be so certain, but she did get a boost of confidence when Niall finally returned, triumphantly flourishing his bag of replica caps.

"Oh, well done," she said, taking one. "They are very like the others."

"She'll never tell the difference," Gyda added. "Especially

since it will be dark."

"It was easy enough, once I found a supply of the right-sized square nuts."

"And Harold helped?" asked Kara.

"That he did. And he was thrilled to get his hand in, as you'd expect."

"Where is he now? Did you send him home?"

"No, I took him back to Stayme's. That place is a fortress. The staff knows how to handle a threat. Turner is there alone. I reminded Harold about Petra's tendency to harm you by hurting the ones you love. I tasked him with keeping Turner safe. He is taking the assignment seriously."

"It's a relief knowing they will both be safe."

"Stayme had sent word back to Berkeley Square. He thought perhaps that Lord Palmerston would like to be present as we lay our trap for Petra, seeing as she meant to murder him, but his lordship declined. He said it is much more important for him to round up support tonight in the Lords. Then he is off to a special cabinet meeting afterward. There he will propose his plans to warn off Russia. Stayme said that he and some of his best men will stick close to the home secretary's side all night."

"I sent word to Wooten," Kara said. He's been in on the hunt for Petra from the very beginning, so I thought he would want to be there."

"And that we could use the reinforcements?" Niall said wryly.

"Exactly. I have yet to hear back."

"I did send him word about the Russian assailant we left with the constable at Chiswick. Hopefully Wooten did not trek out to retrieve the man himself." He glanced about. "Where is Preston?"

"He went to the tower site to set the stage. He'll return to fetch the box of caps. Come." She pulled him over to a table, where a set of drawings lay. "See? He means to position a bricklayer's cart at an angle here, just outside the sovereign's entrance. And on this side, a pile of mortar bags. Both should provide excellent cover, should we need it."

"Very strategic."

"Tell him about the trapdoor," Gyda said.

"It's an interesting idea." Kara pointed to one of the sketches. "Do you recall when we first met Preston, he was repairing a winch? One that lifts supplies up to the upper levels above the sovereign's entrance?"

"Vaguely."

"Well, it turns out that it sits above an octagonal trapdoor in the roof of the entrance. Preston said it is going to stay. It's meant to be used as a lookout, as someone posted up there can peer down into the space and will be able to note the exact moment the queen enters the palace—and they can send word to raise the royal standard, to signify her presence." Kara shrugged. "At first, we thought to post Lord Palmerston up there, so he could observe from a safe distance, but now we are not sure how to make use of it."

Niall straightened. "Oh, this is perfect," he breathed. "I know just how we can use it." Kara's eyes widened as he reached into a pocket and pulled out a smaller, rounder version of one of Petra's devices.

"Is that—?"

"Yes. It is."

GYDA LEFT FIRST, heading to Westminster to sneak in through a little-used entrance that Preston described in detail and gave her a key for.

Niall and Kara followed a short time later, both dressed in black. They entered through the gate that Gyda left unlocked and made their careful way to the sovereign's entrance in the tower. The area was dark and deserted, and Preston had successfully set it up as they had discussed. Niall saw Kara tucked behind a wheel of the bricklayer's cart, then crossed over to duck in behind the stacked bags of mortar. They settled down to wait. Niall drew up his knees, put his face down, and mentally ran through all the ways this meeting could go, trying to prepare for anything.

Eventually, Preston arrived, driving a small cart he had borrowed from the site. He left it standing a good distance away, then removed the tall box of percussion caps from the cushioning bed of straw in the back. He carried it carefully, as if it still contained the original, delicate caps. Setting it in the middle of the entry space, he stood behind it, waiting beneath the beautiful, vaulted stonework.

Nearly thirty minutes passed while they waited in the cold, dark silence. No one moved or made a sound.

At last there came the rattle of an approaching carriage. Niall rose into a crouch as it approached from the supply entrance that he and Kara had used before. It was a finely appointed vehicle. The craftsmanship and the coat of arms showed clear in the light of the lanterns it sported. He did not recognize the crest, though he got a good look as it passed. The carriage swept on, right into the spot that the queen's carriage would eventually use.

How very like Petra Scot.

Niall peered into the entry. He'd chosen this position for the angle of the view. He could see everything.

Preston lifted his chin and maintained his position behind the box.

Petra stepped down from the carriage. She strode toward her childhood companion, smiling. She was dressed all in black, her skirts loose.

Kara was dressed similarly, Niall knew. Both women were expecting physical exertion tonight.

"Good evening, Robert," Petra said with a nasty smile. "Have you brought me what I need?"

He merely indicated the box.

She gestured. "Show me how they work."

Preston's surprise showed in the flickering light of the carriage lanterns. "After all this effort, you would waste one?"

"It won't be too much of a risk for one device to have eight pins instead of nine." Her eyes narrowed. "Do it. Show me now."

They had anticipated this. Preston had an original cap tucked into his sleeve. Kneeling to open the box, he made the switch. He stood and held up the original cap so that Petra could see it. With a swift motion, he tossed it to the side.

The cap struck the stone floor. Instantly, a bright flame flared up.

Petra's face lit up as well. "Excellent." She waved a hand. "Come and fetch it!"

The man standing at the back of the carriage climbed down and came to fetch the box.

Preston moved to block him. "No. Not yet. I want your promise first. After all these years, you have finally roped me into your scheming." He nodded toward the box. "I know these are going to bring death and destruction. Now I will become a part of it." His gaze hardened. "I want your word, Petra. You will stain my soul. In return, I want your guarantee that you will leave Tom alone. I don't want you involving him in your dirty work. Don't ask him for favors. Don't contact him or talk to him. Don't even look at him. Leave him alone. Forever."

Petra's mouth quirked into a twisted smile. "I'm afraid I can't do that." She spoke to her minion. "Take it. Start putting everything together, but for God's sake, be careful."

Preston struggled to keep the man away. "It's what you promised, Petra! It's what you owe me!"

"What I owe you is a bullet between the eyes." From a pocket, she pulled out a pistol.

Preston froze. The henchman pushed him aside and took the box of caps to the back of the carriage, where a crate was strapped.

"Not there, you fool!" Petra told him. "One slip and you'll blow the carriage sky high!"

Shoulders hunched, the man moved the box and the crate to the farthest corner of the stone entry. Now he was closer to

Niall's position. Niall could just make out the back of him as he bent to begin to assemble the devices.

"I should shoot you," Petra said to Preston. "It is no less than you deserve for betraying me. Worse, for constantly, continuously underestimating me." She raised her voice. "Bring him out!"

Niall cast his worried gaze all around. Then he heard it. Footsteps. The sound of a short-lived struggle. From somewhere beyond the front of the carriage came a big man. He dragged a cursing, resisting Tom Hawkins with him.

"What are you doing?" Preston raged. "Let him go!"

Tom's hands were tied, but he yanked free of the other man's grip and stepped away from him.

"Did you think I wouldn't know you snatched him from Bluefield?" Petra demanded. "That I wouldn't notice Levett's stray pup spying on you? That I wouldn't notice all of you colluding against me? Come out, Your Graces!" Her mocking tone echoed into the high, arched ceiling. "I know you are here."

Niall didn't move.

Petra laughed. "I admit, you made me work a little harder at this one. I still haven't managed to break through Stayme's defenses. I had to get a bit creative. Still, I think I managed well enough." She threw her head back and shouted, "Bring the other one!"

Niall ducked as someone moved in the dark on his side of the entrance. Another henchman emerged from the shadows and moved to stand near the back of the carriage. He also prodded a captive along, bound like Hawkins.

Niall clenched his jaw as he saw who it was.

Wooten. The idiot woman had kidnapped Wooton.

"Come out right now," Petra called. "Do not force me to put a bullet in the head of your pet inspector from Scotland Yard."

KARA CLENCHED HER fists, along with her jaw. *Damn the woman!*

"Come now," Petra called. "I must assume you have caught on to my game by now. If you know I mean to annihilate the home secretary—and as Stayme is babysitting him so thoroughly tonight, I assume you do—then you cannot think I will hesitate to destroy a lackey like Wooten. A lackey who once had the temerity to put me in a government cage."

Kara knew she spoke the truth. Petra wouldn't hesitate at *anything*. They had underestimated her. It was a lesson well learned. It was time to confront her.

Face to face.

She crawled out from beneath the wagon and walked calmly around to the edge of the entrance.

"There you are." Petra sounded gleeful. "But where is your dear husband? Surely he will not allow you—"

She stopped as Niall stepped out into the flickering light. He sent Kara an encouraging glance, and they both turned to face their enemy, from either side of the entrance. And they both took care to keep well back from her.

Petra looked around with obvious satisfaction. Preston and Hawkins huddled together on her right, with the henchman covering them and Kara standing off to the side beyond them. To her left lay the other henchman and Wooten, with Niall behind and to the side of them. "So much revenge to be had at once," she said happily.

Kara held her silence, but much as Petra might know, it wasn't everything.

"You first," Petra said, beckoning Kara nearer. "Interfering bitch. How did you get to Gibson's farm? How did you know?"

Kara held her silence.

"So smug," Petra said with a sigh. "I know you were not in that tavern when Dalton was crying to your husband." Her eyes widened. "Oh, yes. Dalton. I suppose I should mention Dalton—and the fact that we found him lurking outside. He's currently trussed up near the gate, so if you thought to rely upon him, you'll have to think again."

The horrid woman watched Kara avidly for a reaction. She refused to give it to her. She was very careful not to look up, where their last hope of support waited.

But Petra kept poking at her. "You hid in the hay cart, didn't you?" She rolled her eyes. "I'll have that livery burned to the ground."

Kara caught a slight movement from the corner of her eye. Niall was taking advantage of Petra's attention being focused on her. He was moving ever so slowly up behind the henchman holding Wooten.

She tossed her head and curled her mouth in contempt, hoping to keep Petra focused squarely on her. "Speaking of smug," she said wryly, "I followed *you* to that livery, Petra—and I didn't squeeze into that farm cart until after you left the place. They had no part in it. There is no one to blame but yourself."

"No one to blame?" Petra laughed. "You dare to say so, after drugging me? There is plenty of blame to go around, but you share the largest burden of it. If you had just done as you were meant to and kept yourself and your interfering crew at home, we wouldn't be so very crowded here tonight."

"Don't be such a child," Kara sneered. "Are you not woman enough to face up to your own mistakes? Not mature enough to acknowledge your own desires? You wanted this, Petra. All of it."

"You don't know what you are talking of," Petra said.

"I do. You know I'm right, too. You could have come into England again and crept quietly around with your Russian conspirators and we might never have known of your presence."

Petra gestured toward Wooten. "Your pet would have kept you appraised."

Kara shrugged. "You are likely right, but there was no need for us to meddle."

"You are an inveterate meddler!" Petra scoffed.

Niall was nearly behind Wooten's captor, but the man, like everyone else, stood captivated, listening to Kara and her temerity in verbally sparring with Petra Scot.

Kara took a step closer, hoping to keep the woman's attention firmly fixed on her. "Perhaps. But we have never tangled with you except at your instigation. The last time, you meant to use Niall. You forced our hand. This time, you could not let us be. You taunted us. Goaded us. You threatened my family to force me into action. All because you could not stand the thought that we won our last encounter." She lifted her chin. "We are all here at this crossroads, Petra, because you led us here."

The other woman stared at her, her brow furrowed. She started to speak, then stopped. Her lips pursed. She put her hands on her hips. "Damn you. I think you are right." She nodded. "You *are* right. I threw sticks at the lioness. I injured her cubs. Because I wanted to best her. I wanted the trophy on my wall." Turning, she took a step toward the carriage, then stopped and looked over her shoulder. "Do you have those devices ready?" she called out sharply.

Someone else spoke out from the carriage, his tone just as sharp. Kara missed the words, but she knew the voice.

The Russian. He was in the carriage.

Petra ignored him. "The devices?" she asked her henchman again.

"Two are ready," he answered.

"Bring one to me," Petra ordered him.

"No." This time the order from the carriage rang clear. "Enough of this. We have real work to do."

"No! She is right," Petra said. She kept her gaze locked on Kara, but held out a peremptory hand.

The man assembling the devices obeyed the summons, holding one gingerly out in front of him as he came.

Behind him, Niall struck Wooten's guard in the head with the handle of his blade. The man slumped, and Niall eased him silently to the ground. He cut Wooten's hands loose, and the inspector immediately began to creep toward the coach.

Petra took the device. It looked larger in her grip. She gazed down at it. "Such a strange-looking thing. And yet it is going to bring me so much satisfaction. For you are absolutely right, Levett."

Niall was trying to tug Wooten away, but the inspector resisted. He clearly wanted to see who waited in the carriage.

"I did want you here tonight." Petra took a couple of quick steps toward Kara, leaving the shelter of the entryway's stone buttresses to confront her. "Because my victory would not be complete…without your death." With a grin of pure evil, she tossed the device to Kara and turned to run.

It was pure instinct. Without thought. Kara reached out and caught it. It didn't go off, of course, despite the multiple pins that struck her palm and fingers. Holding the thing, she looked up.

Petra had reached the middle of the sovereign's entrance before she realized something was wrong. She spun around, her triumph fading to shock—and then to fury.

Kara didn't wait for the woman's further reaction. They had set up several emergency-level, prearranged signals for Gyda—and Petra tossing an ineffective bomb was one of them.

She turned to sprint away, then spun back in time to see the object failing from the trapdoor above. Niall's makeshift bomb, with a functioning percussion cap, fell to the stone floor and landed at Petra's feet. Unfortunately, it landed with the pin pointing up. Without contact to it, nothing happened right away.

Also unfortunately, Petra was quick to grasp what it was— and all the implications. Before the ball could turn and the pin strike the ground, she kicked it away. Niall's bomb skittered across the stone toward the carriage, where the pin struck a wheel.

Kara threw herself on the ground. The explosion roared. Heat washed over her and small, stinging sensations struck her arms and hands where she had flung them over her head.

She lay there, gasping while smoke and other particles swirled in the air around her, before struggling to sit up. "Niall!"

Her ears were ringing. Her arms and hands stung. She stared.

They were full of splinters. Climbing to her feet, she looked back at the carriage.

It had been ripped apart. Parts of it were burning. It listed on shattered wheels into a hole in the stone. The horses… She looked away, swallowing back the horror. "Niall!"

She headed for where she had last seen him. As she passed the back side of the carriage, she saw the blood dripping from it.

The Russian, whoever he was, was no more.

She found Niall just beginning to stir on the far side. He had clearly been pushing Wooten away and managed to get him behind the stack of mortar sacks. His hand still reached out toward the inspector, but Niall had been caught out before the safety of their shelter.

Kara flinched to see a great, long shard of wood impaling the muscle of his calf, several inches above his ankle.

"Niall!" He was groaning as she threw herself down beside him. "Don't move," she ordered him. "Be still."

"Wooten?" he asked, coughing.

She moved to put her fingers on the inspector's neck. "His pulse is steady. I don't see any wounds." Wooten began to stir. "He will be fine."

Coming back to Niall, she threw up her skirts and reached for a petticoat. "That leg is going to bleed when we pull that out. I'll need padding—"

"Kara, wait."

She stopped as Niall grabbed her wrist. He nodded toward the entrance hall. She turned her head to see Petra on her feet, stumbling through the wreckage. She paused in the corner, standing over the box of trigger-less devices. Her face contorted as she pounded the stone wall in frustration. She didn't glance their way or check on anyone else's welfare before she walked out into the cluttered construction site. Kara heard her footsteps stumbling, then quickening to a run.

"Don't," Niall said as Kara reached again for her petticoat. "Kara, you are right. It's going to bleed. It will slow me down.

Damn it, someone needs to go, and it can't be me."

"What are you saying?" She stared. "I cannot leave you!"

"Gyda will already be after her," he said roughly.

"Oh, yes." She looked back up toward the trapdoor in the ceiling. "She'll be facing her alone."

"She shouldn't do it alone," Niall said urgently. He gripped her arm. "Petra has just lost. Again. She will be in a rage. A frenzy. She'll feel like she has nothing to lose." He tried to shift off his hip, but grimaced and cursed. "Damn it!"

"No! You are right. I'll go. I can do this."

His lips thinned. "You *can* do this. The both of you." Reaching into his coat, he handed her his pistol. "You know where she is going."

Kara frowned. It took a moment. "Oh, Brougham."

"Yes. She will need to salvage something from this disaster." A spasm of pain crossed his face. "Odin's arse. I cannot believe I am sending you after her."

She grabbed his face, gripping it between her two hands. "You are not sending me. I am going. You are right. This has to end. Tonight."

She kissed him fiercely. And then she stood. "Preston," she shouted.

"Kara?" The engineer limped into view on the other side of the carriage, cradling an arm and looking wildly about. "Are you all right? Tom and I are bruised, but fine. But where have they all gone? Have they all fled?"

"Niall is injured. Get over here. Don't pull out this shard until you are able to apply plenty of pressure to stop the bleeding."

She glanced down. "I love you. I'll be back."

"You damned well better."

Their gazes met for a long, intent moment. Right before she slipped away into the dark.

Chapter Twenty-Six

NONE OF THE hacks she passed were willing to pick her up, a disheveled woman alone in the night. Kara walked grimly toward Mayfair, picking splinters from her hands as she went. Fortunately, she recalled the address from their research into Brougham, when they had been debating whether to interview Petra's real father. Grafton Street was not far.

She slowed her pace as she turned the corner from Albemarle Street. There were street lights here, but she kept to the shadows, stepping carefully, watching for any sign of Gyda or Petra.

Brougham spent a great deal of his time in France, Stayme had said. There was no saying whether he was even in London right now.

But he was. His home was lit up, both within and without. Kara ducked into a doorway and studied it. Five stories. Brown brick. Not much opportunity for hidden surveillance. There was only a short staircase leading to the front door. Everything else was lined with black-rod iron railing. Perhaps in the back? But even as she thought to turn away, Kara spotted a mess spilling onto the pavement directly across the street. She crept closer.

There she was.

Petra had pushed over a planter on the stairs of the house across from Brougham's. She sat now upon the narrow ledge and gazed at her father's house.

Kara moved closer. Brougham was entertaining. The drapes were open and the small crowd inside was clearly visible. The man himself must be in the front room, where gentlemen were gathered with cigars and brandies.

"I know you are there."

Holding still, Kara didn't answer.

"Where is your husband? Dead, I hope." Petra's tone was flat.

Kara hung back. "No. Injured, though."

"Well, that is something."

Kara sighed. "Do you never tire of it?"

"Of what?"

"Of all of it. The plotting. The vengeance. The killing. The endless anger."

Petra surprised her with her answer. "Sometimes." But then her tone hardened. "I quite hated you the first time I saw you."

"In the warehouse beneath your Seven Dials lair," Kara said with a nod. "I remember."

"Yes. There you were, fighting like a fury with my men, all to rescue Niall Kier. I despised you for freeing him, of course. For complicating my plans. But mostly I hated that you were risking life and limb for him."

"I love him," Kara said. "There was nothing else to be done."

Petra snorted. "We are not so different, Kier and I. And yet no one ever willingly risked themselves for me. Not without promise of payment or threat of punishment. Not even Clémence. Not William, who has taken huge sums of money and disappeared somewhere."

"That is the thing you don't understand," Kara said. "Your circumstance might bear a slight resemblance to Niall's, but you are nothing like him. He *cares*, Petra. He gives of himself. He treats people with respect and kindness and, yes, love. You have to give love if you have any hope of receiving it."

"You are hopelessly naïve," Petra said with a sniff. "It is a woman's fairy tale you spin, you fool. Men do not believe in such airy nonsense. Money, influence, and power—that is what they respect."

"Those are not the things that bring the sort of devotion you speak of wanting. And not all men are like that. Niall is not."

"Perhaps Kier is the aberration, then." She gestured toward the window across the street. "He was my mother's trusted advisor. For years. He fought for her. He defended her publicly, but he never truly cared for her. About her. She was just a means for advancement. A way to make his name."

"You cannot know that. Not for sure."

"She knew it. I have some of her journals, you know. At the end, she knew." A glint of light flashed as Petra tossed a knife and caught it. Once, twice, again. "And what of me? He knew about me. He might have claimed me. Taken an interest. Visited. Learned to know me."

"And your sister." Kara grew exasperated with the woman's relentless self-interest.

"At least my sister got something out of him," Petra said, sneering. "She blackmailed him, you know. Everyone in her life knew she'd been adopted, yet they seemed to care for her. I don't know how she discovered who sired her, but when the waterman who raised her was injured, she came here and met our real father. Confronted him. She convinced him to purchase the cottage in Kingston upon Thames for her parents." She stood. "Now, it is my turn."

"It's too late," Kara said gently. "You have gone too far. He cannot give you anything."

"He can give me the satisfaction of watching him pay for his indifference." Petra hefted her blade, but instead of stepping into the street, she whirled and threw it at Kara.

She had been expecting something of the sort. She pivoted and the blade flew by, missing her completely. She pulled the pistol from her pocket, but Petra was on her, knocking it away. She heard the clatter as it skittered into the street.

It was only a moment before Petra had another blade in hand.

Kara ducked away from her swing and reached for the knife Niall had once gifted her. It had scarcely cleared her pocket before Petra seized her wrist and cruelly wrenched it. The knife dropped from her suddenly useless fingers, but Kara didn't hesitate. She tightened her other fist and swung hard, boxing Petra's ear.

The other woman staggered back. Kara knew she could show no mercy. She kicked out, hitting Petra's knee. The leg gave out and Petra went down on her other knee. She did not hesitate a second, though—she lunged back up, grabbed Kara by the hair, yanked her head back, and pressed the point of her blade beneath her chin.

But Kara had managed to pull one of her pointed lockpicks from a hidden pocket. She fisted it in her left hand and pressed it to Petra's neck.

"We've come to a pretty impasse, haven't we?" Petra asked with a smile. She sounded eager. Elated. "Whatever shall we do?"

Suddenly she stiffened. Her eyes widened. Kara jumped back as the blade beneath her chin dropped away. Petra staggered, stepping toward her.

"Die," Gyda said from behind her. "At least, that's what you will do. At last."

Petra fell forward. She lay on the pavement without moving. Two of Gyda's blades protruded from her lower back.

"Through the kidneys and into the diaphragm," Gyda said. "Just like her League killed poor Sally Doughty. There's no coming back from it. It's over."

Between them, Petra twitched, then stilled.

Gyda's expression crumbled. She started to tremble. Kara stepped over the body and enfolded her friend in her arms. She held Gyda tight while she cried. The walls of her friend's fury and need for vengeance fell away, and she shook with the force of her grief.

Gyda's knees buckled. She sank down next to Petra, racked with emotion. Kara went down with her and just held her.

It took a while, but when the first wave of Gyda's grief was over, she lay silent for a few minutes. Moving slowly, she sat up. Her hand still had a tremor as she wiped away her tears. She stared dully at Petra's still form, then looked at Kara, her expression blank. "What now?" she asked.

"Now we go and make sure Niall is all right." Climbing to her feet, Kara went to fetch her weapons.

"What of her?" Gyda spared Petra's body another dispassionate glance.

Kara looked across the street. In the window she could see Petra's father drinking and laughing with his friends. "Let him deal with her. For once."

Together, they walked away.

When they reached Albemarle Street, Gyda stopped. Her expression was bleak as she blinked at Kara. "I can scarcely make one foot move in front of the other. It had to be done. But now it *is* done. And Charles is still gone. Kara, what now?" she repeated.

Kara sighed. "Now, you grieve. You cry. You rail at fate. And eventually, you heal. But you won't do any of it alone."

Gyda reached out and squeezed her hand. "I know. That much I know."

Kara started walking again. Her pace increased with nearly every step, she was so anxious to get to Niall. When they arrived back at Westminster, they found a large group of men milling around. The House of Lords had obviously closed their session. They must have been drawn to the tower site by the smoldering carriage.

Kara pushed through them. She caught sight of Wooten surrounded by a circle of gentlemen, talking fast and gesturing. From several feet away, she saw Dalton had been set free. He was winding a bandage around Niall's leg. He looked up, saw them coming, and gave Niall a nudge.

Her husband looked at her with boundless relief. He held out his arms and she fell into them. "Well?" he said over his shoulder to Gyda.

"It's done. Over. She's gone."

"It was a close thing, but Gyda saved the day," Kara told him.

Niall reached out a hand to his friend. "Thank you. Are you all right?"

Kara turned her head in time to see Gyda catch her breath and shrug.

Looking between them both, Niall asked, "What now?"

She and Gyda both laughed a little.

Leaning in to kiss her husband, Kara answered softly, "Now, we let the madness recede. We stick together. We heal. We live. We all enjoy a bit of peace."

I admit to fudging the history a little bit with Petra Scot's incendiary device. The design I described is based off an Orsini bomb, which was not known until several years later.

In 1858, Felice Orsini was an Italian revolutionary living in exile in England. He designed the device and he did hire an English gunsmith to create the casing. They tested it in Sheffield and Devon, before shipping it off to France, where Orsini and his fellow plotters used several of the devices in an attempt to assassinate Napoleon III. Their attempt failed, but eight people died and one hundred and fifty-six were injured.

One of the first hand grenades, the idea caught on and the devices were used by violent anarchists throughout the end of the century and also by the Confederates in the American Civil War.

I hope the inaccuracy will be forgiven, but it felt right that a mind like Petra Scot's might have come up with something so terrible.

ABOUT THE AUTHOR

USA Today Bestselling author Deb Marlowe grew up with her nose in a book. Luckily, she'd read enough romances to recognize the hero she met at a college Halloween party – even though he wore a tuxedo t-shirt instead of breeches and boots. They married, settled in North Carolina and raised two handsome, funny and genuinely intelligent boys

The author of over twenty-five historical romances, Deb is a Golden Heart Winner, a Rita Finalist and her books have won or been a finalist in the Golden Quill, the Holt Medallion, the Maggie, the Write Touch Reader Awards and the Daphne du Maurier Award.

A proud geek, history buff and story addict, she loves to talk with readers! Find her discussing books, period dramas and her infamous Men in Boots on Facebook, Twitter and Instagram. Watch her making historical recipes in her modern kitchen at Deb Marlowe's Regency Kitchen, a set of completely amateur videos on her website. While there, find out Behind the Book details and interesting Historical Tidbits and enter her monthly contest at deb@debmarlowe.com.

www.ingramcontent.com/pod-product-compliance
Lightning Source LLC
Chambersburg PA
CBHW060346310726
48976CB00003B/734